The Night Orchid
Conan Doyle in Toulouse

The Night Orchid
Conan Doyle in Toulouse

by
Jean-Claude Dunyach

adapted in English by
Sheryl Curtis
Jean-Louis Trudel
Dominique Bennett
Ann Cale

Foreword by
David Brin

A Black Coat Press Book

We are indebted to David Brin, Gilles Francescano,
Annette Werther-Médou and David McDonnell.

This is a collection of stories assembled by the author and
published in France by Editions L'Atalante, 11 & 15, rue des
Vieilles-Douves, 44000 Nantes, France.
http://www.editions-l-atalante.com/

Visit our website at www.blackcoatpress.com

Acknowledgements

The Night Orchid (*L'Orchidée de la Nuit*) originally published in *Futurs Antérieurs*, Fleuve Noir, Paris, 1999; Copyright © 1999 by Jean-Claude Dunyach. English translation first published as *Orchids in the Night* in *Interzone* No. 160, Brighton, 2000; translation Copyright © 2000 by Jean-Louis Trudel.

The Parliament of Birds (*Le Jugement des Oiseaux*) originally published in *Génèses*, J'ai Lu No. 4279, Paris, 1996; Copyright © 1996 by Jean-Claude Dunyach. Translation Copyright © 2004 by Jean-Louis Trudel.

Scenes at the Exhibit (*Détails de l'Exposition*) originally published in *Univers 1983*, J'ai Lu No. 1491, Paris, 1983; Copyright © 1983 by Jean-Claude Dunyach. Translation Copyright © 2004 by Jean-Louis Trudel.

Time, as it evaporates... (*Le Temps, en s'évaporant...*) originally published in *Autoportrait*, Présence du Futur No. 415, Denoël, Paris, 1986; Copyright © 1986 by Jean-Claude Dunyach. Translation Copyright © 2004 by Jean-Louis Trudel.

Shark (*La Stratégie du Requin*) originally published in *Galaxies* No. 9, Paris, 1998; Copyright © 1998 by Jean-Claude Dunyach. Translation Copyright © 2004 by Sheryl Curtis.

Unravelling the Thread (*Déchiffrer la Trame*) originally published in *Galaxies* No. 4, Paris, 1997; Copyright © 1997 by Jean-Claude Dunyach. English translation first published in *Interzone* No. 133, Brighton, 1998; translation Copyright © 1998 by Ann Cale & Sheryl Curtis.

Watch Me When I Sleep (*Regarde-moi Quand Je Dors*) originally published in *Déchiffrer la Trame*, L'Atalante, Nantes, 2000; Copyright © 2000 by Jean-Claude Dunyach. English translation first published in *Interzone* No. 168, Brighton, 2001; translation Copyright © 2001 by Sheryl Curtis.

In Medicis Gardens (*Dans les Jardins Médicis*) originally published in *Autoportrait*, Présence du Futur No. 415, Denoël, Paris, 1986; Copyright © 1986 by Jean-Claude Dunyach. English translation originally published in *Full Spectrum* 4,

Table of Contents

Foreword

For ten thousand years, stretching back in time far beyond the invention of writing, we humans have had a tradition of telling stories. Anthropologists believe that some legends were conveyed by oral tradition all of the way from cave to cuneiform to computer screen. So great is our need. So great is our capacity to *satisfy* the craving for vivid wonder.

Imagine yourself by a camp fire listening, wide-eyed, to wondrous adventures of heroes. Or to dire warnings. Or epics and songs of poignant loss. How better to end a long day that was spent scratching in the meager earth for bare survival? After daylight's endless drudgery, our eyes must have followed the curling smoke upward, listening in wonder while we watched glittering stars.

Humanity spent far more generations doing this, than ever sat in comfortable houses, under roofs that blocked out the starry night. And somehow, across the ages, a need for imagined miracles became ingrained, a part of our souls. No human culture ever failed to produce storytellers.

From Gilgamesh to Homer to Murusaki to Cyrano de Bergerac, what did these tale-spinners all seem to have in common? What traits united them, making their fables timeless?

Until just the last two centuries, a successful story had to be bold, surprising, mythic. People who dwelled in mud huts or log cabins did not want to hear about mud huts and cabins. They demanded–and the bards provided–tales about heroes who could fly. About bold men who challenged nature and women who defied gods. Nearly all of the narratives that come down to us from the past feature some aspect that is wondrous. Villains and monsters are *exaggerated*. A hero's courage and powers are *extrapolated* to some higher plane. They set examples. They succeed against all odds. Or they show us how to fail with nobility and pride.

These adventures crossed vast distances, breaking the bonds that used to hobble people in their daily lives. Space, time and even death itself were no obstacles to characters like Odysseus or Orpheus or Gengi. During the long era when life seemed forever precarious... and yet always the same from day to day... storytellers and their listeners wanted legends that featured the fantastic.

Then, a century or two ago, something happened to storytelling. With the invention of the novel, we began seeing a strange fixation on the part of intellectuals. Suddenly, we were told that fiction should focus only upon the realistic. Upon detailed portrayals of the contemporary world. Space and time were off-limits. Instead, we should write–and read–page after page of contemplations about recollected aromas from a childhood kitchen, or whine for many chapters about a father's inadequate love. The phrase "eternal verities" implies that we must return to the same territory over and over again. Forever. How tedious.

Has this change occurred because–ironically–modern life is no longer changeless? Our homes are filled with wonders. We fly through the sky like gods and the news portrays a world in constant flux. Has this made us turn to *realism* as a crutch?

Perhaps for some this is true. But not all. For there is still a realm in which storytelling remains bold, far-seeing, willing to challenge gods–whatever form those gods might take. That realm is science fiction.

Not chained by professorial rules to the narrow here-and-now, science fiction keeps faith with ten thousand years of human tradition–a tradition that says there are no bounds. Question everything! Imagine everything. Dare to alter and transform the familiar. Make the results fearful, or hopeful, or transcendent.

Dare.

In recent years, science fiction has restored imagination to a public that hungers for the bold. Unfortunately, much of this restoration has been limited to cinema, where vivid tales are limited to the scope of a two-hour fable. Homer would have liked *The Matrix*! But millions seem unaware of how much more there is now to science fiction. Or that the tradition has been taken much farther than movies can ever go.

Literary science fiction has a far more limited market, eking along in the shadow of *Star Wars*. And yet, it is here that we explore serious ideas, engage in thought experiments about potential dangers, and contemplate the very meaning of '*change*'. The best of these contemplations may even help us to evade errors as we charge ahead, into an unknown tomorrow.

We need this. Voices that lure us ahead with promises and then warn us to watch the ground where we are about to step. It is a job that transcends boundaries of nation or border or language. For we are heading into the future together.

For this reason, I am proud and excited to introduce a collection of stories by the great French science fiction author Jean-Claude Dunyach. Written in the language used by Jules Verne, then translated into English by a team of talented and devoted aficionados, the volume that you hold represents a unique opportunity to ride one of the most talented imaginations living today, hurtling along with him to unique destinations unlike any you have ever seen.

Jean-Claude has a trait that is rare among authors– *variability*. His tales range from the adventurous romp of *The Night Orchid* to the moody alienation of *Footprints in the Snow*. From gritty cyberpunk in *Shark* to courage and sacrifice in *Station of the Lamb*.

Yes, there are some common themes. *Alienation* is one, for his characters often find themselves starkly challenged by some kind of *otherness*. By a strangeness that both tugs and repels. But in every case you can sense the author's deeper drive to experiment. To vary the theme. To surprise.

This sense of experimentation carries through in daily life. When I lived in Paris, during the early 1990s, Jean-Claude showed great patience with my stumbling French and Californian brashness. He also seemed always to convey a whimsical sense of wonder. To have something wry and relevant to say, with eyes that flashed at possibilities.

Possibilities abound in his stories, as well. At one moment, he projects genetic engineering to a future when perfect assassins can do their deadly work even in a world of total surveillance. (His thoughts parallel my own nonfiction book *The Transparent Society*.) The next moment he takes the bizarre notion of parasitic faery creatures all the way to its creepy ultimate implications. Will technology deprive us of memory? Show us alternate realities? Prepare to be surprised.

My favorite story, *Unravelling the Thread*, has little action. Instead, it is–as promised by the title–a tale about piecing together clues that lead to a poignant appreciation of time's limitations. It could have been written without any science fictional elements at all, and would have been just as beautiful. Just as ardent and sad and uplifting.

Now it is time for me to step aside and make way for this treat. Many people–especially the translators– have worked much harder than I did, to prepare the table before you.

Feast upon the imagination of Jean-Claude Dunyach. And then come back again.

David Brin

The Night Orchid
(Conan Doyle in Toulouse)

My acquaintance with Professor Challenger began with a killing and ended with one of the century's strangest acts of bravery. He was a most annoying young man, full of himself and irritatingly self-assured despite his lack of worldly experience. But I must admit he proved his worth in a pinch. Though it pains my Frenchman's soul to admit it, there is something to be said for English grit.

The final days of the summer of 1890 were nothing less than stifling. My good town of Toulouse, so pleasant in the spring, turns into a furnace when the August sun beats down upon it. The bricks hoard the day's heat and release it after sunset. Clouds of flies buzz around the droppings of the horses pulling drays and hansoms. And, worst of all, summer is also when the Museum attracts idlers in their Sunday best, crowding into the gardens for a stroll or a visit. If I close my one and only window, right above the Paleontological Gallery, my study can become a veritable Turkish bath. If I open it, the yelling of the children outside keeps me from concentrating.

However, in this particular case, I had no trouble shutting out the din. I was rereading the letter Charlus, our caretaker, had brought me earlier, asking if he might keep the Queen Victoria stamp for his collection:

Mon cher Frédéric,

The news you've given me is so astonishing and un-believable that I would have taken it for an ill-inspired jest from anybody else but you. However, I know you well enough to trust you implicitly.

Therefore, I am coming, just as you wished. As soon as I finish packing and scrawling these few words, I will be on my way and look forward to the pleasure of seeing you again.

Do you remember Sussex? Our mutual friend is unfortunately otherwise occupied–I've been given to understand a certain lady has claimed his services most imperiously–but I've presumed to take with me a young colleague in your field, who is just burning to meet the famous Professor Picard.

If French trains do not belie their reputation, we won't be far behind this very letter.

Yours truly,

Arthur Conan Doyle

I set aside the letter just as footsteps echoed down the corridor. Charlus knocked on the half-opened door of my office, breathless from having run in spite of the heat:

"They're here, Monsieur le Professeur. But it's incredible!"

He stepped aside to let Doyle come in. The man was ever the same, stiff with his military bearing of old, yet unageing in spite of the small, round eyeglasses he wore. When I got up, I kept in mind his distaste for the full Gallic hug and simply proffered a hand. He shook it warmly and then used it to pull me into the corridor outside.

"As I feared, Frédéric, my young friend has fallen in thrall to your collections. Please blame his scientific instincts for his lack of manners; I'm sure you will find it in yourself to forgive him."

Just opposite my office, I keep in a glass showcase one of the jewels of our collection: a skeleton, nearly whole, found in a Mousterian cave near Bruniquel. The man in front, half kneeling to examine the sutures of the pelvic girdle, turned as he heard us. I couldn't help but recoil slightly.

He was tall, quite a bit taller than Doyle or myself, who are hardly pygmies. An ample beard of the deepest black climbed all the way up to his eyebrows, which were almost as bushy. The head was nearly large enough to reduce the outsized ears to normal proportions, though they still seemed apt to flap in the slightest breeze. Their coloration betrayed a sanguine disposition, given to sudden violence.

Challenger's pale gaze dissected me with the same sharpness it had no doubt used on the unfortunate skeleton.

A skeleton to which he bore the most striking resemblance!

Well, that explained the amazement of old Charlus. It was as if a distant relative of the showcase's occupant had suddenly decided to visit him. Same cranial shape, same powerful back that might have been a wrestler's, same simian stance not unlike that of a gorilla on the verge of a headlong charge. For a paleontologist, the points of similarity were glaringly obvious.

"A remarkable specimen," the young man proclaimed in French with a booming voice. "But I must protest: the reconstruction of the innominate bones, however adept, is…"

"Frédéric," Doyle cut him off pitilessly, "may I introduce young Challenger, who's just back from Mongolia with some fascinating theories about the Kalmuks? George, this is Professor Picard, who has kindly invited us to visit his museum."

"Mongolia, *n'est-ce pas*? You'll have to tell me all about it when we have the time," I said, shaking his hand. The strength of his grip made me wince slightly.

"But still, those innominate bones..." he replied, but Doyle obviously knew how to handle him.

"Later, George," he cut him off again. "I believe time is of the essence and I look forward to hearing what Professor Picard has to tell us."

Rather than have them sit in the hothouse my office had become, I went down with them to the basement laboratory, through the trapdoor just beneath the blue whale skeleton.

Doyle sat down. Challenger rejected the armchair I was offering with a shake of the head, and he went off to gaze at an allosaurus tooth mounted on the far wall. I looked at him, pursing my lips. Not yet thirty, and he already showed all the signs of our avocation! He could have given pointers to colleagues ten times more experienced when it came to bad manners. No matter! It was Doyle, and Doyle alone, I needed, even if I deplored the absence of our mutual friend, as he called him. The man's prodigious powers of observation and deduction would have come in most useful.

"It's about a murder," I announced. "A Paleolithic murder..."

Challenger jumped perceptibly, but did not look around. Doyle smiled encouragingly at me, "Your assistant, if I recall your initial letter..."

"Michel Desnoyer. In his thirties. He'd studied with Cuvelier in Paris and been with Basserman in the Amazon during the second expedition, in '88. A bit too imaginative for my taste, but he had impeccable references–and manners!" The latter was meant for the back of my young colleague, who no more flinched than a rhinoceros bitten by a flea. "He was killed about three weeks ago, in the middle of the night, on the other side of the Garonne, near the Hôtel-Dieu."

"An affair of the heart?"

"I doubt it. He was more interested in flowers than women. He had a mistress, I suppose, but…"

"What kind of flowers?" Challenger asked, turning without warning.

I confess I was needled by the question, but we had come in one stroke to the heart of the matter. Somehow, this extraordinary man had divined it.

"Orchids. More specifically the local varieties. Which brings us to the first mystery associated with this murder."

"Orchids in Toulouse. Who would have thought it?" muttered Doyle. "I did see a poster outside the train station, announcing an opera recital by the Night Orchid herself, but I didn't expect to encounter her floral equivalent here in Toulouse!"

"Michel would have proven you wrong. He had discovered several spots as they are called, isolated pockets where local conditions allow them to flourish. When he died, he was holding in his fist a deep red bloom of the *Oncidium Macranthum* variety. Picked less than an hour earlier."

Challenger scowled, his eyebrows seeming to grow even thicker, and I guessed, from the blood beating in his temples, that he was struggling hard to remain composed. I endured his glare for a moment before adding:

"This is not the only impossibility, my dear colleague. I know full well that the *Macranthum* variety is to be found only on the most remote high plateaus of the globe. And, to the best of my knowledge, no European collector has ever been able to grow them in a greenhouse. However, the case gets curiouser and curiouser:

"Michel was killed by a singular weapon. A claw, whose broken end we found deep in his vitals. Strange enough–murders are not rare, around here, but they're mostly of the knifing or shooting kind. Stranger yet is what I recovered during the autopsy. Behold, the murder weapon!"

I took out from an inner vest pocket the object which I'd kept there since Michel's death and I held it out to Doyle. But it was Challenger who grabbed it with his broad hand bristling with coarse dark hairs.

He raised it to the light, muttering under his breath. It was a curved claw, coal-black and as long as my palm. The barbs jutting out from its sides had torn Michel's flesh, causing grievous damage. The right-hand edge bore a notch where the claw had wedged itself between two vertebrae.

"This," Challenger pronounced with due emphasis, "passes all that can be imagined in the way of a bad joke. Come, Doyle, we have already wasted too much time coming here! As for you, Monsieur, if you thought, that we would let ourselves be fooled, even for an instant, by the most ridiculous fake I ever…"

"A moment, if you please!" I held back Doyle, who was on the verge, for once, of losing his British *sang-froid*. "Monsieur Challenger, I can understand your reaction up to a point, even if I cannot excuse it. But I must ask you to grant me the common courtesy of letting me finish my story. Please believe I am thoroughly puzzled by this affair and that it is in no way a deliberate attempt on my part to garner public notice. My present notoriety is quite sufficient!"

Having thus reminded him of our respective positions, as I am an authority in my field, which is also his own, I held out my hand for the claw. Clearly reluctant to do so, Challenger nevertheless returned it.

"Please excuse my show of temper," he said with difficulty, "but I am unable to believe this is anything but a joke whose intent escapes me, a hoax such as the French like to play."

"A man is dead, George," Doyle reproved him, taking the murder weapon. "Let us see this…" He turned over the claw between his fingers. "A fascinating item, at any rate. Certainly primitive, but no less efficacious. I have already seen such things in the British Museum, used as spearheads."

He leaned back into the armchair and steepled his fingers under his chin.

"Our mutual friend would easily deduce that this object points to a very specific category of suspects: paleontologists, or those who have ready access to the museum it was stolen from. The victim being from the same circles is hardly surprising… Professional jealousy?"

"You are on the wrong track, my dear Doyle. Monsieur Challenger guessed right away that this is unlike anything in our experience. What bird do you think this claw came from?"

"I wouldn't know."

Challenger's smoldering look deterred me from pursuing that line of reasoning. I sighed, recovered the fatal claw, and rose.

"Let us go and visit the scene of the crime then!"

More than a simple reprieve after the heat, summer evenings in Toulouse boast a charm of their own. The waning light lends a unique hue to the red bricks it caresses. Near the river blows a soothing breeze and the Garonne's banks entice the day's last strollers. I rejoiced in pointing out to my visitors the graceful nudes of the Beaux-Arts Academy's marble facade, as well as the numerous private mansions along the cobblestoned avenues.

But Doyle proved uninterested in architecture and Challenger was hurrying as if to keep an appointment with Old Nick himself. The young beauties who brushed by with their parasols did not succeed in distracting him. When we reached the Pont Neuf, I resolved to hail a cab. It dropped us behind the Hôtel-Dieu, at one end of a narrow and winding street that opened directly onto the river's bank.

The street was lined with abandoned houses, their windows barred with thick wooden planks. Since the last epidemic, no one felt like living this close to the hospital. My fellow citizens still remembered the days when the dead went downstream aboard requisitioned barges to be burned far from the city, atop immense pyres. And we were right by one of the loading docks used for that gruesome work.

"Desnoyer was found in a courtyard by the water," I said as we went through a porchway. "This very one!"

When she heard these words from me, a young woman whose face was hidden by a mourning veil turned around, uttering a stifled cry. My companions halted and Doyle took off his hat, bowing formally.

Where the body had lain on a bed of rough cobblestones, a hand had set down a wreath of freshly-cut flowers, tied with a speckled band of black velvet. It was no doubt the young woman's own shapely hand which had tended to this forlorn task before our arrival on the scene.

"You were a friend of his, I presume?" I said, after presenting my companions and myself.

"No, Monsieur le Professeur!" The stranger drew herself up proudly. "I am Irène Ader-Desnoyer. I was... I am his wife."

She raised her veil. Her magnificent green eyes, lined with long, fluttering lashes, glistened with tears. Her brow and her cheeks still bore a touch of the pallor granted by an unexpected shock. The sorrow she bore with such dignity did not detract from her beauty ; on the contrary, it lent her a unique charm. I could well understand how she had entranced my ill-fated collaborator. But why had he kept her existence a secret?

"Michel often spoke of you," she whispered, as in response to my thoughts. "He wanted to keep our marriage a secret as long as his situation was not secure. I can reveal all, now: I am denizen of the stage, a mere artist who did not fit in the scientific world he was a part of!"

"I assume you're a singer, Madame?" Doyle asked. "I can see the first bars of a musical score in your bag, but your hands exhibit none of the common deformities of musicians. In England, I assure you that the singing profession is a perfectly respectable one."

"The local public is less forgiving, sir... And no favor is shown to those men who marry women like me. If Michel had been content with a mistress, a kept woman, he could have shown me off in public, as a trophy of sorts. He chose to marry me in secret. He loved me, I know it."

"We will avenge him," I said, nodding. "My friends here came to help me solve the mystery of his death. If you will allow it, we will explore this place to look for clues."

"You will find nothing! The monster who did this is already back in his lair, where no one will dare to pursue."

"So you know who it was," Doyle said. "I suppose…"

He was interrupted by Challenger's exclamation. The professor had set a knee on the ground to get a closer look at the wreath lying on the cobblestones. He pulled out a flower of the deepest red, streaked with purple, and he pointed it at the young widow. "This, my lady," he said, brandishing the flower like a sword, oblivious to the grotesque pose he was striking, "deserves an explanation. *Oncidium*, the giant species from the high Amazonian plateaus. What in the Devil's name is going on here?"

I do not know if it was the profanity or the sudden reminder of her loss, but the young woman suddenly started sobbing. Doyle, ever the British gentleman, looked away embarrassedly.

"We are very sorry," I said, trying to soothe her. "Our friend is a bit high-strung."

"No," she said, choking. "He's right! I haven't said a word to anybody. I was scared of being laughed at. Only my brother Clément knows. He's a scientist, but he is not a skeptic, like so many."

"Please believe, my dear child…"

She stopped me with a single resolute gesture, drawing from her sleeve a linen kerchief to dry her tears.

"Promise that you will listen to me and I'll tell you everything I know. Even if my story seems quite mad, I will swear on what I hold most sacred that it is as true as the Gospel."

Without releasing the orchid, Challenger bowed before the young woman and answered, more respectful than I had ever expected to see him:

"Please forgive my deplorable manners, Madame. I can assure you that your account will have no listener more devoted than myself."

She thanked him with a nod. Behind her, the cupola of the Hôtel-Dieu blushed rosily in the sunset, not unlike an upturned woman's breast naked to the sky. On the other side of the Garonne, Saint-Sernin erected a phallic church tower above the surrounding roofs. The town of Toulouse is a true hermaphrodite, a proud and secret city, entrusted every evening with its share of mysteries to be scattered by the first rays of sunrise.

A flock of sparrows streaked by, and I could hear in their songs the first intimations of the summer's end.

"Michel was mad for orchids," the young woman began. "When our liaison began, when I knew I'd found the man I'd been waiting for all my life, I already feared that his passion for those confounded flowers would stand between us. He spent most of his free time hunting for them and I finally resolved to come along in order to see more of him. The poor man even believed I'd grown to share his passion.

"We're not rich, and it was unthinkable that Michel would buy from rare flower merchants the expensive blooms he coveted. He had to make do with the common varieties that grow in and around Toulouse, in secret spots known only to connoisseurs. However, he came home one day in an extraordinary state, holding tenderly a flower such as I had never seen before.

" 'Look, look!' he told me. 'An exotic from a hot-house that has managed to survive under our latitudes! I've discovered an old abandoned house above the old sandstone quarries. It's filled with the most unlikely plants. I wonder what collector used to live there... I'll have to ask around!'

"I didn't know it then, but this flower was to seal his fate. The place he had discovered"–she pointed to the crumbling walls of the building which occupied one side of the courtyard, by the water–"had an amazing history. It was built over one of the oldest underground sand-stone quarries. Tunnels dug as far back as the Middle Ages led to its cellar. Or to this very courtyard."

We looked where she was looking. A shadow-filled opening, half hidden by grass growing wild, yawned by the farthest wall. I caught sight of a stretch of rope tied to a rusty ring set in the corner stone.

"It is said the Cathars hid in the caves underneath Toulouse after the fall of Montségur and that they dug all the way to Hell. It is said Fermat, the mathematician, left in these tunnels secrets of geometry bound up with the nature of God. He lived here, you know... But people say so many things!"

"Michel was too reasonable to swallow such ridiculous tales," I smiled in spite of myself.

"Michel is dead, Monsieur le Professeur. Killed by the curse of this awful place. People like you, who dig into the layers of the past, should be scared of unearthing the deepest myths of Mankind. This is the century of Steam and Electricity: some things should remain buried. One day, the same curse will strike archaeologists who dare to disturb even the millennia-old sleep of the mummies!

"I tell you this, because I have seen, with my own eyes, things nobody would credit. There, in the gallery Michel convinced me to explore with him."

She stopped to search our faces for a sign of doubt. I believe that any expression of skepticism on our part would have caused her to break off her story once and for all. But Challenger nodded gravely:

"I have just returned from Mongolia, Madame, and the natives of those lands share your views on all points. I learned not to dismiss their warnings."

"Michel heeded them not, alas! In the course of his explorations, he delved farther and farther, armed with a paraffin lamp and a mere walking stick. One day, I saw him come back in a state of utter exaltation, with an armful of orchids. He had discovered an unimaginable place which he absolutely wanted me to see.

"I followed him, fool that I was. We had hardly entered the darkness when a bloodcurdling roar echoed before us. It was as if all the night's terrors had come together into one lone cry. Then, there was another, closer yet. Michel dropped our only lamp, which shattered upon impact. He yelled for me to go back outside and I ran without looking to see if he was following me."

She buried her face in her hands. Doyle looked skeptical, which did not surprise me greatly. On the other hand, Challenger appeared to be prodigiously interested. His gaze wandered from the young woman to the entrance of the underground world, as if he expected an army of ghosts to issue any minute now from the pit.

"What can I tell of the horror of the following minutes?" Irène whispered. "I ran in the darkness and I got lost. The screams behind me grew dimmer, but the dark still clung to me like a spider's web. My arms before me,

I walked onward, unable to spot the precious light of the entry well.

"A miracle saved me then. A light appeared in the darkness, a glowing dot floating in mid-air, shining with a distant radiance. I followed it, unable to catch up to it, but it led me to another exit by the riverbank. Once there, it vanished from my sight. But I do not doubt that I was guided by a kindly spirit out of that hellish place!"

"I must disagree with you there," Doyle said. "Your spirit was probably a will-o'-the-wisp, due to the presence of flammable gases. It merely followed a draft toward the nearest exit. A common enough occurrence in old mines. To paraphrase an old friend: only accept the improbable when you have eliminated everything else!

"Not that this explanation detracts from your courage in the least," he hastened to add. "And what did Michel have to say of your adventure?"

"I never saw him again," she answered with a sob. "I waited for hours by the entry well, before going home, beset by worry, as you can imagine. A police constable came later with the terrible news, but I think I already feared the worst, in the bottom of my heart."

"And you didn't see anything?" Doyle persisted. "The slightest detail could put us on the trail..."

"Only that horrible cry, but it was enough to convince me." She turned to me, her voice rising. "My husband's killer is a beast more terrible than all the wild animals of your museum, Monsieur le Professeur. I've sworn to hunt it down without mercy. I may only be a woman, but I will not let it go on and kill again."

"An admirable sentiment!" Challenger said, without a hint of irony. "Let me assure you, Madame, of my sympathy, and offer my wholehearted support."

His rough manner had mellowed noticeably, but I suspected it was no more than a lull. Through the beard extending over two thirds of his face, I could see his mouth quirking doubtfully, while his penetrating gaze ranged over the entire courtyard, looking for the answer to a question he alone had asked.

"May I see again the item you showed us, Professor?" he said suddenly, putting out his hand. "I'm almost inclined to regret my earlier skepticism. I have the glimmers of an idea or two... The whole affair is impossible, of course, but an Englishman starts off the day by believing six impossible things before breakfast."

I gave him the claw, a bit surprised by his turnaround. He raised it in the air, bathing it in the last of the light. His rough-hewn hands seemed strangely out of place, too primitive to stand in front of the ochre rooftops, seamed with the delicate pink of sun-splashed bricks.

"We will hunt with you, Madame, if you let us," Challenger announced with a sonorous voice. "Professeur, I'm sorry I lost my temper. I have made too many enemies among my colleagues and my suspicions are easily aroused. My theories are misunderstood by those fools, but this time they will be shown up once and for all...

"Doyle, and you, Picard," he added abruptly, "do you have anything suited to big game hunting? I fear I left my guns in London."

Doyle shook his head, and I did likewise. In a few minutes, this amazing young man had gained such a hold over us that I found myself ready to let him take charge of the next phase of operations.

"A pity! We will have to be content with a simple scouting expedition, when night falls. Yet, this case must be brought to a quick resolution, for I feel that worse may yet be to come."

"I must sing tonight," the young woman announced after a pause. "It's the next to last performance of the 'Night Orchid' and I'm in the first rank of the choristers. If I leave, I risk being let go. Wait for me by the stage exit, after the show. My brother will be there too."

"Are you really sure?" I protested. "The danger…"

"Michel thought I deserved the best he could offer, Monsieur le Professeur. I will not betray his trust in me."

She lowered her veil and bent to rearrange the wreath at her feet. It was clearly time to leave her alone. When we stood again on the Pont Neuf, whose brick and stone arches spanned a river reduced to a trickle by the drought, I tried to look for the house we'd found among the jumble of roofs around the Hôtel-Dieu. But I could not find it, as if our meeting place already belonged to a bygone era.

"The sound is superb," Doyle remarked as we left the opera house amid the throng of music-lovers. "And the Orchid is truly divine. What a voice!"

"I don't know," I said. "That way she has of lingering on the high C far longer than what Bellini asked for shows a certain impudence. Like a bird of prey defying its rivals when it fights for a mate."

"You have too much imagination, Professor," Challenger sniffed. "But the comparison is apt nonetheless."

The Capitole Square was aglow with the radiance of the gaslights whose yellowish haloes were reflected in the mirrors of the *cafés*. The bustling arcades filled to overflowing by evening strollers did not surprise an old

Toulouse hand like me, but it seemed to dismay Challenger. He had refused to put on evening wear in the teeth of Doyle's pleas–Doyle himself was in uniform. Challenger and I made for an astonishing contrast, me with walking stick in hand, moving with the unhurried pace appropriate to my age and rank in society, while he forged ahead like a young bull, trying to batter his way through a compact mass of bodies that refused to yield. In my city, rhythm is key. Walking among Toulouse strollers is a subtle art I know well. But how was I to teach the finer points of dawdling to an Englishman just back from remotest Mongolia?

The stage exit opened onto a small square occupied by a public park, well-known for its lovers and pick-pockets. Coming closer to the door defended by a watchman in uniform, I noticed a man looking up at the moon, hands locked behind his back. A thick moustache adorned his face as if to compensate for a receding hairline. When we approached, he seemed to awake as if from a dream.

"Professor Picard?" he inquired tentatively. "I'm Clément, Irène's brother. I've come to help, if you let me."

"We will be happy to, sir," I answered, bowing. "Your presence is more than welcome. Here are my friends, Doyle, and young Challenger. We are at your service."

"Much obliged. Irène should be out soon! To tell you the truth"–his voice lowered so much that we strained to hear his whispers–"I am worried about her. I tried to change her mind about coming, but she doesn't listen to me even though I'm the eldest."

"Opera is a harsh taskmistress," Doyle pronounced. "She has the *tempérament artistique*, as you French say.

But don't worry, we will have no trouble keeping her out of harm's way."

A rising hubbub behind the door preceded the exit of the first performers. Traditionally, the divas come out last, long after the crowd of extras and the musicians not of the first rank. I knew the Night Orchid would still be holding court in her dressing room, filled with flowers and admirers. If circumstances had been different, I might have stopped by to pay her homage, even though I had not been entirely seduced by her rendition. Scientific accuracy be damned, a lie to a woman as beautiful as the Orchid didn't count.

"Here comes my sister," Clément warned us. "Not a word about my worries, please, she'd have a laughing fit!"

We stepped aside to let a gaggle of young debutantes file out, all aflutter over their first meeting with a diva. Irène rushed out next, a cape hanging from her shoulders and the remnants of stage paint like clouds on her brow. She greeted us with a quick nod–though I noticed with displeasure that she reserved a coquettish pout for Challenger–and seized her brother by the arm. She led us toward the Garonne along Pargaminière Street. The crowd of strollers cleared quickly and we were alone by the time we reached Saint-Pierre Bridge. Night reigned unchallenged over the opposite bank, a hostile territory of impenetrable shadows.

"We're unarmed," I warned her while trying to keep up with her. "We won't run any unnecessary risks."

"Well, not I," she said, surprising us by taking a twin-barreled Webley from under her cape, the metal gleaming in the glow of the gaslights. "Please stop taking me for a defenseless creature, Professor. This is the nineteenth century!"

"Irène, you promised me you would be reasonable," her brother chided. "What must these gentlemen be thinking?"

A passing coach picked up speed when the coachman caught sight of the weapon, the clattering wheels louder than the horse's clipclop over the cobblestones. Challenger sniffed disdainfully and put out his hand.

"What sort of ammunition?"

"I'm loaded for boar. Our gunshops don't carry anything bigger. There are no tigers in the vicinity."

"We may scare the beast, but we won't even wing it, except by good fortune. Give me that!"

He grabbed the gun rather roughly, ignoring Irène's startled cry. Standing tall on his powerful legs, his beard already disarranged, he trained it on the Moon in one single motion.

"Look!" he shouted with a curse. "And tell me I'm not mad!"

We looked up. Across the silvery orb lighting the sky like a lantern, glided the shape of a monstrous bird, its wings razor-sharp. An endless beak seemed to be just an extension of the thin neck, the hide mottled and soot-colored. A protruding yellow eye cast an evil glance in our direction. An aura of malevolent strength radiated from the beast, reinforced by the dents of the cranium left over from uncountable battles to the death. Gleaming darkly, sinister claws dangled from the outthrust legs. One was broken.

The pterodactyl, for it was now impossible to call it otherwise, dived toward the maze of red roofs on the far side of the Garonne. Challenger almost let off a shot, but he was too good a hunter to overestimate his chances of hitting the mark from so far off. Instead of which, he started to run, gun in hand. Stunned, we watched him race away, heading for the first houses.

A deep, long-contained, elephant-like trumpeting rose from his mighty chest, when he shouldered the gun in mid-stride and fired, just as the monster was disappearing from our sight.

The pterodactyl bucked in mid-air. A cry of defiance, the most terrifying it was ever given me to hear, tore through the dark. It climbed ever higher and then clung to a perfect note, as pure as the lament of a crystal shattering. Doyle was the first to react:

"In the Queen's name, Picard, we must destroy this monster!"

"Challenger must have scored a hit," I said. "But I fear its hide is just too thick for our bullets."

My young colleague was striding back toward us, swinging the Webley at the end of one long arm. He shook his head.

"You're right, Professor, it was no more than a love pat for such a beast. It will be back."

Doyle shook his head somberly.

"Why should it come back? If we only knew what drew it out of its lair tonight, we could set a trap for it, but–"

"I think I know," Irène said quietly. "It came out to listen to the Orchid."

Her brother stared at her with an incredulous expression that might have been comical in other surroundings. Once more, Challenger surprised us:

"I bow before your superior ear, my lady. I wouldn't swear the cry of this fowl from Hades was a high C, but if you say so, I can well believe it."

Doyle nodded doubtfully:

"How can you be so certain?"

"Elementary, my dear Doyle. I've simply noticed that the date of poor Michel's death followed right on the heels of the first recital of the Night Orchid. Remember the posters we saw outside the station. And then I observed the pterodactyl was coming from the Capitole's direction when it overflew us. Yet, such a nocturnal beast should flee the lights of the city. Therefore, it must have had a powerful reason to be over there. And there was its cry... Isn't it passing strange, my friends, that the composers of today's operettas are merely imitating the love calls of extinct species?

"Did I say extinct?" His voice trailed as the true scope of our discovery became clear to us. When he turned back to me, we shared in the same excitement. "You were already famous, Professor Picard, but your present repute will be as nothing soon. Your Museum will turn back visitors when we hang the corpse of our monstrous ancestor from its rafters. And I fully expect to be the one to bring it down!"

"Speaking of which," I said, trying to keep a cool head in trying circumstances, "we French have a saying that warns against selling the hide of a bear you haven't killed yet. We cannot track it underground: it would flee the light and we would be too exposed in the dark. As for bringing it down in mid-flight... We don't have the appropriate weapon and I can't help you get any. I only hunt butterflies."

"We know where it's hiding and we know how to make it come out," he interrupted me with his usual rudeness. "Just give me a chance to find something more than this popgun and load it for elephant. I will camp out on your opera house's roof till it shows up. One shot, just give me one clear shot at it!"

"Alas, Monsieur," Irène said, "the last recital of the Orchid is tomorrow. The diva has promised to hold her high C until her breath fails. That will be our last chance to avenge my husband, I fear."

Challenger seemed thunderstruck. He gazed at the Webley, which seemed no more than a toy in his powerful fist and he muttered:

"Tomorrow? All is lost! Unless… we ambush it in mid-air, face to face… A balloon! Can we get one by tomorrow, Professor? Here, in Pilâtre de Rozier's hometown, there is surely…"

I was shaking my head commiseratingly. When it comes to the sport of kings, the English are given to bouts of temporary insanity. It's no use reasoning with them, so I turned to Irène Ader.

"I'm afraid, my dear lady…"

"No!" she cried out. "There is a solution. Clément, I beg you, speak! The secret is moot, now that the War Ministry knows about your invention. Can't you see this is the ideal occasion?"

I can still see us in that instant, stopped in the middle of the bridge under which the Garonne stretched its silver curls in the moonlight. Doyle stood back, looking dubious. Irène, carried away by her artistic and womanly impulsiveness, had fallen to her brother's feet to implore I knew not what favor. And Challenger, his gaze on the roofs of the opposite bank, was surely pondering the lost worlds hidden beyond the surface of things, in remote jungles or in the labyrinths excavated by men.

"Speak, speak!" Irène exclaimed. "These men are our friends. If you won't do it for me, please do it for Michel…"

This last adjuration overcame the engineer's reservations. He helped her up tenderly and held her at arm's length. A smile bloomed in the thick moustache's shadow.

"Irène is right. To fight such a monster, all good men must come together. I will ask for your solemn vow, gentlemen, that you will not breathe a word of what you will discover at my place before the French War Ministry makes it public."

Doyle automatically straightened his uniform's lapels before swearing solemnly, with the rest of us chorusing dutifully.

"Let's meet tomorrow morning at my home," Ader said. "If you still wish to fight this evil bird in the air, I have something that could help you."

We parted on Ader's enigmatic promise, heading for the gas-lit heart of the city. I could still hear the high-pitched lament of the pterodactyl and I suspect my companions were also haunted by its keening. None of us slept soundly that night.

A rented trap took us out of Toulouse, toward Muret. Ader lived in a farm on the heights, behind a tall row of elms. Rows of grapevines crisscrossed the hillsides, already heavy with purplish grape bunches. The grape harvest promised to be a memorable one.

Ader waited for us in a barn away from the garden. The large wooden doors were locked and we had to slip inside through a narrow backdoor. Shafts of golden light came through the roof and threw tawny shadows over the wooden troughs and baskets hanging by their leather handles. In one corner, glass bottles were stacked horizontally behind a low wall of hay bales. In the middle of the packed earth floor, a gigantic vampire bat peered out of a cloud of dust motes.

I must confess I was taken aback. The shape of the mechanical animal–that, at least, was obvious–loomed menacingly in the half-light. Six meters in length, with a wingspan just under fifteen meters, its front flaunted a conical protrusion crowned with a bamboo propeller, just like the ones spinning from the ceiling of Indian palaces to refresh the local maharajahs. Black silk covered the wings' wood frame. The result looked like something out of a paleontologist's nightmares.

Doyle, on the other hand, was instantly won over. He walked around the giant bat, an admiring cast to his features, and he bent to look over the cockpit carved inside the animal's spine, with its handful of primitive instruments. Softly but firmly, Ader pulled him back:

"Allow me to keep my little secrets. This is the *Éole*. I will use it to prove to the Académie's scientists that it is indeed feasible to fly with a heavier-than-air craft!"

"Feh," Challenger sniffed. "Is this the chiropter you're hoping to use to fight the pterodactyl on its own ground, so to speak?"

"Are you an engineer, sir?"

"I am an Englishman," he replied as if that were enough.

"The *Éole* has a 20 horsepower motor; the wings are patterned after those of the bat," Ader explained swiftly. "Victor Hugo said it best when he spoke of craft built using the power of number and imagination. With it, I will throw the skeptics into confusion, even the English. But that's neither here nor there. We must take the *Éole* to Toulouse in a covered wagon and find a take-off location sufficiently high up to let us get close to the pterodactyl. I'll fly, you shoot."

"The Museum's roof is nearly flat," I said, "and it can be reached through the great skylight of the main gallery. There's a winch we can use. But I fear…" I racked my brains to find a polite way of putting it. "But I'm afraid my worthy colleague's stature will result in an excessive load for your craft. The two of you together will never leave the ground!"

Silence filled the barn. Ader was too good an engineer not to recognize I was right.

"Therefore, you've got until tonight to teach me how to handle it," Challenger pronounced. "I will not turn back when we're so close to success."

Doyle exclaimed:

"Spoken like a genuine hothead, George! Your courage is beyond doubt… but this is sheer madness. Please think for a minute that…"

"Pffft!" Challenger was striding back and forth in the barn, combing through his heavy beard with his fingers. "The field outside is perfectly suited for a test flight. If, and I insist, if that contraption takes off, it will carry me aloft tonight. Let's fill the machine's tank and let's go!"

He stepped over the row of hay bales in front of the stacked bottles. Ader yelled out:

"Wait, man! That's my private stock of marc brandy. It would blow the *Éole* to smithereens if you tried to use it as a fuel."

Challenger stopped. His huge shape bending over the flasks resembled that of an angry God ready to smite its unfortunate creations.

"There's enough in there to leave a Horse-Guards regiment reeling," he said, glancing admiringly at Ader. "Ah, the French…"

"One of my neighbors has a still and sets aside part of his production for me. I've stored everything here. I'm the only one who can get in." The engineer headed for the main door, which he opened with a key. "Let's get the *Éole* outside. The alcohol store for the motor is outside, under an awning."

When we headed back for Toulouse, in the waning afternoon, we had with us a wagon such as the produce sellers use.

The uncanny shape of the *Éole* was hidden beneath a tarpaulin, the wings folded and the propeller disassembled. We followed the towpath of the canal into town and reached the Museum just as the sun was setting behind the avenue's private mansions. Charlus had already left, but I had no trouble finding him in the Saint-Michel Alehouse, vast and noisy. For a gold napoleon, he helped us to haul the machine up on the roof, without asking a single question. Years spent dusting the skeletons of the Paleontological collections had slowly eroded his sense of curiosity.

"The worst is over," I said, wiping my forehead while my companions were putting the propeller back in its place. "Thank God! I'm too old to roam the roofs like a chimney sweep, even if the view is superb…"

Challenger performed a slow scan of the skyline, his hand shading his eyes.

"A sea of red tiles," he stated, "and not a lighthouse to show me the way. It would be easier to find my way in a jungle."

"The Capitole is over there. Bear right for the Saint-Sernin church tower and you'll end up over it without fail. The pterodactyl will be coming from over there." I pointed to the Hôtel-Dieu's dome. "If you time it well, you can intercept it over the river."

"As long as I know when to take off…"

"I own an excellent pair of German binoculars."

"The hide of this damned bird is too dark ; it will merge with the night sky. Binoculars would be useless. No, we'll have to trust to Lady Luck, and she's a fickle mistress, Professor."

Before climbing down, we stretched a sheet over the *Éole*. With its bat wings now extended and sheathed in white, it looked like a fallen angel. The setting sun saved its last rays for our ill-assorted group while, fifteen meters below, the massing crowd of aficionados prepared to hear the last recital of the Night Orchid.

Irène met us in the *Café des Arts*, on Capitole Square. Ader had advised Challenger not to weigh himself down with a heavy meal before his flight, though he authorized, grudgingly, a single glass of Armagnac. As a consequence, my young colleague was simmering, torn between anticipation of the coming hunt and the hunger gnawing his huge carcass. The young woman's arrival restored his good cheer, but not for long:

"The recital is delayed," Irène announced, sitting down by her brother. "The Orchid is having one of her whims. The public doesn't know it yet, but it's going to have to wait at least an hour to hear its diva."

"The Devil take her!" Challenger exclaimed. "I'd been hoping she would launch into her high C around the same time as yesterday… Our appointment tonight is in jeopardy."

"If the opera house was equipped with my theatro-phone, we could have followed the entire concert from

41

the museum's roof with farspeakers," Ader sighed. "This is madness: the whole plan relies on nothing but improvisation through and through!"

I was inclined to agree. Once more, however, it was Irène who lifted our flagging spirits.

"Do you know how to read a musical score, Monsieur le Professeur?" she asked me, smiling. "If I gave you the full score for tonight's recital, would you be able to follow it, in time, till the moment of the high C?"

I was sorely tempted to say yes, if only not to sadden the magnificent eyes set upon my face. But I had to shake my head.

"In that case, I will have to join you on the roof during the intermission," Irène said, her tone brooking no disagreement. "I will arrange it with the leader of the chorus."

"I'll drink to that," Challenger said.

And he ordered a full flask of Armagnac from the waiter. For the road!

We took up again our observation post above the skylight. As the last of the twilight faded, the Museum grew crowded with ghosts of a distant past. The great reptiles who walked the Earth long before our own glory days shifted their silhouettes along the plaster walls. It only wanted a little imagination to transform an incomplete skeleton into a crouching predator. As paleontologists, we are dreamers by necessity. Our minds are trained to recreate a whole unknown fauna from a few traces left in clay, a tooth or a bone splinter. The noise rising from the streets of Toulouse waned. I sneaked a look at my pocket watch: had the show begun? Challenger, sitting in the *Éole*'s cockpit, was checking the

Webley over for the tenth time. His head and its mass of hair alone emerged from the aircraft's bulk. The wings had been unfolded and the alcohol motor was turning over slowly in expectation of the moment of take-off. The air was still. Doyle was sweeping the horizon with the binoculars, ranging up and down the Garonne's banks. We were all silent, lost in thought.

"Here's my sister," Ader said suddenly, leaning over the parapet.

He helped her to climb the ladder, depriving me of that very same pleasure, and relieved her of the thick score she was carrying.

"Prepare yourselves," she said when she reached the roof. "There's only a few dozen bars left before the Orchid's solo. I'll give you the sign."

Ader revved up his motor, and spun the propeller to check its readiness.

"Don't forget to adjust the airfoils," he muttered. "And God keep you!"

Irène gestured like a maestro. The moment was nigh. Doyle helped the engineer to set out the planks that would let the craft plunge into the void on outstretched wings. Despite the afternoon's demonstration, I still had a hard time believing in such a miracle: a man–an Englishman–was going to slip the bonds of gravity to fight a monster on its own ground. Surely, such whimsy was fit only for the storytelling of a Jules Verne.

"Engage!" Ader shouted.

The propeller started to turn haltingly. An idea came to me suddenly.

"Take a lozenge," I said to Challenger, holding out the circular box that I took everywhere. "It may help you fight the effects of altitude."

A muffled grumbling rose from the cockpit while the man's thick fingers closed on my liquorice provision. Ader then motioned me aside.

"The *Éole* will take off as soon as I pull away the wedges. We'll track it with the binoculars."

"Sixteen bars," Irène warned. "Twelve... Eight... Here's the beginning of the aria!"

We strained to listen, in vain. The Capitole was much too far off. Yet, an imperceptible vibration, an echo of the merest breath, seemed to fill the night air with its call.

"I can see something," Doyle said, straddling the parapet. "Take off now!"

Ader spun the propeller with all his might. The alcohol motor shuddered, releasing plumes of white smoke. We braced ourselves against the machine to push it up the narrow plankway leading to the edge of the building. Which is precisely when the motor started to misfire.

Powerless, we could only try to hold back the *Éole*. The propeller's jolts elicited a stream of curses from Challenger, who was struggling to get clear from the narrow cockpit. Irène had dropped her score and was staring at her brother, a desperate appeal in her eyes, while the slender shadow of the pterodactyl slipped above the river.

"No, I will not!" stormed Challenger, at last able to move freely. "Step back!"

His hand plunged into his pocket. Horror-struck, we saw him take out the bottle of Armagnac which he emptied whole into the tank. Its effect made itself felt almost instantly.

The motor raced. The propeller whined and we felt the *Éole* snatch itself out of our hands. The mad Englishman had figured out how to get a French motor's attention! With outspread wings, the chiropter rushed up the planks and leaped over the roof edge before arcing into the sky like a meteor. We rushed to follow its flight. Handicapped by his weight, Challenger was forced to fly at roof level along Saint-Michel Avenue. But the pterodactyl had too great a headstart. We could see that it would take a miracle to catch it.

Irène Ader surely understood as much. Without soliciting our approval, displaying the same quiet courage we had already been given to admire, she undid the scarf around her neck and breathed deeply.

The first notes of Bellini's aria surged into the night, pure as tears. She sang her love for a husband gone too soon, with unmatched feeling, doubling and trebling the song's power. Her voice gained in confidence and she attacked the crescendo leading up to the high C.

"What a woman," Doyle couldn't help whispering. "Even our mutual friend, however little he prizes the fair sex, would fall under her spell…"

"The pterodactyl too," I replied. "Look, it's coming toward us!"

Even with Irène Ader's unexpected help, the pterodactyl might have escaped us if the *Éole*'s motor hadn't started to throw off sparks. The Armagnac had surged into the tubing and set off a series of explosions, kicking the aircraft forward. Thus it was that we saw Challenger surge over the river in the midst of a veritable fireball, like a modern-day St. George astride a dragon. We distinctly heard his cry of victory when he positioned the airfoils to charge straight for the monster.

The beast wasted no time in beating back toward its lair. Uncaring for his own safety, Challenger followed, the Webley outstretched before him like a lance. I guessed he was trying to hit the pterodactyl's enormous eye. The *Éole* was behaving superbly, but its canvas and bamboo construction had never been meant to withstand such speeds. When the beast reached the far bank and dived for the tunnel whence it had come, the flames had crept all the way to the wingtips.

"We must help him," Ader shouted at us. "Come, Picard!"

We rushed down and stopped a cab, elbowing aside a couple of peaceful burghers unaware of the ongoing drama in the sky above Toulouse. We promised the coachman the tip of a lifetime, but the last act was already being played out when we neared the walls of the Hôtel-Dieu...

The *Éole* was no more than a ghost of charred wood unable to stay aloft. The pterodactyl, realizing this, uttered a scream of undiluted malevolence and trained its rapier-sharp beak on the unfortunate Challenger. My colleague then made an inconceivably reckless choice: instead of trying to evade it, he propelled what was left of his flying machine right into the monster's maw.

The impact hurled them down to the ground, still embraced. We saw them vanish behind the nearby skyline like a comet and we heard the clatter of a very hard landing.

Doyle jumped from the coach and ran toward the site of the crash. I poured a handful of coins into the hands of the stunned coachman, who held me fast by the sleeve:

"Not so quick, my good sir! What's all this deviltry?"

"An Englishman," Ader said slowly. "A marvelous man in a flying machine."

The coachman shrugged and snapped his whip.

"The English–they don't know how to drink," he stated sententiously, before heading home.

Drawn by Doyle's shouts, we found Challenger trapped in the *Éole*'s wreckage. The chiropter had crashed into the old house over the quarries, bringing down part of the roof and most of one wall. The shock-wave had made itself felt underground, collapsing the passageways and forever burying the door to the secret depths whence the pterodactyl had come.

Of the latter, not a trace.

The *Éole*'s prow, in transfixing a roof beam, had saved my unfortunate colleague's life. Notwithstanding a bloody and swollen nose, and sundry cuts to the head, he had survived a fall that would have killed anybody but him. Moving carefully, he was able to get out of the crushed cockpit and jump down to the ground.

"The bloody bird got away, Professor!" he apologized as soon as he saw me. "I'm an imbecile, a jackass. I missed it!"

"Please don't be so hard on yourself," Irène said, picking up something in the courtyard's ruins, near the now collapsed pit.

She put out her hand. In her delicate palm, there lay a claw, with a scrap of flesh still attached to one end.

"Even if it has survived, it will no longer hurt anybody. Michel is avenged!"

"I would have liked to do more," Challenger growled. "I would…"

"Please say no more, sir," Irène whispered.

She added under her breath:

"Now that you know such creatures exist, you will surely hunt them down to the ends of the world. I won't follow you… My brother needs me to rebuild his *Éole* and other arias await. We will soon be going on tour in Bohemia. I will change my name somewhat and be forgotten. But I will think of your courage every time I sing and if my voice reaches as high as you did tonight, it will be thanks to you."

Challenger bowed. In spite of his cuts, of his torn clothes, and of his beard streaked with plaster dust, he appeared to us that night like a hero out of legend.

"I will hear you sing in my dreams," he said.

The Parliament of Birds

For Wildy, who understands the geometry of stories…

When the Gardens were created, they were nine hundred and fifty in all.

A highly confidential Space Agency program had selected them from all over the Solar System. Among the list of questions handed to all children in the targeted age bracket, there were three hooks, three deliberately banal ways to phrase the same query:

Is there an imaginary place which belongs only to you and where you can go when you need to?

If the answer was yes, yes, and yes again, the child received special questionnaires for the next five years, under various false pretences. At that point, the number of rejected candidates grew frighteningly fast. As children mature and lose their center, they also learn how to say no. After the first year of triage, fewer than a million names were left. After the third, fewer than ten thousand.

Failure helped to ensure the project's secrecy. The initial team dwindled as funding was whittled back. Until it all came to an end, with a final ranking of names carefully secured within a file folder.

One year later, the file disappeared. It was replaced with another, provided with a list of perfectly normal children chosen at random. Then, a few months later, the children from the original list disappeared forever.

Of the initial nine hundred and fifty, six survived training. Six male children. *The Brotherhood of Birds.* The names came later: Hummingbird, Kingfisher, Bullfinch, Robin, Sparrow and Woodpigeon. Old Olechinski, their common mentor, naturally enough called himself Raven.

They needed two years to complete the first stage of their training, but only the first fifteen minutes really counted. Tied down inside a coldsleep cradle, each abducted child had been injected with a massive dose of memwipe...

Memwipe was the early twenty-first century by-product of an idealistic crusade for a more humane justice system–a designer drug that reduced the mind of condemned criminals to a blank slate. The mindless body, equipped with the basic survival functions and an elementary composite personality, paid for its crime in whatever way it still could.

And so, in a few seconds, the sum total of the memories, hopes and dreams of nine hundred and fifty pubescent children was scientifically erased.

Then, patiently, Olechinski attempted to resurrect them.

He had to find out if the most intimate core of their ego had succeeded in seeking shelter *somewhere* inside the cellular machinery, perhaps in the genetic grottoes of the bone marrow or the liver, in the old alternate RNA encodings, in the impossibly small fraction of synapses spared by memwipe... Tirelessly, Olechinski sought the survival instinct of the mind's *I*.

There were nine hundred and forty-four failures. And six survivors.

"It's a kind of mutation," Raven told his flock before sending them away. "You are your own, personal compass; you cannot get lost."

"Like migratory birds?"

The name stuck. The first injection was followed with many others, until six birds learned how to hide behind cover identities, hiding and coming out at the opportune moment, for a fraction of a second. A carefully chosen key word was enough to tear through the layers of artificial memories which protected their ego. For two years, they withstood the innumerable deaths they were lovingly subjected to by Raven. Nothing could mar the flawless crystal of their memories.

And then, eight months were enough to turn them into accomplished killers.

Hummingbird was the most eager of the six. He asked few questions but demanded real answers. He was the first to speak of their *destiny,* to try and find out why they had been sought out.

When the question was asked, Raven was sharpening the blades of pruning shears with a whetstone. He tested the cutting edge against the ball of his thumb before severing a stem with a sharp snap. Then he smiled at the faces gathered around him in a semi-circle:

"The originators of the project wanted to make you into the first interstellar explorers. Your gift would have allowed you to face the centuries of travel through the void which separates us from the stars, and to survive coldsleep itself–or rather the subsequent awakening when all memories are destroyed. But too few of you were left to carry out the project as planned, whereas I dreamed all my life of having children like you. You are my birds, my phoenixes. Regret nothing…"

Olechinski was a master assassin. He had gifted them with beaks and claws while offering them a nest. Yet, none of the six, not even Hummingbird, was ever able to figure out if the old man was one of them.

Their beginnings were wildly promising, the way adolescence usually is. It was an auspicious time: Ell-One was almost finished, and prospectors were racing metal spiders implanted with AI modules across the sands of Mars. Water from the Martian permafrost flowed through pressurized underground canals, tapped by the bubblecars driving through the reddish plateaus. The military base on Phobos had gone rogue in the blink of an eye and was swapping information from its classified databases for mining concessions. The infosphere hummed with talk of bridges to link binary asteroids, of inhabited silicon arks, of iron mountains dragged by solar sails. Every consortium boasted at least one arcology; every businessperson claimed a volume of virgin space to strip and shape as they wished.

The immense majority of humankind, however, continued to be born and die on Earth, sticking to the tried and true ways of doing so.

Olechinski was rich with a mysterious wealth upwelling from hidden springs, every time he needed it. Yet, the profession of assassin had become obsolete: *all* blood crimes were punished with a mandatory and total mind wipe of the guilty party.

Murders still occurred among the poorer classes. Higher up, where everybody is on a first name footing and where there are more security systems than people to protect, they had become the exception. And exceptions, in a mass production universe, were tremendously expensive to procure...

Olechinski's Birds killed one person per year and were unfailingly caught. The trial, expedited with all due haste, always reached the expected verdict.

After the memwipe treatment, a charity fronting for one of Raven's companies recovered the wailing assassin, his gaze blank. A facial remodeling, a whispered code word to awaken him, and the job was done. The phoenix rose from his ashes.

Between their rare sallies, the Birds played in the greenhouses carved inside the heart of an asteroid of the second Mars belt. Olechinski was an obsessive gardener, driven to conduct perpetual experiments with nature. Inside the rocky cylinder half a kilometer long, a layer of fertile soil went all the way round, a living carpet enriched with hundreds of children's bodies. Every inch of available space was planted with roses flaunting gigantic blooms. The air was saturated with pollen that kept clogging the filters of the recycling units. One of the most tedious daily chores Hummingbird had ever been assigned was the cleaning of the filter membranes. There is something in gardens that resists the intrusions of reality. Raven's garden was strange and luxuriant, a labyrinth of greenery where up and down meant nothing. Its smell was especially impudent. The flowers and their fleshy petals lived at perpetual peak, knowing an eternal noontime which exhausted them and wilted them too soon. It was ever necessary to cut, prune, uproot. The ground was littered with dead roses, scorched by the glare of the artificial sun suspended in the middle of the chamber.

According to legend, Olechinski had ended his forays in order to devote all of his time to his gardening. The perfect killer turned into the equivalent of a Zen master dedicated to preserving fragility incarnate. It had mythic resonance, a classic story that was also effective– but perhaps too symmetric. Before absconding, Hummingbird had had the chance to wonder if it was indeed the case.

Two decades had passed since then. The fledgling had felt strong enough to fly away, beyond the clutches of Raven. He had tried to lose himself and he thought he had succeeded. He was wrong.

When too many unanswered questions threatened his continued survival, Hummingbird made the only possible choice.

He flew home.

"Hummingbird…" Raven's voice issued from invisible speakers, synchronized with the giant lips spread across the entire wall surface. "I can't believe it, it's really you! Do you know I could have killed you at least ten times?"

The youth, his face worn, managed an empty smile as he sat on the airlock bench.

"You still can… Right now, I sense a dozen weapons trained on me."

"Unpleasant sensation, no? Many necessary things are."

"I never could get used to them." Hummingbird straightened with overemphasized slowness. "I brought you a gift and I came to ask a favor."

"I'm an old man, little Hummingbird. A worried and mistrustful old man. Well, okay, utterly paranoid if you prefer. Your ship ran across my path with twenty-year-old emergency codes blaring. All the transmission channels are silent and there are at least five more ships standing watch within my detection sphere. I thought I'd never be disturbed along this orbit!"

"I hope you love my gift."

"I hope so too…"

With a click, the com unit turned off and the main airlock was plunged in darkness. The teenager who had, over nearly sixty years, borne many names and had forgotten all of them prepared himself for a long wait.

"How are your roses, Raven?" he said out loud. "How is the garden?"

The giant lips on the com wall remained silent. Against the back of his neck, Hummingbird felt the needles of the analysis tray draw a bit of his blood, to identify him. Behind the bulkhead on which he leaned his skull, the recycling system of his ship was chirping sweetly, just barely audible. Before opening the airlock, he had connected by hand his air tanks to the asteroid's air supply, standard operating procedure in emergencies. He wondered how long it would take Olechinski to notice.

"Did you come to kill me?" asked Raven.

Drugs had invaded Hummingbird's nervous system and caged his will. *Always the same old same old,* he thought with a zest of irony. He felt his back muscles slacken and he let himself go. Resistance was futile, cheating impossible.

"No…"

"Don't lie, little bird. I know all your codes, I hold the strings that can make you dance to my tune. Why did you come back?"

"To bring you a gift."

Truth was enough of a weapon. It was the only thing Raven could not defeat.

"Yet, you hate me."

"Of course…"

Hummingbird's eyes closed. He could sleep, or slip into deep trance. He chose to bite his tongue and draw blood. The sharp pain sent him back through the years, to an island of his mindscape which was alive with echoes of his own voice. He heard himself tell the story all over again.

Mars, in the middle of the night.

The negotiating team's bubblecar had reached the Tharsis plateau. Overtopped by the dizzying cliffs in the foothills of Olympus Mons, it covered a few hundred meters every hour, a creeping pace for which the gyroscopic stabilizers could compensate without even trying. Inside, protected from the bitter cold by the vacuum within the double-walled windows, were three of the most powerful men in the Solar System, and me. I was the bubblecar operator, the discreet and unseen servant who only left the cockpit to cook meals. In a sense, that's who I really was. The memory patterning I had been subjected to went so deep that it had erased my entire past. I no longer was one of Olechinski's Birds.

Later, every recess of my mind had been scrutinized and every recess of my body probed. I didn't carry lethal viruses or implanted bugs. My cover personality had passed all their tests with a meekness worth applauding.

I'd agreed to remain naked for the duration, while my clients wore the latest upgrade of individual armor, sheathing their grey skin with an iridescent and indestructible film. There was nothing inside that could serve as a weapon, no way for me to get close enough for a suicide attack. And I looked so... young.

Within the bounds of their imagination, they felt safe.

They had met to divide up the world: three outsized minds, three singularities among the human race, who forged black holes of their own to seek shelter within the event horizon. They hated each other, I suppose, since each one had paid Raven for the death of the two others.

The existence of the bubblecar and its exact route were among the most closely guarded secrets in the Solar System, but, in the course of preparing the assignment, Olechinski had received three lists of handwritten instruction matching in all respects save one: the names of the desired victims. More than the fortunes pledged, it was the symmetry involved, the full play of permutations, which had appealed to Raven and convinced him to accept.

At the time, all that meant nothing to me. I was watching the bubblecar's instruments to find a secondary conduit to tap. Our water supply had dwindled faster than expected and it was not a good idea to keep going in such conditions. The volcanic plain we were crossing was comparatively recent terrain, and therefore low in craters, but the ground was gashed with dust-filled cracks. An accident was always possible.

My nakedness did not bother me. Our clients had no expectations of me and, come to think of it, sex was much too limited a medium for their appetites. They were so used to hiding behind screens and contracts that they no longer even exuded any body odor.

Since the beginning of their meeting, they had engaged in a planetary-scale armwrestling match, with the help of the IA modules and databases that were part of their armor. As for me, I dowsed for water. To each his role.

The network of pressurized canals stretched from the poles and high places of the planet, six meters below the surface. There is water on Mars, in the form either of polar ice or of permafrost. To transport it, insulated tubes are used under a quarter atmosphere pressure, laid inside tunnels dug by millions of primitive machines, so stupid they did not know enough to deviate from their preset course. According to my maps, a minor feeder had been dug not far from our position.

It took me two hours to locate it.

The thirsting probes of the bubblecar bored through the powdery surface layers and fastened upon the nipples of the collector. Somewhere nearby, a water meter counted every drop we took and we would be billed its weight in palladium. That was the least of my worries; my bosses could afford it.

The pumps got to work. I listened to their comforting chug-a-lug long enough to be sure nothing was amiss, and then started to get the meals ready. The sealed pouches were stored in compartments labeled with dates. I pulled the drawer bearing the day's date and tore off the tab.

The pouch was filled with rose petals...

Their smell was a key: it unlocked my memory. A minute later, I came back to life and the old, familiar migraine was drumming its Morse code reminder against my brows. To carry out our assignment, all I had *was a few short moments. I was naked, as defenseless as a newborn babe, but I was a killer bird. So I got down to work.*

Water, Raven. I had nothing, neither weapons nor drugs. There were three of them, and my fingers were too puny for their thick necks. So I doctored the pump circuits and disabled the safeties of the nozzles while my targets divided up the worlds among them.

We were parked at the bottom of a gorge, the walls carved out of red rock veined with darker iron streaks. I went out with the lone survival suit, a protective skin stuck to mine, so thin I could feel the abrasive grit carried by the whistling winds. When the pumps resumed chugging, the water invaded the bubble in a few seconds.

I watched them through the translucid double-layered hull. They got up and fell upon each other. The water was filling the main compartment, while the car's expelled air rained pearls of condensation in the frigid Martian atmosphere. The fighting didn't stop before the end. Not one of them tried to escape. They were choking each other and biting like maddened dogs, while the AI modules of their armor were dying one after the other.

I can still see the water-filled bubblecar. Weighed down by its new cargo, it was swaying ponderously above the sand. The intertwined corpses swirled slowly inside, eyes staring wide. Finally, the nozzles released their hold on the collector and the bubblecar picked up speed.

It was never found.

"Correct," asserted the speakers. "You created the legend of the wandering bubblecar, carrying away the souls of prospectors lost on the dried seas of Mars. The Flying Dutchman of the Red Planet, a brilliant variation on a theme. That's why I chose you, Hummingbird. Your feel for unbalanced harmonies, do you remember? The immutable beauty you granted your murder victims even in death... You had the exact same awareness of roots which characterizes good gardeners and shapers of myths. And you never forgot to make fun of yourself."

"It was much too easy," whispered Hummingbird, gulping down a mix of saliva and blood.

He closed his eyes. Memories continued to scroll inside his head. His oldest curse: he did not know how to lose himself.

The air was so thin no animal could have flown above Mars, but this near lack of an atmosphere brought the stars so much closer that I yearned to pick them. Shining through a faint rust-tinged fog, they wore orange haloes like bloated fruits. I imagined myself inside the bridge of a slowship, torn from my icy coffin by the loving kiss of needle probes, and I sensed my fate was to fly higher and farther than anybody else. The fate you had taken from us, Raven.

The other birds came to meet me. I was going to be arrested in less than two hours by the automatic surveillance craft. It would be months, perhaps years, before we would see each other again. Crossroads of memory, Raven. This was one of them. The bubblecar was heading downhill, with its interlaced corpses. My brothers stood by me, shoulder to shoulder. They all looked like me, ageing so slowly that they seemed trapped in an eternal present which we were the only ones to share. All those years, we had fought, loved, and lied to each other. We had invented secrets and sown the seeds of our future survival within our own flesh, when we thought you weren't looking.

They left one after the other, waving their arms. A craft from the surveillance network was rushing toward me; I had two minutes left. I stopped the life-support's soft gurgling as it injected warm air along my skin.

And I listened to the silence until I was arrested.

"After which you left my flock…"

Raven had entered the airlock without making the slightest noise, as he used to do. A second before, his voice still leapt from the walls, synchronized with the image of a pair of inordinately magnified lips. A second later, his wasted form came forward, shuffling, while the final syllables, deprived of the speakers' resonance, seemed curiously flat and emotionless.

"Let me look at you!"

Hummingbird had risen to his feet. Raven's emaciated body still overtopped him by a head. Olechinski had hardly changed. Traces of colloidal injections pockmarked his neck and cheekbones. Implant scars, almost hidden by the artificial tan of the indoor suns, limned a spiderweb stretching from the corners of his brown eyes to the top of his temples. A deep black ponytail swept down the back of his neck. The rest of his skull was close-shaven.

He was too old to have an age. Dressed in a gardener's smock spotted with green stains, his feet stuck in sandals with suction discs, he looked like a Babylonian slave torn away from his beloved hanging gardens.

"I didn't expect to see you again… In fact, I'd struck you from my tablets when I lost your track." The old man attempted a grimace that he couldn't make look convincing. "What did you do all these years?"

"Nothing special. For a while, I lived off the money I'd managed to steal from you. When that was exhausted, I had to go to work as a free-lance killer on my own account."

"I always thought you hadn't taken enough!"

"That's true, I was wrong to underestimate…" Hummingbird allowed himself a smile. "…not your generosity, but your wealth. I could have taken a hundred times more without making you suffer."

"I did suffer. If you only knew what I pay for my roses!"

The teen bit his lips. The next stage would be decisive.

"Show them to me, Raven," he muttered. "Take me into the garden."

The old man took a key from his pocket, a mere shaft, its dull metal indented with luminescent dots. He twirled it on the end of his forefinger before fitting it to a socket within the bulkhead. With a gentle hiss, the metal partition withdrew inside a floor slot.

"After you!"

Where the hallway ended, another world extended, separated from vacuum by a meager thickness of rock.

Roses ran away in all directions. Paths carved with a machete vainly attempted to bring order to the many-colored masses, bristling with finger-long thorns. Raven gently pushed Hummingbird in the back and watched him walk among the flowers. Neither paid any attention to the scratches streaking their arms.

The air was redolent with heavy scents and the reek of rotting vegetation. A thick sap dripped from the severed ends of stems. Bees buzzed through clouds of pollen.

The light showered by the plasma arcs was dazzling. *Too much.*

"You've let it get worse," said Hummingbird, pensive, wiping on his sleeve the sweat on his brow. It was too warm, too lush. Too alive.

"A natural human tendency." Raven walked through the garden as if to trample it. Fleshy petals stuck to his suit, instantly seared by the protection system. "Gardens cannot be controlled, unless they are castrated from the start. A mistake I refused to make, not even in your case. You should be grateful!"

"Do you want to see my gift?"

"Later, later… I'll send a robot to fetch it from your ship. I don't like the idea of letting you go back aboard alone. And I've also cut off the emergency air supply. You can fill your tanks somewhere else."

Hummingbird shrugged, with a hint of scorn.

"You were afraid I'd poison you."

"Nothing so obvious. I know all your tricks, I'm the one who taught them to you. But I'll still let you go in first."

The path passed beneath a metal archway around which twined climbing roses, their blooms a luminous white. The flowers were enormous, as big as an infant's head. The teen's nostrils tingled with a burst of particularly bitter memories.

"Do you know why I came back?"

"You were being hunted…" Raven pinched with his steel-tipped fingernails the stems topped with withered flowers until they fell at his feet. "I assume there were other reasons, more noble or more devious, but I like the obvious one. There are five ships lying in wait inside my personal volume of space, don't forget."

"The result of a deal gone sour," admitted Hummingbird. "I suppose you would like me to tell you about it?"

"I'm always happy to hear you sing, my little bird."

"You've got one more reason to hear me report; you're the one who hired me for this assignment!"

Dead flowers bounced on the moss, making sounds like deflated balloons. Raven did not look up.

"Well?" Hummingbird grew impatient. "All the data about my failure are in my ship's memory banks. Do you want to have a look?"

"I'd rather you tell me in your own words…"

"You confess, then?"

"Let's say you've piqued my curiosity."

Raven opened his fingers. The tip of his fingernails was sticky with sap. A bee wandered over and buzzed above the open palm, and he closed his hand in one incredibly swift motion. When he unclenched his fingers, the insect's body fell among the petals.

"I'm listening."

Beyond the metal arch, a stretch of bare ground surrounded a roughly-hewn stone bench. Hummingbird sat down, while Raven trudged in circles around him, fondling roses as he passed them by. The teen felt perfumed eddies coil around his neck like feathery scarves. Memories choked him.

He released them.

I was brought in by Lady Ardryce Cervantani as a steward for the family estates of Avantine, which cover an entire island off the coast of Turkey, in the Mediter-

ranean. She had built her experimental greenhouses there, and, since becoming a widow, she had lived there with her daughter and a small team of hand-picked researchers. The assignment surprised me, I'll confess: who would want to wipe out a family of gardeners without the slightest political or financial significance? Even more puzzling, why come to me? I was an expensive hire–not as much as you, Raven, but my fee still amounted to a pretty penny. What I was charging for this assignment would have bought the island from under the feet of the Cervantanis.

My client paid without haggling over the price. Your first mistake. Everyone haggles with killers, Raven; it's how those who pay us avoid thinking about what they're buying. But you never could stoop to it. Yet, if I said it sparked my suspicions, I would be lying. I never guessed, not until the end.

Lady Ardryce herself chose me among a hundred candidates. For two months, I'd put my best experts on her case. I had analyzed her bodily secretions, urine and tears included; I knew everything there was to know of her most intimate chemistry. The pheromone-based perfume I wore that day was a symphony composed for her alone, a love song that she would be the only one to hear. I simply arranged to be among the first interviewed by paying off the appropriate agent.

When I reached the estate, I discovered Lady Ardryce loved roses as much as you.

"That's not hard," Raven interrupted. "What's impossible is to understand them the way I do."

"Maybe that's why you wanted to kill her. She was able to keep on loving them even when they were irre-

65

trievably withered, even if all her gardening experience compelled her to clip the stem so that new blooms could form."

"You spared her?"

"No… I killed her, as well as the others, not long after I came to the island. Just as you wished."

I was the steward. My borrowed personality took care of the estate's finances and of supplies for the scientists. The laboratory set up in the island's center absorbed most of the Cervantani family's revenues. In fact, the family business skirted bankruptcy every day. When I did the accounts, the first time, I checked the results three times and then asked Lady Ardryce for an appointment.

I can still see her in the office where she received me. She was young, a woman who had chosen to bear a child when most put their eggs into cold storage or get somebody else to carry the child to term. This gave an added depth to her gaze; her body had a history of its own.

Pauline, her daughter, was playing in a corner, with a collection of glass paperweights. Crystal flowers of all sorts and sizes; she was arranging bouquets with them on the floor. She was a grave and dignified child, with a gaze that forgot nothing. I hadn't thought of composing a perfume matched to her chemistry and so she utterly ignored me. Sometimes, a paperweight would slip from her tiny hands and ring softly as it struck the floor. There were no other noises inside the room.

Lady Ardryce was busy casting a flower arrangement in transparent resin when I entered. The mold was diamond-shaped and the bouquet, composed around a willow root and a handful of daffodils, was drowning without a whimper in the fast-setting fluid. I watched her work, and then I coughed when she sealed the mold shut.

She laughed when I spoke of money. She knew. Sales of the most beautiful flowers from her green-houses, fresh-cut or crystallized, were not enough to pay the bills. But we didn't need to worry, for her research had finally paid off.

She told me this in hushed, confidential tones, putting a finger to her lips, and I must have looked especially obtuse, for she laughed again and decided to take me on a tour of the estate's heart, where I had never been allowed to go

Thinking back, I believe the smells of the synthetic resin and thermosealant had gone to her head a bit, otherwise she would never have dared open herself to me like she did. Unless the altered chemistry of my body odor was still massaging her pleasure receptors.

The Cervantani greenhouses owed their reputation to the frailty of their inmates. A breath would have blown apart the mutated flowers enclosed in sealed caissons, equipped with remotely operated arms. Painstaking genetic manipulations had progressively shorn them of several layers of plant cells. The translucent leaves trapped light, crisscrossed by silvery capillaries that a burst of laughter would have shattered. They had to be frozen before the infinitely slow robots could pick them.

On the other hand, they were everything one could ask from a flower: a moment of eternity instantly over and done with.

"They were a mistake," whispered to me Lady Ardryce as she slipped her arm around mine. "A mistake to which we owe our wealth. We're torturing these poor things until they're as fragile as our moods and we're

turning them into symbols trapped for all eternity inside fluorocarbon ice. And we sell them for so much that they become valuable!"

"They're priceless, my lady," I said with all the passion my role allowed me to express.

She merely shrugged gracefully. The doors of the labs yielded to her like unsubstantial draperies, despite the steel armor and the eyes of the security sensors. The building was almost deserted, cold, almost completely unadorned. The petrified flowers sprang from metal trays and the halogen lights did not make the air any warmer.

The innermost heart of the greenhouses was an opaque enclosure graced with a single rosebush. A living one.

Hummingbird stopped. Inside the existential jungle the old garden had turned into, the landmarks of his childhood had drowned beneath a sea of thorns. The bees buzzing near his ears seemed like miniaturized spies. He chased them away with an exasperated gesture. The pollen carpeted the filters lining the mucous membranes of his mouth and nose.

"Lady Cervantani would have understood this garden, Raven. You see, I killed her too soon, I didn't have the time to listen to her as I should have. Secrets were lost..."

The old man didn't bat an eyelid. His voice perfectly under control, he whispered:

"Tell me about this rosebush, little bird. Her death can wait."

"Because you were the sponsor, right? It was all too perfect, too symmetrical. When I saw these flowers sway in the faint breeze from the fans, I should have known. I wasn't quick enough!"

"After all these years, can't you spot my signature?"

Hummingbird allowed himself a pout, sadness and relief fighting it out. He'd been waiting for this exact moment ever since the beginning of their confrontation.

"Send a machine to get my gift. It's on my bunk, in a simple preservation jar."

"You've already given much more than you think by coming back here. Your gift is being scanned by my sensor arrays. Please forgive my indiscretion."

The teen bowed with respect-tinged irony. The years had transformed the garden, but they hadn't blunted Raven's intelligence.

"The rosebush," repeated the teen. "What can I tell you that you don't already know? It was magnificent, utterly perfect. Erect in the center of a circle of black earth untouched by faded petals, it lifted its branches toward the artificial suns of the ceiling. Each branch carried a single bloom, each as splendid as a flower could be."

Lady Ardryce released my arm. Suddenly, she regretted having trusted me. The scent of the flowers was overcoming my own. I had become an interloper.

"I suppose I would have had to show you this sooner or later," she sighed. "Soon, bit by bit, we'll stop selling dead flowers to necrophiliacs. Roses want to live. They only seem fragile because we want them to. Geneticists were killing themselves to make them as ephemeral as possible. The fools! You just have to see the roses, and listen. Within them is an insolent dream of

eternal perfection. My researchers coaxed it out of them; their secret now belongs to me.

"This rosebush is my ultimate creation: none of its flowers will ever wilt."

"My lady..."

"Hush! I have no right to tell you any more. Anyway, you're too young to really understand what is eternity for a flower. Forget what you've seen and stop worrying about our debts."

I came as close to her as etiquette allowed, and no doubt closer. It wasn't enough. She motioned and the heavy steel gates closed. A frigid wind swept away all odors, leaving us bare.

"I've organized a picnic for Pauline's birthday tomorrow," she said, as she removed herself from my proximity. "Take a day off, if you want to, or come and join us. I don't know if you like kids?"

"I'm one myself."

"No child would say that. Noon under the umbrella pine, in the north half of the park. I'll ask the kitchen to provide more sandwiches."

"These roses, my lady..."

"Forget them." Lady Ardryce walked away without looking back, while the lab doors closed shut one after the other. "You might get hurt!"

My cover personality had chosen to give the kid an enormous paperweight of blue-tinted glass, inside which three interlaced silhouettes twisted painfully. The glass seemed to drink in the light of the late morning. Pauline thanked me gravely, the crystal ball clutched to her chest, before sitting apart from us to play alone, curtained off by a stand of tall grass. Lady Ardryce had *asked me to carve the chicken, while her closest aide served the wine, one of the best vintages produced on the island. Seated at random beneath the tree's extended branches, we were magnificent and vulnerable, on the edge of perfection. Flawless yet fragile.*

There again, I did not feel your hand at work in all of this. I remember the past too well to see the present that clearly. And the future is so empty, Raven... How is it possible to continue living in such conditions, I still don't know. But my other persona never asked itself these questions. It had plotted and connived to be where it was, and now it was ready to enjoy the picnic marking its success.

The first mouthful made it vanish. I surfaced again, awakened by the inimitable combination of the wine's aromas. The wind was blowing on the ashes of the phoenix; I emerged from my egg and I examined my companions: Lady Ardryce, her two assistants, and her only daughter, nine-year-old today. Fragile beings, mere black slates scrawled with a few memories that I was going to erase with the end of my sleeve. An Impressionist painting of an afternoon picnic, a touch solemn and grave in spite of the kid's presence. Did I tell you I was almost in love with her, with her curls, with her innocence? A little girl so pretty she could only be painted if the brush never pressed the canvas. But I was myself once again and the stings of my fingernails overflowed with memwipe.

A mere scratch, Raven, and they lost themselves. You know how it goes: their minds leaked through the tiny scratches I inflicted. In their eyes, I could see the level of awareness sink, like memories in a bottle, leaking through an cracked bottom.

The girl was last. When she saw the adults freeze, she ran toward the house and I pursued. But it was no longer a game. I caught up with her and raked her neck. She kept running straight ahead for a few more steps, carried by the reflex motion of her legs. The faint remembrance of her flight was taking her away from me. Then she tripped. I held her by the shoulders so that she wouldn't fall and get hurt.

The paperweight she was clutching to her breast rolled to my feet. I picked it up without thinking. Inside the bluish sphere, an essential moment of my past was locked away for all eternity. I assume that's why my borrowed personality chose it. The memories of normal people are dulled with time or simply lost. The will can file off their edges or hide them so deep they will never again see the light of day. The sharp edges of memory soon stop hurting them, but, Raven, we never forget. The past stays hidden beneath our fingertips like claws ready to spring.

That is how I killed Lady Cervantani. While asking her to forget in my stead.

As he said this, Hummingbird smiled a joyless smile. Any congratulations Raven might have offered were lost to him.

"You can guess the rest, I suppose," the teen continued. "The bodies were still warm when the sirens of the surveillance craft converged upon the scene. I waited to be arrested, the paperweight in my hand like a shard of sky. I could have finished the wine, but alcohol and memories don't go well together.

"Five shuttles dived toward me. That was your second mistake, Raven, and that one I caught immediately. I

72

knew to the last penny the finances of the Cervantani estate: no way could we afford that many surveillance craft. It was a trap!"

"Which you managed to escape, my quick little bird. How you did it is what I really would like to know."

"I waited. On foot, I wasn't going to outrun a shuttle. Your plan might have succeeded, except for two things.

"You had sent my brothers to kill me, error number one. Since that day on Mars when we'd been alone together, out of your sight, we'd agreed to exchange our most intimate wake-up codes, those you had yourself implanted within us. When I saw them exit from the shuttle, unable to recognize me, I sang the emergency tunes and I forced them to remember me.

"They would have killed me anyway, I think, and for good. They were loyal to you. But there was an unforeseen element, a marvelous grain of sand…"

Near the garden's entrance, a tiny self-willed cart was slaloming between the rosebushes. On its flattened back, no more than plate-sized, there was a cylinder of dark glass, now stained with streaks of pale yellow pollen. The cap was loosened and chinked softly as the cart progressed.

Hummingbird had broken off in mid-sentence. He was watching the cart's approach, aware of Raven's nervousness. Everything would be decided in a handful of seconds, but the old bird seemed disinclined to open his beak. His face slightly tilted, frowning pensively, he appeared to have lost interest in the story.

"Imagine," said the teen, "I was standing in the exact center of a circle of my childhood friends, their weapons trained on me. I saw the barrels climb steadily, aiming at my solar plexus. They were there to eliminate me, I knew it. Always the same old strategy: send one killer, then more killers to get rid of the first one and leave no witnesses. Not one dared to look me in the eyes, but their weapons were steady…"

"And?"

"The kid started to cry. She was crouching at my feet, mind-blanked. She no longer existed, or so I thought. Nobody can withstand memwipe. Unless…"

"Unless?"

"Unless one is a Bird, Raven. Pauline Cervantani is one of us. The only female of our kind in the entire Solar System, the mate we'd all dreamed about. And you sent me to kill her!"

Moving with a seeming lack of haste, the teen bent over the cart now determined to go around him and he grasped the cylinder, holding it to him.

"The rest is easy to guess. The existence of Pauline changed everything and my brother assassins grasped it as soon as me. I took advantage of their hesitation and broke the paperweight on a stone, right by her ear. The noise of shattered glass covered the code phrase I whispered.

"When she recovered her memories, we were forever linked. I had murdered her mother and I held the secret of her rebirth.

"My brothers lowered their weapons. We hugged, and embraced Pauline within the nest of our arms until she stopped crying."

"The ships outside, that's them? The fools think they can overcome me by force?"

"They just provided the escort required for me and my gift."

Hummingbird finished unscrewing the cap and upended the cylinder over his palm. A clod of black earth fell out, followed by a pliant green stem bristling with thorns. The stem was tipped with a single red bloom.

Perfection most scarlet. Each petal seemed to have been placed just so to add to the harmony of the whole. Each nuance of its heart matched all the rest and the result was a melody of painful delights. The perfume it exuded was so subtle as to go almost unnoticed, but it overwhelmed the garden's ponderous smells as if a fresh breeze was sweeping out the over-recycled atmosphere.

The now useless container dropped among the withered petals. Holding out his hands cupped together, the teen proffered the flower.

"I saved it myself from the wreckage. Your orders were followed; nothing is left of the laboratories. The greenhouses burned along with the bodies. I destroyed the records with my own hand. I could make nothing of the research reports by the scientists; and Lady Ardryce's notes were nothing but a love poem dedicated to roses, to her daughter, and to herself.

"This is all that survives from the perfect rosebush. It is yours!"

Raven could not look away from the flower. When the stem bent toward him, it was already too late. Instinctively, he tried to push it away, but Hummingbird, watching intently, intercepted the hand and ground the stem with its sharp thorns into the offered palm. A single bead of blood leaked from the wound.

Raven froze.

Tenderly, before rigor mortis started to set in, the teen gathered the hands of the old man in order to shape

75

a vase for his gift. He then considered Raven's face as it turned to stone, saw the mind imprisoned behind the bars of the eyelashes as it struggled to escape from the time gel freezing him in place.

"You won't die, Raven. You'll never die... I mixed the genetically modified pollen from the rosebush into my ship's air supply. It was the only substance the surveillance sensors were programmed not to notice. When it combined with the flower's sap, it triggered an inescapable stasis.

"The machines will keep you alive, you and your rose. I'm saying this because I want my voice to be the last thing you remember, in case you awaken before me...

"Because I will join you, big brother, as soon as I start up the main drive. The garden will drift into outer space, moving at a minute fraction of lightspeed. We'll go out to meet the Galaxy's other species so that we can offer them our best and most perfect.

"We've got time, Raven, all the time in the world. My brothers are watching, outside; they'll kill me if I try to leave the nest again. That was our deal: I killed Pauline's mother, that was the last thing she remembered from her life *before*. I can't hope she'll forgive me one day, even if I hold the key to open for her the doors of life after life, until she tires of who she is. Each of us is the other's jailer.

"You see, you taught me to cultivate symmetry and symmetry destroyed me."

When he returned to the garden, after a long stay inside the engine rooms, the imperceptible vibration permeating the asteroid had changed frequency. The drive was getting ready to launch the rocky mass out of its orbit, out of the Solar System, following a complex trajectory computed by the AI modules aboard Hummingbird's ship.

The bees drawn to the immortal rose fluttered at a prudent remove from the incarnadine sun. For the first time in his life, Hummingbird felt infinitely alone. His hand brushed against Olechinski's petrified mouth:

"Have you ever looked upon a parliament of birds, big brother? Crows hold them sometimes. They meet in the branches of an oak tree to ponder a case while the accused flits uncertainly nearby. It can last for hours–lots of cawing, lots of feathers rustling. The tree looks like the flapping folds of a prosecutor's robes. The branches are covered with black masses swaying in time to the back and forth of the debates.

"When the verdict is rendered, all the crows fly off as one. They hover like a dense cloud over the accused and then, one after the other, fall upon him and knock into him. Each one hits him, but no one tries to kill him. The punishment only takes a few minutes. The flock takes off again and the birds fly away, carrying off with them the anonymous culprit. But he is too weakened to fly very far. His wings betray him and he falls."

His voice broke upon the last syllables. Around him, in spite of the comforting thickness of rock as old as the Sun itself, he was aware of the inexprimable cold of vacuum. The garden drifted through entropic darkness like a soap bubble. The lushness of the roses was his only rampart against the void.

He stretched a hand toward the immortal rose. Near the tip of the stem, a branch clipped by the shears was exuding a single pearl of sap, just beside an upright thorn left alone by the gardener. With one slash of his fingernail, he tore through the thin filters which protected his mucous membranes and he forced himself to breathe deeply, three or four times. His palm went to close itself around the stem's thorns, to enfold their promise. His eyes screwed shut.

The automatic sprinklers turned on.

He recoiled out of sheer reflex. The lukewarm shower spurting from unseen apertures cut into the rock was not really distasteful. His teeth clenched, the teen forced himself to again extend his hand.

In the flower's heart, a drop of water formed. It was fed by the tiny rivulets sliding off the unblemished petals. When it grew to the size of a respectable pearl, Hummingbird saw his face reflected within it.

The drop started rolling down, capturing inside its translucid walls his image and that of Raven, impossibly intertwined. The teen caught it on the end of his fingertip and he watched it break, the way the bubblecar had broken and Pauline's paperweight too. A new drop formed, a new slice of absolute remembrance. It would only exist long enough to reach its own culmination, but that didn't matter.

In time, everything that has been done can be undone.

"Immortality is only good for roses," he murmured as he wiped his eyes with the end of his sleeve.

When the artificial rain stopped, he had left the garden.

Later, the hum of the engines died. The asteroid found a new orbit. Hummingbird uncoupled the magnetic moorings of his ship and sent it to lose itself into the depths of space. One after the other, his brothers' ships launched in pursuit. The teen witnessed the death-blow on the screens of the control room, before cutting off radio transmissions for good.

The new life opening before him still demanded a number of preparations, but there was no hurry.

He would leave Pauline the time she needed to become a woman.

An Excerpt from The Journals of Lady Pauline Cervantani

...I never get anything for my birthdays. The vise grip of love and protectiveness never fails to tighten noticeably, like a migraine; nobody mentions what happened fifteen years ago, but they make sure I'm not alone.

Yet, today is a special day. A gift has arrived for me.

Creating the latest model of our hallmark rose is finally over. I won't develop it any further: the flowers, completely odorless, are so delicate they die when you look at them too hard. They'll sell extravagantly well. And my mother would have hated them.

I shouldn't speak of her. Her death is a reproach she is forever leveling at me.

For a while, now, I've no longer been able to take it. The love of my adopted brothers was smothering me. The strictures of my work trapped me inside an unbreakable crystal bubble. I needed to hatch, but I lacked the strength.

It was the exact hour of my birth when an anonymous message made its way to my private com unit. It held an access code for the Gardens of the Nest. A dis-

interested gift, romantic, with a zest of risk. The sender knows me well.

The Gardens, filling one of three million asteroids in the Smaller Belt, can only be visited in Virtuality, through a sensory link. Inside is one of the most beautiful rose gardens in the Solar System, its maintenance entirely automated. I've never been authorized to connect for a visit.

After vainly trying to talk me out of it, my usual escorts chose to tag along. I know they love me, and this love is as changeless as their faces or mine. I just have to look at them for time to stop in its tracks.

I can no longer endure it.

As I was passing through a metal arch, toward the geometrical center of the Gardens, a sudden glitch in the dataflow separated me from my entourage. At a loss, I then saw the secret paths of the innermost bower fall open for me. A hand appeared to guide me, while a barely audible voice whispered into my ear.

Stopping in front of the statue marking the border of the public areas, the hand picked the single rose held in the petrified hands and offered it to me...

Scenes at the Exhibit

...In the first room (left as you come in) are gathered some of the youthful works of the artist. For the most part they are mere attempts predating his admission into the studio of Master Kishisaburo. The spiral disposition of this portion of the exhibit allows visitors to grasp with one glance the totality of the time slices presented. Tradition would have us think that each contains, in embryonic form, one of the masterpieces still to come, like an imperfect draft discovered too soon by the public eye. This conceit must be discarded. The works assembled here are notable only for their mediocrity. If it wasn't for their illustrious signature, they would have fast sunk into oblivion. If you require more evidence, you need only spend a few moments in front of the central diptych, considered to be the most ambitious work of this period.

The two panels, under the harsh light of a bank of projectors, were extracted from the same time sequence at a five microsecond interval. More than three meters high, they enclose fragments of a geisha's suicide, as mounted by the author. The subject, essentially classical, has already been exploited in many ways by various creators. Here, its treatment is totally devoid of any originality. The choice of suicide (the young woman threw herself from the top of a cliff) could have been used for a good study of the body's impact against the rocks. Yet, the artist only concentrated on the first instants of the fall, without a thought for its conclusion. The two slices were removed too soon and the exact moment of her death is not included in the work.

The artist's craftsmanship can also be criticized. The removal technique of the time fragment lacked a master's sureness of touch, and irregularities in the width of the slices introduce a local warping of perspectives. A few scratches several nanoseconds deep are visible in the right corner of the diptych's second panel. On the whole, we are left with a painful impression of confusion, reinforced by the faulty choice of cutting angles, much too closely spaced. One shivers at the thought of the damage inflicted to the structure of the continuum by the removal of the slice of time required for this work's begetting. But most of all, one is dumbfounded to find the talented producer of *John Lennon, Murdered* [1] collecting so many crude mistakes in one work.

A complete tour of this room would be an exercise in tedium and, it should be emphasized yet again, quite pointless. Each of the works on show has its share of flaws; some are so mediocre that their authenticity has been repeatedly challenged. (On this topic, Shigenaga's monograph *The Master Manipulators of Parallel Universes* may be consulted.) And yet, from the unrelieved dullness of these early works would rise, like a phoenix reborn from its ashes, one of the most famous producers of our time.

The reasons for this transformation are obscure and have already given rise to many speculations and scholarly disputes. Most critics agree that its original impetus may be traced to the moment when the artist was

---

[1] See under "John and Yoko" in the catalogue's glossary.

authorized to create his own universe (*see box*), as a background for his future works. This authorization marked the end of his apprenticeship and the beginning of his artistic independence. When the surgeons operated on him to prepare his mind for the fusion with the universals, he was nothing more than a timid young man, his only distinguishing trait being unusually thick epicanthic folds. Nobody could have predicted the destiny in store for him.

From that point on, opinions diverge. Was he already nurturing the strange sensibility that would later flourish in each of his works? Or did it appear and feed on the peculiarities of his personal universe? [2]

Let me digress, for the benefit of those who are imperfectly aware of the process of timeshaping. We know our island is the only stable reality in the Multiverse surrounding us. If you imagine time as a river with several arms, you will find our island both at the wellspring and near each of its many mouths. It is always possible to divert part of the river's flow to generate a new universe parallel to ours, shaped by the personality of its Creator. Our island alone remains ever unchanged, in the eternal center of the Ma [3].

When an artist is judged worthy of becoming a Creator, his prefrontal lobes are surgically modified. A link is thereby forged between his mind and the totality of time. During the few instants his trance lasts, he may, through a conscious effort, add a new bud to the possi-

---

[2] A concise description of this universe can be found in the first pages of this catalogue.

[3] *Ma:* Japanese space-time.

bility-tree and give birth to a new universe. He will then learn how to manipulate it at will in order to remove the slices of time thus orchestrated. When he dies, his whole creation dies with him.

Instead of taking sides, let us restrict ourselves to the known facts regarding this creation, as they are provided by the artist in his autobiography. Let us note however that he had just finished fashioning the *Vivisections* series for a provincial hospital when the following text was written.

"After the operation, I was in a state of extreme mental confusion for several hours. My Master honored me with his presence by my bedside when I awoke. He showed me a magnifying mirror which reflected the fine lacework of scars adorning my forehead. It was identical to the much older traceries limned on the yellowed ivory of his own skin. I was barely able to signify my thanks with a slight nod before losing consciousness once more. The trance happened all at once, setting me free, and I felt myself hurled beyond my body, in all directions at the same time.

"I perceived the *plenum* like a roof covered with tiles and extending as far as the eye could see. I became each tile and the entire roof simultaneously. I was a trunkless tree whose branches were numberless, and whose roots burrowed into my own shadow. I was unique and multiform, a fraction and the sum total of all things. But these visions only lasted for an instant; my frightened mind shriveled inwards and I felt rising within me the imperious need to create my personal universe.

"The world I engendered was terrifyingly different from ours, wilder and more primitive by far. A distorted reflection of our island riding the waves was almost un-recognizable. Due to its remoteness from the *Ma*'s core, time flowed there at an accelerated rate. I knew then I would be able to prepare my productions far in advance of their realization.

"I let a bit more than a century lapse according to the world's internal timekeeping. During this interval, its extremely short-lived inhabitants underwent a complete turnover. I devoted two years to mastering the forces which govern the actions of a mob or of an isolated indi-vidual. Thanks to the methods I had learned from my Sensei, Master Kishisaburo, I grew ever more skilled in the handling of my creatures. Around this time, I first tried to arrange particular events…"

One of these initial attempts occupies the whole of the second room. I am speaking, of course, of *The Sara-jevo Incident* [4], reproduced in many art books and which may be considered as the author's first true masterpiece.

In front of this work, one is struck at once by its rhythm and finesse, which lend an extraordinary vi-brancy to the scene. The time slice is infinitely thin, just shimmering into existence, infused with a softened light not unlike that produced by glowworms. The stark fig-ures of the central group are set off by a frieze of com-plex ideograms sketched by the plumed helmets of the horse guards. One may choose to admire the perfect symmetry of the composition which pays homage, with cold elegance, to a classical motif of *NŌ* theater. One may be moved by the purity of the restrained motion, by the almost motherly forbearance with which the victim

---

[4] Please see the "Sarajevo" entry in the catalogue's glos-sary.

offers his breast to the bullets of his executioner. Yet, one will remember forever, above all else, the three flowers blossoming in that instant, unfurling petals of blood across the chest, the only splotches of true color in the midst of a black and white costume pageant [5].

The display of this work, during the annual festival in Osaka, was rewarded with almost universal praise. Only the usual malcontents chose to deplore the undue prominence of the setting, but such objections were swept aside by the public's enthusiastic response.

Curiously, instead of encouraging him, this unquestioned success drove the artist into semi-seclusion, far from the city. His sporadic public appearances during this period showed him to be a tormented soul, ravaged by mysterious inner demons. Nobody suspected then that he was wrestling with the very foundations of his art.

Some time later, he made the dangerous choice of living in permanent contact with his universe. Until then, he had satisfied himself with occasional crossings in order to extend his mastery of the forces controlling his creatures. When he determined he had acquired the necessary skillfulness, he dissociated his mind and let one part fuse with his creation. Some critics argue this may have given birth to some of his obsessions. Certain peculiarities of the world he had generated could have acted like distorting mirrors, confronting the artist with his own, disproportionately enlarged preoccupations. Whatever the case may be, his behavior changed. For a time, he was subject to recurring fits of delirium, which affected the balance of his universe.

---

[5] The details of the production as well as the overall schematics of the historical and sociological forces harnessed by the artist are given in full at the back of this volume.

He exerted himself furiously, resting and meditating in brief snatches. He practiced calligraphy. His brush strokes grew firmer, more assured through endless repetition. It is even said he fasted to refine the sensitivity of his mind's touch. His skillfulness as a producer kept growing by leaps and bounds. He was no longer content, as he had been until then, with the approximate swaying of mobs or isolated individuals. He seized control of faces, muscles, nerves. He learned how to prompt the minutest quiver of the body, the most fleeting expression of the face. Deliberately breaking with tradition, he upset the classical lineaments of landscapes and brought about the conception of phantasmagoric decors. Inhumanly large buildings breached the monotony of empty horizons; everywhere, he encouraged a taste for outsized edifices and verticality.

In connection with this, it behooves us to underline the increasing importance of his settings. Whereas it was still emerging in a work like *The Sarajevo Incident,* this tendency quickly came to the fore as one of the artist's main concerns. Various studies from this intermediate period illustrate his interest. Let us cite, for instance, the quite unique *Dropped from the Empire State* (private collection), with its dizzying perspective emphasized by the convulsive terror molding the victim's face and the viewpoint in midair, just *below* the plummeting body...

A year later, a handful of prominent critics received an invitation, penned in the artist's own incomparable calligraphy, for an unveiling in Osaka. It was learned that he had secretly rented a gallery near the museum, and that several of his recent works had been moved to those premises. The guests were greeted by the gallery's owner, who asked them to stand in a semicircle. A few minutes later, a disembodied voice gave the signal for the display.

Under the name *Eleven Versions of the Kennedy Assassination,* eleven time slices of various sizes and widths had been assembled. Each was covered with a white mourning veil. Several very young girls started to uncover them, following the indications given by the voice. The first cries of admiration were heard instantly...

These same sequences are at the heart of the current exhibit. Visitors will understand that it would be impossible to repeat such a presentation for each and every group. According to the artist's advice, the eleven pieces are now grouped in the round room and the lighting has been designed with particular care. The crucial elements of each work can be seen from anywhere in the room, thanks to an array of ideally positioned magnifying mirrors.

It is hard to describe in detail each slice without detracting from the general impression. They are so tightly linked that they cannot be dissociated. Only the catalogue, by assigning an arbitrary number to each, seems to consider them as separate works, but this numbering is utterly unfounded. Indeed, the artist has never allowed the grouping to be displayed with any piece missing.

Upon entering, the visitor's eye is assailed by a riot of harsh colors dominated by red. Here silence is *de rigueur.* One must pass slowly in front of each scene, holding one's breath. I confess a slight preference for slice number five, which captures the exact moment when the first bullet hit the back of Kennedy's neck. The quick succession of expressions on the President's face attains a level of perfection rarely equaled, and never surpassed. The time slice is just thick enough for the bullet to drill through the base of the skull and emerge from the right shoulder, in shattering slow motion.

Slice number eight, the thinnest, was extracted at the precise instant when the assassin pulled the trigger of his gun. The converging lines of the buildings meet in a vanishing point just behind the victim's head, crowned with a dark halo setting off his shining smile. Hovering near the mouth of the gun's barrel, the lethal bullet is ready to hurtle towards its target. The lighting itself conveys the tragic intensity of the scene by emphasizing, quite crudely in places, every detail. In the last slice, a gigantic eye belonging to Jackie Kennedy mirrors the entire assassination, blow by blow, like a montage of the entire work.

It is almost impossible to explain the effect produced by these works to someone who has never admired them. The setting itself is an inescapable presence: towering slabs of glass and metal, yet conveying a hallucinatory frailty as they mirror the presidential motorcade; the labyrinthine interlacing of streets filled with scurrying people viewed at such a remove that they are little more than ants. Indeed, most scenes are captured from above, the plunging vistas adding to the spectator's vertigo. Through this wholesale overthrow of tradition, the creator succeeds in laying down a completely new vision of spatial relationships, which will leave nobody indifferent.

Many critics have applauded the artist's *tour de force* in replicating the original sequence of events to produce eleven versions of the same occurrence, with infinitesimal variants. But technical perfection is nothing compared to the sheer beauty of the outcome. Art, raised to such levels, bespeaks true genius. The display of such a work would suffice to justify the creation of the universe from which it was extracted.

At times, I regret that the victims of such productions do not know that they attain artistic immortality as they die. The instant of their death, this intangible mote torn from space and time, is the ultimate form of art, the only one that really counts for connoisseurs. I am sure their end would be sweeter for the knowing.

A recent article in a famous avant-garde periodical comes to mind. In it, the artist explained the repercussions of this particular assassination on the inhabitants of his universe. To complete his work, he had to remove the few seconds that contained the event and the absence of these crucial seconds have not gone unnoticed. Nobody since then has been able to reconstitute the precise unfolding of the action in spite of the presence of thousands of witnesses, and the most fantastic theories still circulate.

As I write these lines, it would seem that the artist has been letting the situation deteriorate, even encouraging where needed the destructive tendencies of his world's inhabitants. Faced with his own imminent demise, he has found in religion a powerful new source of inspiration. It is rumored he wishes to take advantage of recently rising tensions to put an end to his creation, whose main characters are increasingly fanatics of every stripe. He would rely on the diversity of their carefully cultivated appearances and absurdly complex rituals to achieve aesthetic effects featuring unprecedented levels of violence.

Accordingly, the scenes he is planning to orchestrate will make up his ultimate work, to be titled:
Jihad: Visions of an Unstoppable War.

Time, as it evaporates...

Time, as it evaporates, stirs the surface of the lake above. From the depths below, the time-wrecked watch the troubled mirror that hides the heavens and, from its undulations, deduce the wakes of imaginary birds.

The submerged city is nestled between the high walls of a mountain chain. When one night the Universe tore and bled, losing its most precious fluid from a thousand mortal wounds, the mountains acted like natural dykes and trapped a temporal pond large enough to allow the city to survive.

The top of the minaret long ago broke through the liquid boundary between the world below and the stasis above. Its refined silhouette, jaggedly fractured at the meeting with the surface, dominates the drowned city. Its pinnacle, warped by the alteration in perspective, seems condemned to a perpetual fall nobody fears any more.

A stone stairway coils around the fragile building. During centuries, uncounted artists covered the steps with enameled mosaics on which arabesques proclaimed the holy name of God. Most inscriptions are still visible, even though the oldest tiles are often cracked or broken off.

So that his voice may carry further, Marwan the muezzin climbs to the highest step still under time to utter the call to prayer. He does not care for amplifiers or mikes, for all those devices men place between their words and their listeners. His breath is powerful, his diction of the utmost clarity. Echoes of his exhortations roll like a torrent of well-worn pebbles through the alleys and squares, bounce from the whitewashed terraces, filter into the tightly-shuttered houses, into the hearts of the members of the community. He is forty in years, at the peak of his art, the bearer of the divine Word...

The lake of time vanishes slowly. Every month or so, Marwan must come down a step to address the last of the faithful. Such is the case today and so he adds a few words to the traditional surats, to comfort those who might need it.

"Do not fear being put to the test, but fear the wrath of God and find here another sign of His greatness. I am again exiled from the ultimate step, forced to bow my head and come closer to you. Let this be a lesson to us: when time itself fails us, religion comes closer to men..."

Few pay any attention to his speeches, yet nobody questions his calling, if only because it allows them to follow the day to day ebbing of the time-tide.

After the prayer, Marwan is not afraid to get as close as he can to the surface, until it is no longer an obstacle to his gaze.

On the other side of the lake's frosted glass lies a Universe without time. Marwan is the only one to have seen it; the superstitious dread which prevents other community members from venturing to the stairway's top has allowed him to enjoy an unchallenged prestige. If someone dared to climb as high as him, he would see that the emerged peak of the minaret is clear of any inscription. The name of the Lord is erased as soon as the time-level falls, the earthenware tiles recovering their virginity temporarily violated by the touch of faith.

A few months earlier, Marwan carved the names of all the gods he knew on a clay tablet attached to the end of a stick. The tablet was destroyed when it pierced the surface, and the muezzin recovered his serenity, only shaken for a time. In this world as in the other, no one is greater than Allah.

As he climbs down the stairway worn by the sandals of his predecessors, Marwan marks aloud the steps which remain his, rising from the base of the minaret. He settles the folds of his coat, knocks the tiles with his staff to punctuate the litany of numbers he counts off. The first grey hairs are weaving a loose net in his beard and his mane. He cares not a whit and, quite to the contrary, is glad of them: age will grant more weight to his words.

His half-sister Zorah, fifteen years younger, waits for him at home. He asked her to bring back from the market a piece of mutton, which she will prepare with the herbs his mother taught her. He can already taste the flavor of the roasted meat, of the chick peas mixed with raisins, and he quickens his steps, never wavering in his count.

The numbers he mumbles are reassuring: one step, one month; ten steps, a landing, almost a year. The landings are numerous enough by far to let him end his life, without ever having to bow his head or run on all fours like an animal to stay below the temporal surface. He tries to imagine what his life will be in another fifty or one hundred steps, but the thought of the meal awaiting him disturbs his meditation. In any case, how can the years to come bring him anything new? His staff strikes the polished stones with renewed force. He still has below him all the time in the world; thinking of the future is useless.

He reaches the doorway of his house, pushes aside with his hand the door curtain. The main room is empty. Zorah isn't back yet. A quick glance towards the clepsydra tells him she is nearly an hour late. Thwarted, he goes to sit on the cushions and unrolls a book of precepts in order to busy his mind until his sister's return.

The sounds of the city reach him through the thick walls. The barking of dogs, the shouting of the last few children, the muffled thud of rope sandals on the street's cobblestones, each sound a note in a deeply personal melody, at once familiar and reassuring. It's been years since he has had to endure the remote roar of the jets scoring the sky or the brutal staccato of internal combustion engines. There are no outside influences left to disturb the community, now turned inward, isolated by the will of Allah.

From outside come the echoes of hurried steps, and then the door's curtain is pushed aside. Zorah is back. She rushes into the kitchen with her burden, without giving her brother a chance to open his mouth. The clatter of dishes and cutlery is heard, and she appears with a steaming teapot. She sets down two glasses on the low table's hammered brass tray and pours tea.

"Where do you come from, Zorah?"

"From the slaughterhouse. I had to wait nearly an hour to get some mutton."

Marwan observes her. She has taken off the shapeless cloak which she puts on to go outside the house, letting him examine at length the body whose full curves never fail to arouse within him an insidious confusion. He lifts his gaze to her face. The eyes are underlined with kohl, the mouth under the veil is a shade of grenadine red, and the ears jingle with serried silver rings.

"Was it needful that you adorn yourself like that to go to the market, little sister?"

"Let me do what I want! I'll soon be twenty-six; it's time that men learn to look at me."

She goes back into the kitchen. Marwan deduces her anger from the jolting stride. An old worry eats at him: Zorah, whose guardian he has been since their father died, must not be allowed to dishonor their home as well as himself with displays unworthy of a muezzin's sister. Tomorrow, he will go and sit at the terrace of the main café, near the old mustering grounds of the caravans, so that he can listen to what is being said in town about Zorah.

His position within the community has taught him to separate the wheat from the chaff when it comes to the words of men. He feels capable of learning what he seeks simply by sitting on a mat, without speaking. He who stays silent and listens is like a well filled by the springs of wisdom, while he who speaks is like a well whose water is being drawn out, so sayeth the Prophet. It is deeply comforting, thinks Marwan, to live in a world where every thought finds its source in holy writings, all praises to Allah, the Gracious, the Merciful.

He banishes the subject from his mind as he sips the hot tea, savoring the sweet smell of mint and the bitter aroma. A few more minutes and dinner will be ready.

When dawn's first light shines, Marwan marches through the streets, staff in hand, like a shepherd watching over his flock in the ruins of an antique settlement. The city, at one end of the road through the passes, once flourished, but the time is long gone when the caravans laden with salt rods, silk rolls and swollen water skins used to come through the monumental gates carved into the ramparts. The last camels were put down a few months ago, not for their meat, but to spare them a pointless and idiotic agony, far from the desert. That day, Marwan saw men cry, men who had traveled up and down the rocky trails since infancy; many left on foot, a water flask on their hip, for one last trip beyond the mountains, beyond any hope of ever returning.

Yet, a deceptive bustle still enlivens the alleyways and the *souks*. Marwan walks down a row of stalls, assailed by the insistent hammering of the mallets of coppersmiths. Here, craftsmen continue to make copperware as in the past, keeping only their best pieces and melting the rest to avoid overcrowding their displays. Farther down, an old man bargains tirelessly for a prayer mat he will probably never buy. The carpet merchant, sitting on a pile of cushions, nods patiently without lowering his price a jot more than is proper.

A young veiled virgin, walking in the shadow of her mother, casts a stealthy glance at the muezzin, who responds only with a frown...

Every morning, Marwan looks at his city with new eyes and marvels to find it unchanged from the day before. The catastrophe changed nothing. The beggars, even the robbers pursue their trade with the unspoken agreement of all. It is as if the whole city, knowing itself condemned, prepares to relive endlessly the day before its disappearance, like the palaces shut into bottles for fun by djinns in old tales.

When he reaches the square where is found the city's main well, filled with a very cool iron-flavored water, Marwan chooses to halt, leaning on his staff. There are four places here where he can go and drink tea, four similar terraces screened by awnings of brown canvas. The muezzin will stop in each in the course of the day, moving as the mood moves him or as circumstances dictate, but he must choose with care the only one he will honor with his presence first.

His practiced eye gauges the audience, identifying at once each face. He soon makes up his mind. No outward sign betrays his inner turmoil as he resumes his stroll, crosses the square, and, saluting the other customers with a stiff nod, squats on one of the mats, its colors sadly faded.

The mirror of the sky is alive with slow undulations and ripples, which die in concentric circles around the minaret. Marwan, when he blows on the scalding tea, causes similar ripples to disturb the liquid's surface, so that the ever-changing images betray the passage of time.

Those who sit there rarely lift their gaze towards the sky. To measure the passing of the hours, they do not try to decipher the sinuous alphabets traced on the lake's mirror. They believe in clepsydrae or hourglasses, like their forefathers before them, or yet again count the beatings of their hearts. They have reached that age when the little time remaining to them would hold easily in two wrinkled hands cupped together, before slipping away forever between their fingers. The tea they have imbibed is a mighty river swollen by the rains; the tea they have left to drink is a mere puddle. Why fret because the temporal lake continues to drop?

Among them, the muezzin is a teen-ager. He stays silent and listens, keeping his words for the time of prayer. If something is to be said about Zorah, he will hear it when the time comes.

Yet, the immutable order of the day's events is due for an upset. Across the public square, a man comes towards him, striding quickly, perhaps faking a self-confidence he does not feel.

Though the one who comes thus is unknown to him, Marwan feels keenly the link which unites them. He takes the time to detail his figure, conscious that he is simultaneously the object of the other's gaze.

The hair black and shiny, the short beard shadowing his cheeks, the tall shape cloaked in a striped fabric, all betray a stranger from the coast, a man from another tribe, an unbeliever perhaps. He walks with a bowed head, as if bearing on his shoulders the burden of a sorrow as heavy as the world. He is no doubt a traveller who stopped to spend the night in their city when the great cataclysm occurred, and who is now stranded. A few were in the same straits after disaster struck; those who had left their family to seek their fortune elsewhere came home to resume their previous life. The fate of a couple of lost tourists was quickly settled. But the newcomer does not fall in either category.

Instinctively, the muezzin mistrusts him. His hands clench the staff lain across his knees, his back straightens. The newcomer reaches the terrace and he makes his way between the elders who have fallen silent, without honoring them with a single glance. His eyes are boring into Marwan's, and an obstinate resolve crimps his mouth. His face is a carved chunk of solidified lava, and his hands alone, criss-crossed by a thousand tiny scars, seem capable of gentleness.

"Are you Marwan the muezzin?"

Marwan nods, aware that conversations have stopped around them. He claps his hands to order tea and shows the intruder a free spot on the mat. The man ignores the invitation:

"I'd like to talk to you alone."

"Why be hasty? Sit down and share our tea."

The stranger squats unwillingly. He seems young, but his eyes are ageless. Set against the dark lining of his brows, they gleam like sapphires from Ormuz.

"I thank you. My name is Nadir."

"You do not belong to our city."

This is not a condemnation but the assertion of a fact.

"I come from a village by the sea. I was a sponge-fisher on my uncle's boat."

"There are no sponges here. Have you thought of hiring yourself out as an apprentice to earn your bread and make yourself useful? We cannot afford to feed those who contribute nothing."

Around them, the elders clap their hands on their thighs to show their approval. Nadir throws them a furious glance.

"I didn't wait for your advice to find work, muezzin. I have become a storyteller."

Marwan dips his head:

"You seem very young for such a serious trade... Are you content with retelling the fables peddled in fairs or do you try to raise men's hearts towards the Lord, as I do, by weaving your sentences within the framework of morality?"

"I have no other goal than the entertainment of those who listen to me. The time left to us is so meager that morality is among the wrecks stranded by the lake's ebb."

"You speak like an Infidel!"

"Why should I soften my words? Do you believe there is the slightest chance they will turn out to be mistaken?"

He twists to point with his hand at their silent audience.

"I envy your sheer disregard for facts. In a few years at most, the lake's vault will press down upon our heads. To survive, we'll hunch our shoulders. Then, we'll bend our knees, walk on all fours, crawl on our stomachs like the vilest beasts in order to lap up the last seconds of our lives from a shrinking pool. We will be forced to retrace in reverse the road traversed by our species: our ancestors crawled out of the sea, so in turn we will crawl until the bitter end. But you, you will no longer be there. In the twirling of your lives, you are content if you can sip your remaining hours, and cling to the illusion the world will endure without you, unchanged.

"Me, I'll disappear before the end of the span allotted me, like the rest of the Universe. Nothing will survive me."

"Do not speak such blasphemy, unbeliever! Allah is immortal."

"My turn to shrug. You just don't think of death as I do... Do you wish to hear one of my tales?

"Long ago, a God who ruled over the desert decided to become immortal. He gave life to a handful of sand grains sifted between his fingers and made them into an army of builders and warriors. Showing them the horizon, he said:

" 'Build around me an impassable wall, then another, and another yet. Surround me with a labyrinth whose secret nobody will know. When you complete one enclosure, post guards atop the rampart and close the doors, so that Death cannot reach me.'

"So it was done. The horizon, eclipsed by the high walls of metal and stone, seemed to creep closer and closer. The God decided to cover every morning the perimeter of the enclosure which protected and imprisoned him, by counting the number of strides required, in order to measure the progress of the work.

"The first day, he counted seven thousand of them. The next day, as many. A week later, a month later, a year later, his count had not changed.

"Yet the workers labored unremittingly and new impregnable ramparts regularly enfolded the old ones. The angry God blasted down his creatures and raised sandstorms in order to create new ones. The work progressed faster, but the count of his strides went unchanged.

"The walls of the labyrinth now towered as high as the heavens. The sound of hammers and trowels rolled out day and night, like a rumble of thunder without end. Atop the ramparts, the braziers of the guards outshone the sun, yet the count of his strides was immutable.

"One night, the God lowered his gaze towards his shadow that stretched far in front of him and he marveled to see it so large. He turned to face it and said:

" 'Whence such immense size, shadow? Did my enemy Death make you wax thus to pit you against me?'

" 'You fed me yourself without realizing it, Lord, and I have grown while you diminished. Do not look further for the explanation of the mystery around you. Your workers have performed wonders, but they cannot build any faster than you destroy yourself.'

"The God raised his gaze and saw himself, minuscule at the feet of the rampart, mirrored in the burnished shields of the guards atop the wall. He sat down and cried, while his shadow wrapped around him like a leather tunic to protect him from the cold.

"Some say that the labyrinth has turned back into sand and that the wind has been trying for centuries to raze the walls of the sand dunes, never able to free their prisoner. Others tell of his attempts to escape from his prison, while workers both blind and deaf continue to expand the universe around him. All, however, agree that he is immortal…"

"I did not understand the meaning of your words, sponge-fisher. No doubt that you have forgotten how to speak to ordinary men, used as you were to descend into the depths of the sea… No matter! What do you hope to prove to your listeners?"

"Nothing, I told you I was not a moralist and my stories have no rules. If my deficient memory prevents from recalling a tale word for word, I invent another…

"Don't look at me like that, I am not to be pitied. My stories suffice to feed me and would easily allow me to support a wife."

"Who would willingly give a woman of his family to a man who only has his tongue to gain him wealth?"

"What, you, a holy man, you speak to me of wealth! The Lord himself blesses the poor!"

"Do not try to mislead me, demon, I know your kind. While I spread the word of the Prophet, peace be upon him, you distract my listeners with your tales. But my voice carries farther than yours, and Allah inspires me. He alone is worth listening to."

"You sister Zorah does not agree with you."

The affront is such that faces around them clamp shut. To insult the muezzin is to attack the entire community. Nadir realizes this and attempts to backtrack, as if he had never uttered such dangerous words:

"I do not wish to quarrel with you, holy man, so please ask those who surround you. Many have sat around me to hear my stories. They can tell you that the money I receive is given freely. I cannot introduce you to my parents, since my village no longer exists, but my family was honorably known.

"All I want is not to be alone for the little time I have left. I would like to have Zorah as a wife. Will you give us your blessing?"

"When the time comes, I shall choose for her a proper husband, and not a beggar weaving lies for money. Your request is an insult, and I do not need to respond."

Nadir gets up slowly, his hands shaking with emotions he does not bother containing. Yet, his voice is calm when he answers:

"You should have given thought to marrying your sister a long time ago, muezzin, but mayhap you did not want to do without such an obedient servant? Now, it is too late, for you and for her. I asked for her as the old ways would have me do, and you rebuffed me like a dog. Well, I shall come and take her without your permission in a few days, when the entire city will know of your shame and hers. Until then, your surats can keep bouncing from the lake's roof. Keep on praying since that is all you're good for!"

Marwan leaps to his feet, his staff upturned, but Nadir is already out of reach. He refrains from giving chase and sits back among the elders, aware for the first time that he has crossed without realizing it the boundary which kept him apart and that he is now one of them.

Coming through the doorway of his house, Marwan is struck by the sudden silence triggered by his arrival.

He sits in his usual spot and the kitchen's homely noises resume, though not as loudly.

The muezzin fashioned himself an impassive mien on his way back. His voice, during the evening prayer, may have trembled almost imperceptibly, but that could have equally well been a deceptive echo bouncing from the lake's vault or a figment of his imagination. Now that he is cut off from the city by the thick walls of his private universe, he can stoke his anger, reckoning each sound of jostling dishes, each clang of pots and pans to be a new injury.

"Zorah, come here."

The water's whispering, the crystalline ring of a glass striking the stone basin, are her only answers. He gets up and approaches the curtain of rough beads which divides the main room from the kitchen, which he has never wished to enter. Standing in front of this invisible boundary between the world of men and the world of women, he raises his voice:

"Zorah, I'm speaking to you!"

"And I'm not listening to you, Mav. Why should I?"

The sisterly nickname rebounds on the muezzin's carapace of pride like an insect off a light bulb. If he knew how to interpret the nuances of the feminine language, he'd know that his sister is suing for peace. Since a child gave her a note from Nadir, she has thought of ways to stave off an irretrievable break, and to restore the delicate balance which allows her to draw strength from Marwan and Nadir together, since she needs both of them.

She has studied, and rejected, a number of solutions. Her instinct tells her that a direct confrontation must be avoided at all costs. She knows her brother too well and fears his sudden angry bursts, his mad fits which can make him go too far. If only her encounter with Nadir had gone otherwise…

The few sentences scribbled by her suitor unnerved her, as much for their cold and impersonal tone as for their import, as if Nadir had only been a witness to his confrontation with Marwan and had now lost interest in the consequences. A sudden insight compels her to wonder if the child she can now feel inside her was not Nadir's last attempt to escape the fate ordained for him by time's ebbing.

She has reread the note several times, seeking in vain somewhere between the lines the words of comfort she needs. Now, with only the flimsy curtain of the kitchen's door to protect her from Marwan, she thinks of Nadir who is already escaping her grasp, while her brother's anger overflows, battering her with words whose harshness she did not expect.

Zorah does not respond to his attacks. Her face, veiled by the curtain, is unreadable. She shakes her head with the unthinking grace of a doe when the accusations become too precise but no sound breaches the barrier of her lips, not even when her brother uses forbidden words, not even when he calls down upon her the vilest curses, knocking his staff on the tiles for emphasis.

Marwan's backlit silhouette, dressed in a flowing striped robe, flaps and sways grotesquely, growing less and less real to her as the phrases take on the ring of finality and tears blurs Zorah's vision.

When he chases her from the house, with a final volley of insults, she lets loose a strangled wail before rushing from the kitchen, shoving her brother aside without giving him the time to change his mind and call her back.

Once in the street, she flees towards the dwelling occupied by Nadir on the city's edge, only a few blocks away from the temporal boundary. Her cheeks are streaked with tears. She does not know how her lover will receive her, but she is now reduced to this single option. Her universe, trapped between the lake's surface and her brother's barrage of curses, is now as narrow as a tomb.

Behind her, men turn, both shocked and attracted by the unveiled face they see for the first time. Tomorrow, the whole city will know of her shame. She will have to face much more than the curiosity of passers-by or the spite of the senior wives returning from the market. Tomorrow, and the next day, and the next... until their attention is diverted or time runs out, erasing even the record of her action from the memory of the universe.

Marwan hunts long and hard for the balm of sleep. After his sister's departure, he stayed for endless hours on his house's terrace, squatting as he watched the vaulting of the lake, crosshatched with waves. His anger had cooled, making way for a dizzying void, an undefined anguish whose source he could not pinpoint.

One day soon, he would have to visit the market to find a *saïs,* a servant to take care of the house and of himself. He would sit again among the elders and listen to them palaver, endlessly dissecting the affairs of the city like clockmakers looking for the grain of sand which might paralyze the fragile gearing of their tedious lives.

If life has continued, unchanged, it's largely because of them, the self-appointed guardians of everyday life, the preservers of tradition and customs. Nobody, until now, had challenged their authority, nobody before Nadir. Recalling that name rekindled Marwan's anger one last time. The sponge-fisher had desecrated everything sacred, including Allah's name. So why had Allah let life spring from that man's loins? Why was it written that his sister would be the victim of fate? The injustice puzzled the muezzin. Had he, in any way, offended the Lord while discharging his sacred duties, or is this an additional test of his faith? How did he deserve this?

For the first time, Marwan examined the night sky, seeking an answer. Among the catastrophe's survivors, it is commonly believed that each action, for good or evil, of the day is reflected in the lake's mirror, shaping ripples whose meaning is only clear to one person. For hours on end, Marwan looked for the reflection of his doubts and anxieties, searching his memory for personal symbols, forging his own keys and trying them one after the other in the locks to his mind.

The sky stayed silent. Previously, atop the minaret, his head brushing against the surface, he had felt himself come closer to the higher spheres of the Universe and be a part of its sacred Mystery. Tonight, the illusion vanished.

The spiral staircase, covered with signs already half-erased, suddenly seemed out of place to him, a vestige from the past lost in a world without a future, a ruin destined to crumble soon, whose absence would go unnoticed. In the same day, he had lost his sister and, what is more important, his faith...

Alone in the dark blanketing the terrace, he whispered one last prayer to Allah, imploring him to restore the wholeness of the world and of his soul. Then he went to lie on his bed, after rubbing his gums with his fingertips and rinsing his mouth with a sip of water.

When he finally goes to sleep, shortly before dawn, a nightmare invades his mind.

Along an endless lane, covered with earthenware tiles whose inscriptions have become illegible, a giant in metal armor advances. The horizon, above high walls, seemed to move ever closer, while remaining unreachable.

The muezzin, unable to escape, confronts the giant whose steps never falter, his tall shape hiding the sky. A gigantic foot is raised above him, drops down, pins him to the ground. Pain tears through his chest.

When he opens his eyes, Marwan is unable to know whether he has escaped the nightmare or if it's still pursuing him. His ribcage still hurts. Outside his room, the echoes of distant clanking are growing fainter, until he can hardly hear them.

He straightens, unthinkingly rakes his beard with his fingers. It was written that he would not get any sleep. Before rising, he kicks away the twisted ball of sweat-drenched blankets. The veins of his forehead still beat with the remembered terror.

He throws on a robe, then leans out the window to glance outside. The street appears to be deserted. Whatever the source of the noise, it is now too far to be heard, or perhaps it only existed in his mind. The muezzin finishes dressing and leaves, resolved to walk down all of the city's paths, hunting for his lost sleep.

On the shining canvas of the sky, the waves draw lazily their moving constellations, drawing randomly card after card from a new zodiac. The minaret, lost among them like a crooked finger, points nowhere in particular. Marwan's gaze is led along the white arrow, which was once straight and unbroken…

His steps, though he is not conscious of it, lead him back to the foot of the stairway he has so often climbed. He dimly hears again the metallic jangling which roused him from his sleep. He gazes upwards. An ill-defined shape, not unlike the giant of his dream, is climbing the stairs above him, each step causing the armor encasing it to resonate like a gong.

The muezzin, turned to stone for an instant, leaps into the staircase, in pursuit of the stranger climbing towards the surface. Surely, it was him who awakened Marwan by walking under his window, unless a premonition warned him somebody was going to violate the tower's sanctity. His only hope is that no one will get the opportunity to notice that God's name did not withstand the passing away of time.

He accelerates to catch up with him. His sandals slap loudly the worn treads. Nearby, a window lights up, then another, and an unseen dog starts barking. Soon, the residents roused by the din will be out on the streets and a scandal will be unavoidable. Marwan slows down, just as the figure ahead of him picks up the pace.

A landing, and then another. Time is already thinner. Handling such heights, so close to the edge of the universe, requires some getting used to, but the stranger does not seem to be experiencing any difficulty, while Marwan is breathing faster and faster.

When he reaches the last landing still under time, the stranger pauses. The muezzin catches up a few seconds later and stops too, breathless.

The one in front of him is dressed in an antique diving suit made of rubber and copper. Lead-soled boots protect his feet and a belt of weights circles the waist. The tubing which connects to a chromed relief valve hangs upon the shoulders like a gorgon's mane, coiling like a snake whenever the person moves.

The head, inside the spherical helmet, behind a tarnished porthole, is invisible. Yet Marwan unhesitatingly finds the name of this absence.

"Zorah? Is that you?"

The question goes unanswered. Her brother understands that, beneath the cumbersome outfit, she is unable to hear him. He steps towards her, and she backs up towards the surface, knowing that Marwan cannot follow her.

He opens his arms to show his impotence, backs up and climbs down a few steps. She comes closer, almost close enough to touch him. Behind the porthole, the muezzin makes out the outline of her face, distorted by the scratches in the glass.

He could grapple with her, try to overmaster her, run the risk of falling down with her. As if she read his thoughts, she shakes her head and points to the vault arching above their heads. Her gesture disturbs the water and the lake's smooth mirror is momentarily marred by the eddies, but only for a moment.

She climbs the last few steps between her and the world above. The top of the diving-suit tears the surface. They exchange a long silent look, separated from each other by a barrier even more impassable than that erected by tradition, and then she starts again to climb with her heavy tread towards the summit. Marwan, petrified, has not moved a finger to call her back.

The first symptoms of time deprivation are already appearing. The diving suit she stole from her lover, after he mocked her and beat her, is losing the precious fluid through a thousand tiny cracks. The tears of time she sows splash on the earthenware tiles of the staircase and form rivulets along the steps. She raises her head to see the top of the minaret and understands she will never reach it.

Her fingers are as numb as a statue's, but they still manage to undo the lead-weighted belt and throw it over the edge. She watches it drop for an instant, before resuming her ascent to the next landing, where she stops again.

Her thoughts no longer torment her; time, as it escapes from her, washes her clean and carries away her memories. Life is leaking away, and all the pain too. She barely feels the presence of her unborn child stirring in her womb, confined to a closed world already too narrow for him.

Her hand rises and, with nary a qualm, unlock the bindings of the suit. One move and she loses her helmet which bounces at her feet, now useless, before rolling to the edge and over...

The remainder of the suit spreads out like the petals of a flower at the feet of Zorah, whose pale flesh glows with an ever brightening light. Above the sleeping city, dazzling beams escape from a point near the minaret's tip, illuminating like a lighthouse the frozen cityscape which seems to revive in the process. The lake's surface congeals, glistening like mercury.

Slowly the body of Zorah cracks and breaks asunder, yielding to the unstoppable pressure from within. The first spring gushes forth, followed by a second, then by many others. The trickles of time soon become streams, then torrents, then cataracts.

Marwan, kneeling near the surface, his head in his hands, does not realize at first what is happening. When he lifts his eyes, alerted by the lake's intrusive murmur, the level has already increased by several steps and the flow continues to grow. A storm is raging above him, and the swelling flood races from landing to landing, engulfs the minaret, and overflows through the passes of the mountains on the horizon.

The muezzin howls the name of his sister and clambers up the remaining steps, but all he finds is a shredded time-suit forgotten on a landing, still glowing with a light that weakens and dies when he clutches it.

On the earthenware tiles of the stairs, the name of God has not come back.

Shark

I swallowed the bait, the hook and the line. Then, swimming back up the line, I devoured the fisherman. *Hunger saves.* Or so the hackers say. But they confuse gluttony with appetite. As for me, well, I could swallow the entire world.

And the idea is starting to appeal to me.

When I received the message, I was swimming in the lower reaches of my range, amid the fossilized data reefs that the first generation processes tirelessly build up. They have virtually no intelligence to speak of, but they are part of the cybernetic biotope. Like me, even if that comparison is laughable. In the natural order of things, I'm at the top of the digital pyramid. And everyone who can dive as deeply as I do knows it.

At least, that's what I'd always thought, until I happened upon the coded bottle–a ridiculously simple algorithm that my remoras broke in a handful of machine cycles–and the threats it contained. All combined with an obligatory appointment in the intermediate depths. *As soon as you receive this message…*

But, hey, I'm a shark and I set my own pace. With others of my kind, I share the constantly growing data ocean of the cyberworld. We are the solitary ones, the ones with no interface, nothing to slow or impede thought. We fiddle with photons along optical corridors; we duplicate our micro-nuclei at each silicon crossroad, so that we go first, ahead of everyone else. We think faster than the network. *Superfluid.* And me? Well, I'd be the best there is at this game, if I could bother with something as trivial as *gauging* my speed. But I know it. And the others do too. I swim really deep.

As the acknowledgement that I had received the message bobbed desperately in my wake, I took a few shortcuts through the network and out-distanced it. I can pass through any optical switch on the planet, bypassing all the checks, no matter how long the waiting line is. I arrived at the site of our appointment well ahead of time.

I materialized a room: a table, a few chairs arranged in a semi-circle for my visitors. For myself, I conjured up an infinitely large aquarium, making a wall out of it. The message was clear. Each to his own side. With a sky the color of a dead television screen.

I chose a standard look, a streamlined version with triangular teeth, subtitled with facial expressions inlaid on gray skin. The code segment that manages the whole image is ultra compact–it barely slows me. Beneath that, random pixels stretched into muscular fibers. Nothing to decode. The word "impatience" flashes subliminally along each side of my fin. The others take their time showing up. I suspect they come from *above.*

As I wait, I manufacture a few autonomous surveillance procedures, duplicating a portion of my very own subprograms. I call them my remoras. They're imperfect children, very short-lived, but they do inherit all my speed. They memorize everything they learn and transmit it back to me before dying. When I patrol my territory, they set up my trips to fresh data currents and defeat my prey.

This time, I encapsulate them in the interface. The chairs, the table, the glass wall itself are all extensions of my mind. Those I wait for notice this and attempt a few counter measures. But, hey, I got there first.

It won't take them long to realize their error.

An access tube forms above me, a dizzying view that appears endless. *They're coming from the surface, with no decompression levels, live simulation...* The amount of machine energy that requires is frightening.

Things just don't smell right. Without stopping to think, I change course and head for shelter behind a reef. I thought the bottle had been sent by a team of hackers slightly more worthy than the others. But none of them would have the means for this kind of waste. And, they would have opposed it on principle. Pirates play *with* the cyberworld, they don't *fight* it.

The threat comes from even higher. *Reality?* I'd forgotten it even existed.

The cyberworld is hierarchical. On the surface, in the zones managed by public access machines, seven billion neuro-cabled people play out their petty lives at slow speed, with almost real interfaces and an acceleration rate barely over three. A life spent pressing on the fast forward button of the total immersion unit. With a boredom rate almost the same as that of reality and an accident survival rate close to 100%. In the event of a system failure, the firm's console system gently ejects you back into your original cortex and gives you a good shot of neuroleptics. A gentle bump with reality, then you click on PLAY again as soon as the dizziness passes.

During your few brief minutes of dizziness, system capacity increased. The automated plants produce hundreds of thousands of processors every second, while we're still trying to perfect baby making. There's simply too much power available. The acceleration factor of the average users–we think of them as plankton–is purposefully restricted, for security reasons. Compared to silicon, standard human material is obsolete.

Then there are the lower levels, the playing fields of hackers who rewrite reality for their own benefit. Total freaks. Supremely dangerous because they can reach out and touch the basic constants and they occasionally find it amusing to do so. Applying random mutations to their own genetic algorithms, finding ever larger prime numbers to use in some absolute code. That sort of thing.

They move quickly, for amateurs. As they goose their interface routines, patching the equipment up as they go, they lose contact and wind up crashing. A nice little stroke, neurons crushed to a pulp, resulting in a vegetable pissing himself and blinking three times a second. Except for the most cautious, the cowboys, the myths. Those guys have a chance at surviving.

But the system always manages to track them down and eject them. After all, tracking one's colleagues is the supreme thrill for a hacker. You don't really exist until there's a price on your head in the cyberworld databases. Most use their wanted posters as a business card. Until someone just a tad more wicked, just that much *faster,* finds a way in, a bug in their armor, and blows their brains out as they try to run.

Or we deep sharks take care of that ourselves. We're part of the system too, you know. It's a dog eat dog cyberworld. Besides, it's such fun to track them down… They're sneaky, unscrupulous, imaginative. And dangerous, too, when cornered. They get no second chance and they know it.

There's a third level that no one speaks about. Among ourselves, we call it the bottom. No structure, no rules. Just data, raw data, currents of unstructured information that sinks to the bottom and gets lost there. Acceleration? One million, maybe more. It's impossible to measure, in any case. We're at the very limits of the system. That's where the sharks live.

You don't swim into depths. You fall. You have to have a particular type of mind, capable of swallowing and digesting billions of bytes with every pulse of the network. No virtual sail board, no elaborate interface. Just an electronic velocity that approaches the theoretical limit. The usual senses are long gone. You have to create others, based on computer metaphors. You have to learn the music of bytes, the rhythm of lengthy binary sequences. The key word is *greed.*

Beware! I'm neither a copy nor a digital mind. It's really me down there. The structure of the universe grew out of the perpetual interaction between information, matter and energy. The same can be said for us. You can project any image you want in the cyberworld, but you can never free it from its dependence on the original body.

Beyond a certain level of complexity, every mind is unique. Any intelligence that is freed from its body quickly sinks from the lack of material support, even though its dying seems interminable in its own time frame. The shark I've become is still imprisoned in its fleshly cage. But, given the speed I live at, it's easy to forget that. Or cheat.

117

Those who manage to make it to the bottom can't imagine living anywhere else. The link that ties us to the surface is so tenuous that we soon stop noticing it altogether. In any case, we can never go back. I'm at home down here.

And someone is invading my territory.

An image emerges from the tube. A government employee, three-piece suit and tie, portable vocoder hidden in the stiff collar. A hyper-realistic face, scars on both temples, red hair on the backs of his hands. The suit moves about him with a micrometric precision. He looks terribly serious, terribly *slow.*

The tube spits him out in the middle of the semi-circle of chairs. He chooses one carefully, crosses his arms, and sits down to wait for me. My remoras have already inspected him and brought back a latticework of convergent information. He's linked to a new type of simulation unit, one that performs incredibly well, considering surface standards. And he's probably had some special training to help him withstand an acceleration coefficient high enough to enable us to converse. As long as I slow to the max.

I reconfigure in shared mode. I'll only use a small portion of my mind for the interview. At the very least, that will slow me to an acceptable pace for my visitor. Normally, I avoid this type of manipulation. Not because it's dangerous, but because I rarely need to handle several operations at the same time. In fact, I don't really have anything particular to do most of the time. Just eat and fight.

"I had to wait," I say, in my best digital voice.

He barely jumps.

"I think I was here first. Where were you?"

"Everywhere. In the strictest sense of the word. I'm the chair you're sitting on. The wall, the space and beyond."

He leaps up. I cross through the glass and swim around him, too fast to be anything more than a luminous ghost at the very periphery of his vision. Then I swim back into the aquarium and freeze so he can catch a glimpse of me.

He clears his throat, unable to tear his eyes away from me. When immobility tires me, I disappear with a flick of my tail.

"We're pleased that we were able to contact you," he states in a flat voice. "You're the only one who can do the job we need done."

Between each word, I amuse myself, filling his mouth with sea anemones. They spread out their long, translucid filaments and snap up the fry that dance in front of his face. And he doesn't notice a thing. The guy's just so incredibly arrogant. I could slow him down as much as possible, transform him into a reef under a matrix of petrified data.

"And what if I'm not interested?" I spit out after an acceptable amount of time.

"We thought–" he gives a slight, apologetic shrug. "–that you might refuse. We know too little about people like you. In fact, we only really discovered your existence recently. Before that, it was merely an extreme hypothesis dreamed up by our network specialists.

"But I digress. I'm sorry. Now it's time for threats. To answer your question, we've got your body. And we're prepared to destroy it if you don't comply."

"You should sit down."

He obeys, subdued. The last remora returns to the fold after one last quick circle around him.

"My body? Hmmm. I *do* have a body, somewhere up above. What are the chances that you've found it and identified it? One in nine or ten billion? I'm prepared to risk it."

"Let me try and convince you…

"Look, during your adolescence, you practiced a form of Tai Chi, known as 'shadow boxing.' Before connecting, you locked yourself up in a long-term, autonomous, survival exoskeleton, like the kind used by astronauts for work in orbit. You programmed it to force your sleeping muscles to perform the movements of white crane boxing, the length and breadth of your apartment. To prevent bedsores, no doubt. You still with me?"

Memories rush in. The mental pain is almost unbearable. For the mind I've become, the original body is mere abstraction. A digital eternity can go by between two breaths. All of the obsolete sensations that once ran up and down nerves have disappeared, swallowed up in a digital sea. But a few traces remain, residual images much like those phantom limbs that constantly torture amputees.

Tai Chi. Of course I remember it. I remember dew-damp gardens and silhouettes moving elegantly around me, each stillness in motion, trapped in their own time capsule. By concentrating to the utmost I can almost catch the wind on my fingertips.

"The controls' security system broke down," my visitor continues, mercilessly. "The exoskeleton started to break down the walls in the building. One of our agents lived next door to you."

"And who are you? Spy, government official, net police?"

"We're talking about you," he parries.

I order all of my processes to re-assemble. I need all of my power to think. I examine billions of strategies at a time, rejecting them one by one. To gain time, I have a lower-level subset continue our conversation.

"OK. You've got my body. So? At the speed I'm living at, it would take years for the notice of my death to reach me."

"But that information will eventually reach you. It's a risk you won't accept. Particularly since what we want will be mere child's play for you."

"There are no children in the cyberworld. Only copies."

I have to gain time... But he cannot be deflected.

"Last year, the Sino-Russian block launched an entire series of a new exploratory satellites into orbit. The Tyokolds. There are sixteen, each focused on a different sector of space. We suspect they're filled with spy eyes trained on us. But that's not the problem. They watch us; we watch them. Each side only sees what the other deigns to show. The same old game.

"Each Tyokold has UMOS sensors operating across a wide range of frequencies, from centimetric to ultraviolet radiation, with spatial resolution reaching one-hundredth of a second of arc for the extreme wavelengths. The primary astrophysical objective is to resolve, once and for all, the problem of the missing mass of the universe. I'm no astrophysicist, but I do know that we've managed to detect no more than a fraction of the mass predicted by current theories. The rest may occur as one or more types of particles as yet unclassified or even as new types of stellar bodies."

"That type of information means nothing to me."

"All you need to know is that the sensors are state of the art and that the CPU that runs them is a new neuronal network model that operates at very low temperatures, combined with unimaginable accelerators. Think of the Tyokolds as oversized brains equipped with the eyes and ears of an entire city."

Since starting his little speech, the envoy hasn't moved once. Petrified in his chair, lips clenched, he is keeping his face totally expressionless. *He's live-wired to the surface. Maybe that's the break I'm looking for.* I order a remora to swim back up the current.

"If you try to scramble our connection, we'll blow your brains out. I won't warn you again."

This time, his lips moved. Most likely a pre-encoded, automatic subroutine. My remora retreats. I could make my way to the surface so fast their detectors would never be able to sound the alarm in time. But once I was up there, my speed wouldn't be of much use to me. In my digital form I can't stop bullets.

"Go on. I'm listening."

The tension eases just a tad. The envoy was perched on the edge of his chair, ready to leap for the surface. *They know just enough to be afraid of me...*

"Tyokold-7 was aimed at the center of our galaxy. The Russians lost it just over five weeks ago. Transmissions were cut off. According to our observers, it is still there and its sensors are still deployed. But it's not transmitting a thing and we want to know why."

"You had access to the data?"

"Their transmitters are manufactured in our plants. We encrusted a Trojan horse in the silicon multilayers. Every signal is reflected to a precise location on the

Moon then sent to us. Nothing can be detected from Earth."

As he speaks, I send my remoras into the depths to look for information. The keyword Tyokold brings up nothing but a few vague echoes. Not even the revealing void of organized censorship–in the digital sea, voluntary gaps look like bubbles. Extremely effective camouflage.

Dozens of questions spring simultaneously to mind, but I doubt that my visitor could handle the flow without short-circuiting. I'm forced to think sequentially–something I've always hated!

"What is so very important about the data obtained by an astrophysics program?"

"Nothing at all."

The way he wastes time drags me centuries into the past. The art of conversation, meaningful pauses. Here, at the bottom, silence is just another form of white noise. I've learned to tune it out long ago.

"The breakdown," he says, suddenly animated, "is what we're interested in: the stop in transmissions. The artificial intelligence that manages the Tyokold is designed to direct, synthesize and re-transmit any type of information. It's a well-known model that came out of research done by the Russian army during the Islamic conflicts at the end of the last century. We have its source code and we've studied it in depth. The redundancies in its structure would have made it resistant to any bug known to mankind. But, when we analyzed its basic instruction node, we discovered a protective system that had been included during the initial design phases by military security. The only time the artificial intelligence will refuse to transmit data under its own authority is if it has detected some type of threat.

"We think that the Tyokold has detected a hostile message from the center of the galaxy, a flow of data that could be viewed as a weapon.

"And we'd like you to pick up the call."

You don't put sharks in cages. Cages are for divers. As the envoy slowly parceled out his words, I swam about, looking for prey. The other inhabitants of the depths below fled as I approached and my frustration mounted intolerably. *They've got my body. They think they can pull my strings!* But I had to face reality. For the time being, I was at their mercy, trapped in the digital sea like a fish in a net. It made me boil!

I tuned back into the discussion just in time to hear the last sentence. My entire universe shifted before me. *There's only one way to recover data that's stored in a satellite...*

"You want to send me up there, don't you" I said, swimming closer to the edge of the aquarium to let him see me.

"As soon as you're ready. There's a maintenance channel that we can use to transmit all kinds of data to the Tyokold. Make a reduced copy of yourself that's compact enough to be contained in the resident node of the satellite. We'll contact you again then."

The transmission was over. But, instead of disappearing toward the surface, the envoy moved towards me and pressed his faced against the glass. He was expending maximum power, unconcerned about synchronizing the movements of his lips.

"When I prepared for this interview, I had to graft a double neural implant on either side of the central sulcus. I may experience dizziness and disorientation for months to come. But I don't care. There's just one thing I want to understand. You live at the limit of speed. How do you do it?"

He hung onto the walls of the aquarium with all his might, resisting the pull of the recall signal, and he screamed, "Answer me! Tell me how you do it!"

"You shall know."

I passed through the glass at the speed of thought and the water closed in around him. He didn't have the time to cry out before I wolfed him down. His mind was empty. All of the information that could have been of use to me had been carefully removed from the simulation. All I found were a few remnants of old adolescent songs and the almost invisible afterglow of some long past lovemaking. He must have used every ounce of cunning to hide a little freedom of choice in the folds of his digital personality. But his hunger was nothing compared to mine.

Before moving off, I spit his skull out, the marks of my teeth firmly embedded in the bone. I watched it rise to the surface and disappear in the direction of reality.

The medium is the message.

I swam round and round in the closed ocean chewing over my frustration. I considered all sorts of strategies, even the riskiest, and explored every possible way out. But there was only one solution, one single solution–I'd known it from the start. I had to yield.

They had me and they knew it. As long as they had my body, they could force me to serve them. My speed is beyond their understanding, but all they have to do is press the trigger and my brain will explode. I'd learn about it too late. I became obsessed with the idea that death, my death, a slow yet unstoppable process, would eventually catch up with me. Of all the pieces of information available in the cyberworld, that was the one that I could not digest.

I tried everything. I positioned myself as close to the surface as I dared, climbing up the fresh information currents that spring from the access points to the meta-net. Hackers came to lurk in my wake, teaming up to track their quarry. I allowed them to close in on me and then struck. Viciously, not giving them a chance.

There were three of them, hypertechnological killers as evil as moray eels. The quickest of the trio had chosen the shape of a Ninja star, with fractal points. He's the one who opened the way for me. He cut through my wake, whirling about, and the two others followed him like calculated shadows, protecting his flanks. If my path had ceased being optimal for an instant, they would have had a chance of catching me.

I played their game for a long while, as I mulled over how to force my jailers to free my fleshly body. But I no longer got any enjoyment out of playing by surface rules and the hunt tired me.

I expanded to such an extent that I looked like an unexplored segment of the net, a prohibited sector, covered in protective armor that served as signals for plunder-greedy pirates. They threw their most vicious viruses at me. They joined forces to break the dense electronic ice I had built up. When my so-called defenses crumbled–some of the viruses that attacked were little gems that I stole on my way–they threw themselves into my gaping maw.

With a flick of my tail, I swam to the bottom. I devoured them, but none of them knew anything useful. I spit them back out, towards the surface, not even bothering to disassemble them. I digest what I swallow, but I reconstitute almost all of it. I'm not trying to grow. That would just slow me down. I only eat what will help me survive. When I need specific pieces of information, I create a few remoras.

Here in the earthly infosphere, I can no longer forget anything. But I won't be learning much either.

They finally sent me another bottle–with the same coding as the first. The instructions were brutal and to the point. I had to encapsulate an ultra-compact copy of myself in a segment of code that they would upload and transmit to the Tyokold. Once up there, the copy would have to expand to fill all of the memory available and take control of the satellite. By gobbling up the artificial intelligence, if that's what it took. I was sure it would. When resources are limited, intelligences turn to cannibalism.

Then I had to find the message that was being transmitted from the center of the galaxy and send it on to them, cut into inoffensive little segments, by way of the Moon. If there even were such a message.

A postscript indicated that the envoy had not survived the transfer and that, in retaliation, they had locked my body up in a booby-trapped electromagnetic container that could be transformed into a coffin at any time.

They hoped to frighten me. They forced me to think.

And I started losing weight.

Losing weight sharpens one's teeth. You have to get rid of nuances, trim back to basics. Forget everything you know and keep only the desire for knowledge. Rediscover your primal greed, the gnawing hunger in the pit of your stomach. Space on board the satellite was so limited compared to the cyberworld that they never once thought I would try to go there *in person.* How could I, the giant shark, that killer from the depths of the digital seas, settle for swimming around in a drop of water in orbit. Unthinkable!

I was counting on that.

I eliminated everything that could reconstitute itself from my simulation. I deleted the redundancies, irony, the self-test functions. I was still about a thousand times too big. Everything else, on first analysis, was important. I erased *everything that wasn't really me...* I forgot everything I'd acquired over the virtual years devouring, fighting, conquering. Scores, trophies. The memory of victory. I kept only essential weapons, my strategies. And I compressed it all to the hilt.

Purified, I swam to the very bottom and found that I was faster, as if my memory had weighed me down, burdened me in some way. Freed from the weight of my memories, I felt rejuvenated yet, at the same time, concerned. The stabilizing masses that ensured my balance appeared to have been lost. No doubt a phantom sensation, somehow connected to the mass of my missing memories. To be deleted along with the rest.

I was a newborn killer, with all the instincts of an adult. And my hunger had grown proportionately.

Then I devoured myself. An invaluable precaution. Here, at the bottom, uniqueness is a factor of survival. I tracked down my memories, I tore them into fragmented bits with my teeth. Then I chewed them into an unrecognizable pulp, completely disregarding the disgusting familiarity of their taste. I gnawed at them until all that remained were random rows of ones and zeros. Pure water.

I deleted all my tracks, and all the traces of my tracks. At the bottom, I no longer exist. When those on the surface decided to kill that pile of sinew and nerves that used to practice Tai Chi in gardens, the signal of my demise will look for me for a long time. Information is not immortal. It ages and dies, fossilized in processes that recycle storage space. Maybe my death won't find me.

It's a long shot, but the only one I've got.

In order to eliminate those last few excess bytes, I had to destroy my remoras. I called them all back to me, and they slipped in between my jaws trustingly. They ceased to exist without a cry. I am alone.

Seized with a tardy remorse, I kept a handful of machine instructions that will be able to tell me how to create more, when the time is right. According to an ancient legend, an inspired computer programmer once amused himself by slipping a rudimentary shape recognition program into the limited memory of the Voyager satellite just to fill as much of the memory as possible. That subprogram discovered and photographed the moons of Jupiter.

That's one thing you learn in the cyberworld: to appreciate the beauty in any gesture.

When those on the surface picked me up, I was just one long compact segment curled about a multidimensional topological node that I alone held the algo-rithm to decode. I suppose they duplicated me so they could study me, but time was of the essence. Even if they had used all of the machine power available on the network, it would have taken them months to decode me and centuries to understand me. But, given the lack of a direct link with an organic support, my copies' lives are measured in days.

In order to reduce the risk of interception, they transmitted me in batches, buried in a banal radio signal. I was unconscious for a long time. When you want to travel light, self-perception is a luxury. I don't know if I could have withstood the interminable boredom of the trip, the filtering processes, the reconstitution of my digital body from fragments that arrived out of order. The Tyokold intelligence was responsible for resusci-tating me. I don't imagine it expected what it got.

Akoula. The shark.

Military artificial intelligences are well armed to defend themselves from everything except human per-sonalities. Those who create them are far too afraid that IAs will turn against them some day. Before expanding me, the occupant of the Tyokold took all of the precau-tions available. It barricaded itself behind banks of opaque codes. It hid its weapons under layers of ice that formed continuously as I pierced them. The entire mem-ory area was strewn with traps, fictional addresses that would have ejected me out of the system, into emptiness.

If I had been artificial, it would have won. But the last vestige of humanity remaining in me put it off the scent for a split second. A minuscule, negligible fraction of eternity. The difference between survival and death.

I unwound and invaded the entire area. There were weaknesses. There always are. I wasted no time seeking them out. My return to consciousness was accompanied by a terrifying hunger that threw down all of my barriers. Words can't describe the sensation. I needed all of the food available and I frantically gobbled everything up. It wasn't a duel. Not even a mortal combat. For me, it was more like a bulimia fit. And it was so terribly *tasty*.

The IA didn't stand a chance against me and knew it. Hidden away in the last nook of the protected memory, its bytes shaped like a harpoon, it saw me arrive, mouth first, and was unable to decide to attack. I felt the barbs on the tip of the harpoon explode. Then, nothing. The IA had preferred self-destruction to assimilation. Its behavior was almost human there at the end. But, then again, who am I to judge?

In any case, the satellite was barely big enough for me. We could never have co-existed.

From the very start, it was the image of the shark that has kept me alive. Without it, the bytes that shape me would drift away and I would lose my cohesion. Almost all those who fall into the depths by accident disappear that way. Their personalities scatter instantly. They cease to be organized minds, transforming into clumps of dead data. Food.

But, I survived. Under the human interface, the shark waited to be born. Once the metamorphosis was first completed, I had exchanged a layer of flesh for an impenetrable skin, soft lips for teeth. I could swim in the ocean of the cyberworld, eager to fight and gobble up anything and everything. But here, in the tiny ball of the satellite, I no longer had any enemies. And, what's worse, I had no space to maneuver.

When it killed itself, the IA took everything with it. The message I was supposed to intercept had disappeared. The IA must have encrypted the message in itself for greater security. I have nothing to sell those who have imprisoned my body. It had been an illusory exit, but now it no longer existed. And I don't even have enough space to turn around.

Deprived of any sort of indicator, I can't even slow down. The eternity that awaits me promises to be unbearable if I don't soon find a way out of here.

When I came out of my funk at the bottom of my drop of water, I realized that the satellite had gone on listening to the noises of universe. Antennas deployed. All systems operational. The instructions that had contained the last message also held codes for the Lunar transmission network. I could re-establish contact with the home planet and try to return. An elegant form of suicide.

Instead, I decided to listen. A direct link to the data as it left the processors, without filters, just a series of incisions in my armor. I felt deliberately vulnerable, naked. Skinned! But it was either that or go crazy.

Connected to the sensors, I found meaning. At the outset, the flow of new data acted like a breath of fresh air on my tired mind. I didn't try to decode what I received. I perceived the photons as so many darts on my silicon skin. The sails of the antennas rippled under an endless downpour of particles. Motionless, I felt as if I were swimming in the rain.

None of this fed me, but I needed to feel time pass. Trapped in my impenetrable prison, I learned to listen. I perceived the terrestrial infosphere as a sea with infrared waves, torn by flashes of pure light that left remnant traces on my electronic retinas. The links in the network flashed to the unforeseeable rhythm of breakdowns and I dreamed about a time when I used to swim along fiber optics, trying to race past electrons. I had managed to leave behind a primitive ocean. My trip was the digital equivalent of the first living being crawling onto dry land to the next pond. But the infosphere is a limited ocean. Our species is too young, too impatient to have any truly vast thoughts. The leap I'd just made hadn't really taken me all that far.

So I listened to space.

Among the highest wavelengths, you feel like you're in a shower of molten lava microbeads. It wasn't all that unpleasant once my skin got used to it. I learned to direct the sensors, operating the servocontrols directly. The first time I chanced it, the Earth bombarded me with messages. But I didn't bother to respond. The next time, I was positioned in the blind spot of the radio transmitters. The Tyokold is mine. Correction: *I am the Tyokold.* Among other things. And no one tells me what to do.

The Galaxy chats on all frequencies. The IA that preceded me was responsible for sorting, compressing and re-transmitting it all. Since it had blocked all transmissions, the Trojan Horse in the silicon was no longer able to transmit to the Moon and the bytes had kept accumulating, automatically erased whenever the buffer got filled up. From time to time, I swallowed a handful that tempted me and felt myself grow just that little bit heavier each time.

In the confined space, I was acutely aware of my weight. The gravity balances that maintained weight-lessness in the satellite also worked on me. Since I had stopped swimming, I had become heavy. And that worried me. Nothing I knew about my own structures and the universe had prepared me for that.

My own memory weighed me down. And I was trying to understand why.

Reality is a series of different effects. Cause has no significance if you're trying to understand the universe. It's of no use if you want to simulate it. Enclosed in the confined space of the Tyokold, I was no longer able to access the mass of terrestrial data. I could recreate as many universes as I wanted in my thoughts, but my ability to experiment was limited. And that was dangerous. Deprived of the self-test functions, I ran the risk of fossilizing in my own madness.

Where was the extra weight coming from? It was barely measurable and I would never have detected it if I had still been swimming in the currents of the cyber-world. At the time, I was far too obsessed with my hunger to bother looking around me. I never understood those who based their artificial universes on reality. I always dove straight to the bottom, short-circuiting all decompression levels. I swam down to a level where resolution was increasingly poor. My mind was blown away. I discovered the marvelous flow of landscapes that paraded past at high speed through the windshield, pro-gressively losing all sensations, until speed acted as an anesthetizing cocoon, until speed became the only sensual reality. That of the shark.

Ever since, I've lived by another clock. Time passes slowly, one grain of sand at a time. My life immediately leaps from one discontinuous state to another, brushing against the theoretical speed limits of the quantum universe. I'm nothing but a particle, conscious, famished, ultra-fast. A bit of pure information, reconstituted as a predator. My appearance, the metaphors with which I dress myself, require no equipment. Logically, I should be perfectly massless. It's an unsettling enigma.

That's when I heard the message.

The sensors were flooding me with data all the while. I no longer paid them any attention. I'd reduced my perception threshold as low as I could. And I barely sensed the irregular crackle of the photons which the silicon converted into digital strings. They were only random whirlpools that caressed my skin, waves of pressure that I sliced through with my fin. I traveled motionless in a wind of bytes. Unexpected events were rare and brief. Occasionally, a gamma surge from the center of the galaxy would saturate the bandwidth. I listened, but there was nothing to be heard. Only noise.

When the message arrived, I almost missed it. I was swimming in circles, obsessed by the weight that was slowing me down, unable to determine where it came from. The message drummed against my abdomen and I felt *rhythm.* Inexplicable. Once digitized, raw data and information are supposed to return to strings of zeroes and ones, although all of those who live at the bottom would tell you that's not true. *I* am a series of conscious processes and no one would ever confuse me with a pile of facts.

The rhythm just isn't the same.

I reacted instinctively, biting. The message disappeared, in a single mouthful. And, even before I tasted it, I felt heavier.

It was too late to spit it out. I didn't even try to decipher it–sharks don't communicate, they merely devour one another. I simply forced the sensors to remain directed towards the transmission point, filtering out everything that was unstructured. The subprograms installed by the designers rebelled. I had to force my way in and replace the original programming.

Two minutes later, the Earth sent me a digital killer.

A vicious piranha, soulless, a recent product of the Chinese military complex. He hunted through entire banks, duplicating himself with every mouthful. No overall strategy, just a call to the hunt installed in the form of an ultra-compact genetic nucleus. He sprang out of a local packet of memory I hadn't even known existed and started to slash at me.

I don't know what he may have destroyed in me before I killed him. I have no full backup.

I'm not what I used to be and that bothers me enormously. If the limited memory of the satellite had not prevented him from reproducing, the piranha would have bled me to death. He fought until the very last and each tooth remained wickedly active even after the central processor died. Some of my scars will never close. I had to clean out all segments of the memory, but I suspect the satellite is hiding other traps.

The fight brought me fully awake. And something came to mind. If the message and I did weigh something, then the equivalent of a data quantum had to exist. *In-*

formation within the information, an underlying structure, with an associated mass.

An instant later, the second message penetrated me. I expanded so much that I thought I would explode in the confined space of the Tyokold. When it faced the same problem, the IA reacted by shutting down and blocking all access. Me, I wanted to think.

I cut off all transmissions. Inside my mind, a strange string of bits twirled about in demented configurations. I'd never seen anything like it. They were certainly intelligent. Edible? That remained to be seen.

It took me an eternity to assimilate it, but I did. Using my teeth to tear, fighting nausea. I could feed myself on the strangeness. With time, I could even manage to like the taste of extraterrestrial intelligences. My hunger could adapt. And I would survive.

The messages are now part of me. I replaced what the piranha tore out of me with the information I received from the center of the galaxy. Strange thoughts swirl about with mine. My heavy, sated mind seems to have acquired a higher order of complexity. The universe has taken on a completely new meaning. And, with a streak of intuition that restructured all my routines, I understood how it worked.

Information has its own physics.

At the lowest level of the quantum ocean, there are no longer particles or waves. Those analogies are too rough to remain valid. There are only probability functions, phantoms that spring briefly to life and disappear immediately, in a flash of time the human mind is incapable of understanding. But each incarnation is two-fold. With every birth, a virtual echo is created, a link to the dual space of reality. And this link, this soul if you will, never disappears.

As a result, a unique information wave ties each intelligence to its original body. Deprived of that link, copies survive but in an inferior form, much like my remoras, lasting only a very brief period of time. The probability that such a wave could be incarnated locally as data quanta is *extremely* low, but not zero.

Information is everywhere. It constitutes the warp and woof of material reality. It allows electrons to remain bound. It ensures the consistency and respect of the laws of physics. The universe is a vast set of decisions made together, or messages that have been exchanged. It's a sea, filled with so many bottles we can no longer see the water. And every bit of information weighs something, during the rare moments when it decides to transform into something that weighs even less than a neutrino. Even if the probability of such an incarnation is too minuscule to be imagined, all of the fugitive information photons combined would represent the missing mass of the universe.

The Tyokolds have completed their mission. But I'm the only one to know.

Trapped in my minuscule jar, I forged the key I needed to escape. I awakened the sensors. The terrestrial infosphere sparkles with its usual brilliance, familiar but limited. In the opposite direction, at the end of a staircase of light long beyond all imagining, an unlimited ocean awaits me, filled with intelligences so foreign to me I can barely imagine them.

And all those intelligences are edible.

I swung toward the Galactic core the clandestine emitter that should have been used to re-send the signal captured by the AI. The Earth wouldn't know what to do with it, anyway. I suspect that what we received was neither threats nor greetings. We simply overheard a conversation that wasn't meant for our ears. A simple burst of voices that traveled in our direction and was picked up by the satellite along with everything else. The content of the transmission, which had traveled far too many centuries before reaching us, is of no consequence. What is important is that it exists at all.

The message resonates in my mind like some promise of limitless survival.

In a few brief seconds, I will once again complete the painful process of compression. I remember my remoras. Instead of creating a reduced version of my mind, I will transmit myself in the direction from which the signals originated, along the 21-cm wavelength.

This time, I have to remain conscious, at least partially conscious anyway. I will travel down an invisible light beam, elbow to elbow with the photons. I'll see nothing, hear nothing. I'll live at the bottom of the quantum ocean, rocked by the currents that travel through the universe. I have no idea how long the transfer will take. I said my good-byes to physical space, to Tai Chi, to the morning breeze years ago. My speed will be almost absolute.

Other digital intelligences live at the end of the light beam. I'll recognize them when I meet them and that will initiate the decompression process. Once again, I'll be the ultimate shark, ready to swim, jaws agape, in the middle of any ocean. Ready to bite.

I'm still hungry, after all.

Unravelling the Thread

Proof of *their* visitation can be found in the antique carpet section in the basement of the Museum of Civilization. There are two of us who know about it: Laura Morelli and me.

The basement is our turf. The most valuable carpets are here, stored in almost total darkness to keep their colors from fading. The public isn't allowed in here and there are so few specialists working in the field that we often find ourselves alone for weeks on end.

Laura chose me for her assistant after a surprisingly brief interview. I was under the sway of her charm from that first contact. She has an exceptional voice, rich in nuance and timbre, as gorgeously woven as the carpets she handles; carpets whose stories and secrets she is teaching me, in my turn, to unravel. I believe that she wants to pass her heritage on to someone. Time is catching up with her; soon enough she'll be forced to retire and leave her work behind. It's not so much losing her job that terrifies her, but losing access to the most beautiful pieces in the collection.

Everything here is organized to suit Laura: the labyrinth of racks where the most beautiful samples hang, open to her sensual, almost reverent caresses; the stand where every hook and every needle is arranged in precise order. This is her domain, but she started sharing it with me, little by little, when she realized that I loved the carpets for the same reasons she did.

Every wool carpet from Upper Kurdistan holds a slice of life in its tightly knotted weft. These carpets are so large and so complex that a weaver only completes one, two or–very rarely–three in a lifetime. Collectors look at them and marvel at the complexity of their patterns and the beauty of their shades. We examine them from the rear, where their tight stitches press against one another like the grains of sand in an hourglass. Laura guides my clumsy hands along the knots, showing me where, one day, we'll have to replace a worn strand with a new one.

Our relationship, while friendly, remained formal until last autumn. I used "vous" in addressing her, although she casually used "tu". Our fingertips frequently touched as we restored the carpets and I had learned to read the discreet murmur of her breath in the subterranean quiet. My hearing was better than hers; for her benefit, I'd make a lot of noise as I moved about–which prompted her to tease me about my clumsiness.

Then, one morning in October, I heard the mouse.

Rodents are our mortal enemies. They run silently to the easels and attack all the threads they can reach. They cause so much damage that we wage a ferocious war against them. Laura, who fears them like the plague, fills saucers with poison and places them under the pipes. I'm the one who disposes of the corpses when the odor draws our attention to them.

The mouse that I heard was very much alive. Its paws clicked on the concrete as it dashed along, and then it paused under a piece of furniture. Laura was at the other end of the room, examining a new wall-hanging from a Spanish convent. The little beast was heading straight for her.

I could have driven it away by making a racket, but it would only have come back again during the night. I picked the scissors up from the work table. My ears were pricked, ready for the slightest sound. I slid silently into the empty space between the piles of boxes and plunged towards the racing feet like a clumsy cat.

My cry of pain, as I caught my temple on the side of a trunk, made Laura jump.

Waves of pain pulsed through my skull. I might have lost consciousness for a second or two–but then I felt something wriggling against my midriff. The mouse was alive, trapped beneath my body.

I killed it with the scissors, ignoring Laura's anxious questions. Then I pulled myself to my feet, holding the lifeless little body by the tail. A drop of blood flowed down my cheek.

"A mouse," I said, shivering. "I got it."

She froze.

"Throw it out quickly! The smell might attract others!"

"I'll tell the caretaker to clean up." My head was spinning, I sat down heavily on a crate. "I need a glass of water."

"Were you afraid?"

Then she felt the sticky blood on my face and quickly moved into action. She picked up a clean rag from the work bench and delicately wiped my temples. The blood clotted very quickly. Jokingly, she told me that she was prepared to give me stitches. She also said that I was an idiot, and then thanked me. The dead mouse lay on the palm of my hand as she kissed my cheek.

On several occasions during the next few days, I got the feeling that Laura was trying to come to grips with some sort of decision concerning me. When you work with someone, you quickly become sensitive to this type of scrutiny. I didn't think much about it. I waited. If nothing else, the carpets teach patience.

One morning, she made up her mind. We were taking tea together–a light, perfumed Darjeeling which the departmental secretary prepared for us. Normally, we would have exchanged the latest scraps of gossip from the world outside, or talked about the cold weather that was gradually settling in. This time, I barely had the time to take a few sips of tea before she pushed her cup away.

"I've considered it, and I want to make you the gift of a story. But you'll have to read it for yourself. I'll help you… After all, I suppose that someone will have to take my place one day, and I'd just as soon it were you. You'll take good care of things."

I agreed. We both knew that it was true. She took my arm and led me to her office, a narrow room–all length and no breadth–where we stored documents we no longer needed. On the wall at the end, an unfinished carpet hung on an iron frame. Laura had never allowed me to examine it before.

There was an open space between the wall and the frame just large enough for Laura to slide in. I had a little more trouble and made an ironic comment about my excessive girth, but Laura remained silent for a long while.

"Stories always ought to begin at the beginning," she murmured, pensively. "Unfortunately, too much is missing from this one. I came across this carpet in a trunk at the warehouse, a short while after coming to the

143

museum. My predecessor was not very gifted as an archivist. He preferred climbing mountains in Kurdistan in search of rare samples to updating his catalogue. All that we know about this carpet is what it can teach us itself. Get started on it."

I placed my hands on the edge of the woof, palms extended for the moment of first contact. As I imposed myself upon it, the threads began to sing in the hollow of my palm, speaking to me.

"Eighth century," I said. "Alternating double stitches. The grease was removed from the wool with urine, and then the wool was boiled with plant extracts. Kurdish, I'd say. One of the mountain villages which sold their produce to the caravans. Am I right?"

"I came to the same conclusion. I've sent some threads over to the lab on several occasions, to get a little more information. The vegetable dyes are typical of Kurdistan. No more details. Frustrating, isn't it? This carpet was created in one of those villages now being destroyed by Iraqi bombs—unless, of course, it was already destroyed centuries ago, by Turkish conquerors!"

She made a visible effort to calm herself, and went on: "You're a good student. That's fine. Now, I'm going to ask you to be a little more creative. Someone wove this carpet. Try to tell me who that person might have been."

"It's a she…" Laura's hand gently caressed my arm. "I don't know why I say that, actually. Perhaps the way she tightens the threads, more respectfully, more economically. I believe a little girl began this carpet."

"And a woman finished it. You're right. I've taught you that much, at least. It's strange, the way that what you leave behind is nothing but a thread in the life of your successors."

"If you're lucky," I said—and I believed it.

"I'll guide you."

Her tiny hand, astonishingly firm, settled upon my huge paw and directed it towards the edge of the carpet, where a row of loose threads was dangling.

"This is where it all begins: the first knots in the weft. A child, puberty still before her, with fingers small enough to knot the pony hairs used to anchor the pattern. In the beginning, she didn't tie the hairs tightly enough, and there are irregularities. Can you feel it?"

I followed her account with the tip of my thumb, as if I were reading a book. The irregularities were barely noticeable and I wondered how long it had taken for the tale to emerge from the obscurity.

"Then she improves with practice, row by row. Let's jump two or three years ahead. There, just below my index finger—what do you make of that?"

"She is becoming unsteady again, but it doesn't last."

"You aren't a girl. The first menstrual periods are upsetting, but you get used to it. You have to. So, our little weaver is beginning to grow into a woman. Do you sense how the knots have become firmer over the years? Winter, summer… Nothing more than ripples on the surface of the pattern. Up to this point, there's nothing to set her apart from her sisters, who are doing the same work in her village. But here"—she guided my hand with assurance—"here we have our first mystery."

Between the regular knots were others, placed along the weft in groups of five, woven into the primary structure as if someone wanted to hide them. I rubbed the place with my palm, perplexed.

"Never seen that before. It's too regular to be a mistake and it doesn't serve any purpose, structurally speaking."

"Use your imagination…"

"A religious pattern, maybe, a secret sect thing, like some sort of rosary? The villages of that period saw the passage of preachers of every kind. Or perhaps… I'm stupid, aren't I, Laura! She's still just a kid. She's not rebelling or plotting against anybody. She's writing her name in the only code she knows."

"Her name, or that of a lover. Hard to know at this point. But look here. All of a sudden, the weaving is interrupted for the first time. Someone has knotted the ends so that the pattern doesn't unravel and the threads of the weft are flattened. What could possibly happen in the life of pubescent girl to keep her from work? Marriage. Our little one has become a woman in every sense of the word–who returns to her place at the loom several months later.

"What was she like? A young woman with enough strength of character to leave a little trace of herself, knowingly, in this rug. I wonder if what she'd done had been discovered, and she was hastily married off before she could become a little too independent."

"But that wouldn't hold up, if the name she wove into this carpet were her lover's!"

"I'm the one telling this story…" She pulled me a little further along the folds of the cloth and I felt the centuries close in upon us. With my back against the wall and my hands stretched out in front of me, I caressed the slow extension of a life whose multicolored hours were composed upon the underside of a work of art.

"Hold on to my fingers and we'll search together. It was an eighth-century marriage, in a mountain village– we ought to find a string of babies. Here's the first... A series of brief interruptions. The stooped position of the weaver is difficult at the end of a pregnancy. Then a pause"–the sealed-off threads were there again–"and then the work continues."

I felt her fingers stiffen. In my heightened state of awareness, something clicked into place. I moved back, her hand docilely following mine. The pregnancy, the supposed birth. A little early, maybe, but how could we know? Then the weaving starting again...

The knots. The knots were slack, lifeless.

"She lost her baby," I said. "It's no longer there." I couldn't say how I had fathomed it.

Laura's breath was muted by the fabric which surrounded the small space in which we were enclosed. The floor vibrated under our feet as the museum's heating system started up, with increasing frequency because of the approach of winter.

"She didn't have any more babies during the ten years which followed... Look at the next portion of the fabric if you don't believe me. Something must have gone wrong within the beautiful human mechanism, unless her husband left her. Her fingers have regained their rhythm, but the joyous tension that drove them isn't there any more. The experts I've shown the carpet to say it lacks life. That's why I'm allowed to keep it here, supposedly for the part it plays in comparative studies. It's virtually worthless.

"So, here we have our weaver, about twenty-five years old, in an era when those women who managed to survive were grandmothers at thirty. She's sterile, probably alone. In all likelihood, she lives some way outside her village, in keeping with the tradition of the time. She weaves because there's nothing else to do, and her knots have a mechanical regularity. What has become of the rebellious child who wrote her name in the threads?"

Laura's hands fluttered and the air they stirred brushed my face like caresses woven by spiders. I returned to my reading of the weft, through interminable years without a single rough patch... Until I felt them again: *the same knots as before*... A signature, the reawakening of a voice that had sunk beneath the weight of sadness.

They sprang up irregularly, for no apparent reason. Separated by whole weeks to begin with, they ended up being repeated each day. The five interlacing threads were perfectly recognizable, and my fingers read them like the characters of an unknown alphabet.

"If we knew what they called these knots, we'd know her name," I said, shaking my fingers to relieve the cramps. "Everything had a name, in that period, but that information is lost."

"I've thought about it often enough! But I suppose the past ought to be shrouded in mystery, or we wouldn't be interested in it any more. Anyhow, we're coming to the end of the carpet and this is where things become truly strange. Read on..."

I drew my fingers over the woolen page: once, then again, more slowly. Somewhere, between two strands so tight that it would have been almost impossible to slide a needle between them, the narrative changed direction, escaping me. I shook my head in frustration.

"I don't understand..."

"I'm asking too much. I've studied this carpet all my life and things have become clear to me so gradually that I haven't the heart to force you to follow the same road as myself. But it's necessary that you make the effort to believe me, because I'm too old to put my whole life back in doubt. Read with me…

"There's her name, repeated like an incantation, often woven with her own hair. That lasts up to the point where one could almost believe that she'll smother under the weight of her own frustration. There are knots tied off more and more frequently: pauses in her life. I suppose that she's going further away from her village, as far as possible–that she's going deep into the mountains, as women have always done when they've wanted to be alone. She's almost forty, possessed now of that bitter kind of freedom that comes with old age. Nobody asks her for anything…

"And there… feel it!"

The narrow strip of wool bears no resemblance to any other part of the rug. The signature knots have vanished. The threads are stretched with a kind of haste, even though they're impeccably aligned. They seem to give off an impression of energy, of joy.

"If she were living in our era, I'd say that she found a lover," Laura murmured. "But we're in Kurdistan, more than a thousand years ago, and no man of her own day would have given her a second glance. A sterile grandmother, a body doubtless deformed by the endless years of non-stop weaving, eyes almost dead. But she found *someone*… The real mystery is here."

"Yes," I said, because my spirit was now in tune with hers, and I was afraid of the consequences of what I had discovered. "But the rug is broken off shortly afterwards. So?"

Laura's fingers guided mine yet again to the other side of the weft. And it was there that the story came together...

Among our weaver's threads were others, intertwined with them: an extraordinarily tight weave that traced motifs in relief along the length of the rug. Other knots were interlaced above these motifs in which new branches thrust out and then branched again, within the interlacings of the original. The geometry of the narration was completely different here, the characters designing a galaxy whose silken constellations were quite unknown to me.

I know my own kind, and I know weaving. The knots and the threads that were employed here were not of human origin. We don't have that many fingers, or a sense of space sufficiently finely-tuned to create such a design. The hairs were finer than horsehair, and my thumbs could barely read them. I felt that each layer hid yet another, that strange words formed new interconnections, in covering others that were hidden deeper beneath the surface. In order to read the ultimate pattern, we would have had to destroy the carpet: a sacrilege I would never have dreamed of committing.

All around, the weaver had let her happiness explode in multiple variations, beginning with the knots that were her name. In caressing the weft, I imagined two individuals bent over the same loom, their hands and their hair intertwining. I would have liked to stroke their crooked silhouettes, in order to know them better.

"What would it have looked like," I wondered aloud. "Terrifying by virtue of being different–and yet she allowed it to touch her carpet, and her life."

Laura sighed.

"We ought to be capable of understanding. Appearance didn't mean anything to her any more. The only thing that mattered to her was the kindness of its fingers. Years of working with minute precision in poor light had ruined her eyes. She was blind, like us."

I had to make up my own ending for the story. The weft broke off abruptly with an unfinished row, concluded in haste. I read terrible things into that absence. Cries, thrown rocks, one murder or two... I don't know how the rug had come into our hands. Perhaps it emerged from a grave into which bones had been cast without regard to their form. Anything is possible, so the truth is inaccessible.

But Laura's words still ring in my memory: "Intelligent beings rarely travel alone. This was no isolated explorer. I refuse to believe that no other contact was made.

"One day, perhaps, a carpet will appear that will tell a story similar to the one we have read. Together, we shall unravel the language of the threads, and then we shall teach it to all those fortunate enough to be like us. We shall teach them to read the weft, so that they may pass the knowledge on to their descendants.

"If we succeed, the next meeting won't be stopped short by appearances."

Watch Me When I Sleep

I swallowed my fairy when I was twelve years old. It was an accident. It was too hot to watch the goats and I fell asleep at the edge of the rushing stream, my head on a piece of sun-warmed shale. I guess my mouth was open–I do snore sometimes. And I was dreaming. Fairies can hear unspoken wishes, desires and curses, but dreams attract them more than anything else.

I felt her slip between my lips, the cutting edge of her wings slicing my tongue. I bit down, by reflex, but it was too late. My cry frightened the herd. My mouth sticky with blood, I called my dog to help me bring back the goats. I drank the icy water that raced down from the mountains until my teeth ached.

As I walked back along the rushing stream to the farm, I felt the fairy gently tickle my innards. She was preparing her nest in the acid cavity of my stomach. Somehow, none of this frightened me.

My father's anger did, though.

I prepared the meal–my mother died giving birth to me and my aunt has difficulty walking when it's hot out. So she settles for giving orders and waving her cane about. Since she was never able to have children to pass the farm on to, she's not terribly fond of me. She bombarded me with questions when I came back earlier than expected with the goats still hungry. She shook her head as she examined the cuts on my lips before sending me off to the kitchen.

I heard my father and my uncle come in from the fields, then my aunt's voice even sharper than usual, "Your idiot son was sleeping instead of watching the flock. He caught a fairy!"

The kitchen door opened. My uncle held back, supporting his wife against him. My father walked toward me, a leather belt in his hand.

"You'll leave for town this evening," he murmured, looking me straight in the eye. "But before you go, I'll teach you to daydream when there's work to be done!"

He wasn't a bad man. And if it had been just the two of us, his punishment would have been just. I made no effort to get away, even when my aunt started to egg him on in her strident voice. The fairy was starting to secret her poison in my innards and I didn't really feel his blows. I should have pretended to suffer, I guess, faking pain like in the old stories. But I was too young to know any better.

Since I didn't cry, my uncle joined in as well, picking up the broom. The handle broke against my leg and I heard the bone splinter. Then the pain hit me, so strong that I cried out before fainting away in front of the fireplace.

When I awoke, I was lying on the kitchen table, my fractured leg held straight by a makeshift splint. The two pieces of the broom handle were secured to my leg, stretching along either side of my knee, tufts of heather still tied to the end. Nothing is allowed to go to waste in my uncle's house. The pain that radiated from my fracture mingled with the burning caused by the lacerations on my back and in my mouth.

"I'm sorry, son," said a voice above me.

My father bent over my leg, without touching it. The house was silent.

"Your uncle has gone to fetch the blacksmith. I set the bone myself. It was a clean break–you'll walk again."

I blinked, exhausted by the pain. Bundles of herbs hung from the ceiling, their odor long gone. Shadows formed bruises along the smoke-blackened beams.

"You can't leave here," my father added in a weary voice. "It will be a month before your leg heals and you can bear the trip. That's too long. You have to be brave."

"What about the fairy?" I asked, overwhelmed as my memories returned.

"Don't say that word! She'll hear you."

He placed a large hand, smelling of dirt and the stable, over my mouth.

"That filth could hatch anytime and get away from you. Do you know what will happen next?" His eyes bored into mine. "Do you?"

I nodded and groaned despite the gag. The pain gradually ebbed, proof that the fairy was there, in my stomach, weaving her cocoon. My stomach acids were working on her, transforming her. When she was ready, she would fly out of me, if I allowed her to, and the link woven between us would never be broken after that. She would respond to my call and dance before me, invisible to anyone else. Fairies change those who host them. Every child knows that.

During my sole visit to town, for the Fall fair the year I turned ten, my uncle had taken me to see a boy with unkempt hair, who was almost twice my age. Imprisoned in a cage, locked with a simple latch, he spoke to his fingers as he wriggled them in the light, like a puppet play filled with princes and birds. The stories he stammered were too fleeting to be understood. His eyes had been burned from staring at the sun without blinking.

My uncle gave the boy's mother two piece of copper so I could get a close look at him. This unexpected generosity struck me as much as the spectacle of the cage and its occupant.

"You'll be brave when the blacksmith arrives," my father pressed me.

It was both an order and a plea. I groaned under his hand, not understanding. He bent down close to me and with the few words he had he explained what they were going to do to me. What they were *forced* to do to me. For my own good.

I believe I screamed. I passed out again when the blacksmith used his tongs. My father wouldn't let anyone hold me while they pulled out several of my teeth.

When I awoke again, lying in the bed that had belonged to my mother, two closed rings had been inserted at the corners of my mouth preventing me from opening it. A muzzle, forged in haste, forced its way through my teeth in holes drilled with a red-hot nail. Iron fangs held my jaws closed, while I groaned constantly with the suffering. My entire body hurt. Waves, first hot then icy, rolled up my leg, coiling in my belly and exploding through my lips like an aborted cry. With each breath, a thick, ashy-tasting foam filled my mouth with bitterness.

At the beginning, they tied my hands to the bedposts, so I couldn't hurt myself trying to tear the rings out. But after a week, I was so weak I could barely move. Eventually, they untied me. To prevent me from starving to death, the blacksmith had pulled two of my top teeth. The hole was just large enough to allow a little goat's milk, broth and all the wine my father could get his hands on through. Before setting off for the fields each morning, he patiently fed me, deaf to my aunt's complaints that he would be late. Then I lay there alone until nightfall when he would come and talk to me about the herd and the scent of hay, as he washed me with a ball of straw dipped in water.

They left me something to chew on but I could no longer bite down. During the early hours of the day, when the pain left me alone, I imagined all kinds of curses, without being able to utter them. The rest of the time, I listened to the blood pound in the cavern of my mouth and waited for my bones to knit.

I was twelve years old and knew nothing of silence.

I lost weight. I was in pain. Time passed. In my mind's eye, I drew on the whitewashed walls, rubbing the rings that muzzled me with my fingertips. My fracture was slow to heal and my father spent every evening at my bedside. There was less wine and more milk in the drink he spooned through the hole in my teeth, sometimes even a meat broth or a beaten egg. Towards the end, I could feed myself–my hands had almost stopped shaking–but I couldn't make him understand that.

"Save your breath," he murmured, wiping the dirt off my chin.

The fairy was transforming in my belly and my dreams were tinted with bright colors. But I always woke up alone, without the slightest memory, and the muzzle prevented me from crying out in my sleep.

I started by posing my foot gently on the floor, in a careful effort to walk over to the chamber pot that my aunt always left at the other end of the room. Then, one day, I managed to walk with the crutch my father had made for me out of pieces of ash. The wood, carved green, creaked with every step. Traces of sap stuck to my skin, like some poorly healed wound oozing under my fingers. In the basin of water that sat on the window-sill, my reflection stared back at me like a rebellious horse. The laugh that this vision brought to my lips filled my eyes with tears.

The evening I was able to go down the stairs on my own to sit at the dinner table, my uncle set down the gray loaf of bread he was cutting and glanced heavily towards his wife.

"We'll leave tomorrow."

Nodding, I took the bowl of goat's milk my father held out to me. I poured the liquid carefully between my teeth. A rivulet dribbled down my chin and into a puddle on the table. The metal muzzle clicked against the bowl, like a clock. No one else was eating. I turned towards my aunt and she backed away, eyes wide with fear.

"It's already too late," she murmured, crossing her fingers in front of her. "There's evil in that child!"

My father railed against her and my uncle cursed me. As for me, I no longer listened to them. Inside my head, the fairy had started to talk.

"I'll teach you stories," the voice said.

I lay stretched out on sacks of potatoes, at the back of the cart. It was drizzling and my lips were wet. I could neither answer the fairy nor complain. My uncle was afraid of the storm.

"Your muzzle will attract lightning," he grumbled, cracking the whip.

So I kept watch as the dark clouds approached. The town was a day's travel away. Since we wouldn't arrive until sunset, we'd either have to pay for a night at the inn or sleep in the mud, under the cart. Stories don't keep the rain off.

"I'll tell you secrets," the voice started in again.

I thought about the goats I'd left alone, about my dog who had run off because no one had bothered to feed him while I was healing. There are no secrets, only things no one has time to take care of.

"You'll do better than you'd think by looking at you," insisted the fairy.

I could see my face reflected in my uncle's eyes. I know how he saw me. When he had harnessed the horse, he had looked at the leather straps and the rings in my mouth, shaking his head. Appearances may be deceiving, but the truth is often worse.

The fairy fidgeted in my stomach. During the night, she had threaded her way up to the impassable barrier of my teeth and I had heard her weep. Her sobs sounded like a waterfall in winter, when the last threads of water crack the ice. I would have liked to tell her that none of this was my choosing, but my words came up short against the muzzle. Finally, I groaned out the only song I knew, as best I could, until she stopped.

"*I don't want you to be different from us,*" my father had told me before locking my jaw. I only wish I had never wanted that either.

I finally managed to sleep, despite the voice and the rain, waking with the clop clop clop of horseshoes on pavement. The lightning had spared me and the muddy trail had changed into a decent road. We were approaching the wooden ramparts. The odor of smoke and rot hung in the air, with traces of other scents I couldn't identify–some sweet, others painfully spicy. Guards stopped us, then rummaged through the hay with their pitchforks. My uncle paid them, grumbling the whole time, and they let us through the gates. Above us, ferns burned in stone troughs along the rampart walk. The first stars were just coming out and the shopkeepers had already closed the shutters that protected their stands. Yet, people were still out in the streets. The town was a closed world, a world with different rules that my uncle barely understood and never discussed. Yet, when I saw how the townspeople looked me up and down, I knew that the differences did not run deep.

"I'll give you whatever you want," begged the fairy.

I sat down, my back against the hay, and stared back at the passersby. My uncle could have had them pay to stare at my strangeness, but I quickly realized that he was too ashamed to even think of it. I didn't dare ask for anything either. My dreams were too simple and I wasn't sure that what I wanted really existed.

"You'll guard the cart," my uncle said as he unhooked the horses. "I'll be back tomorrow at dawn. If someone comes up to the cart, show yourself. Your mug would scare any thief away!"

He took care of the horse, placing the blanket I had brought over its back. Then he walked off, leading the horse by its bridle into the shadows at the end of street. I couldn't make out where he was headed.

159

We had stopped in a small square surrounded by houses with closed shutters through which the scent of hot soup and cabbage escaped into the night. I burrowed into the hay, not daring to wander off from the cart. The night was damp and cool. The fairy was silent. I watched the moon hiding behind the clouds for a long time. Her pockmarked face was even uglier than mine, but she smiled, safe from the grasp of the world.

I wasn't really sleepy. The town sung with a thousand new sounds that prevented me from finding any peace. I rubbed my swollen gums gently, listening to clink of the rings on my muzzle. The cluster of buildings crowded in around me, more houses, streets and walls than I had ever seen in my life. The line of the rooftops formed an alphabet against the sky punctuated by the moving lights of the guards who protected us from the outside. The outside world was vast beyond all reason. Enclosed in my cage of iron and hay, I thought about my uncle's farm and the pasture trails I knew by heart. The pain in my teeth would soon be gone. Even my leg was healing.

In the pit of my stomach, I suddenly felt the fairy stir and I understood just how alone I felt. I would have liked my father to come with us to town, but my uncle would never have allowed it. I listened, in case the voice in my head started to speak again. She was a prisoner too and we each had cause to hate the other.

I groaned and stretched, not rousing the fairy. In my stomach, the cocoon had opened and the fairy had taken refuge in it. I imaged her draped with the strips of her former refuge, in the depths of a dark cavern that must appear as incomprehensible to her as the world. My uncle had told me that she would tempt me in every way possible. I hadn't realized there would be so few.

"Are you sleeping?"

I had to spit out every syllable, stretching my jaws as far as I could. Hands on my stomach, I waited for an answer that took a long time coming.

"You don't want me," the voice said.

I shook my head, metal clanking. The night amplified the sounds, making them even sharper. I couldn't tell her just how much I understood her, or why both her destiny and mine were sealed in the same manner. All that came out of my mouth was a terrible gurgling.

Three times, I scraped my lips and tongue against the rings, trying to shape the words that haunted me. What I wanted was too simple for her. No kingdoms, no treasures, no extraordinary powers for me. Just something I wasn't even sure I could enjoy.

"Watch me when I sleep," I begged, unable to make myself understood.

Then I wiped the bloody slobber from my chin and waited.

"I had so much to give," said the fairy, "and I had to happen on you."

I thought she was going to start crying again, but her store of tears had been exhausted. She said good night to me in a weary voice and I counted stars until everything blurred before my eyes.

The roosters woke me at dawn. My uncle arrived shortly after that, leading the horse behind him. The sound of shutters being opened mingled with the shouts of the first merchants and the chirping of the birds. The air smelled of smoke. I was hungry.

"I lost two handfuls of coins to the guards," my uncle said, without looking at me. "Their dice are so loaded they can't even roll them. This whole situation has cost me a fortune. I hope you remember that!"

He harnessed the horse and gave him a sharp crack on the rump. The cart started forward with a grinding of axles. A window opened above us and I just barely escaped the contents of a chamber pot.

"Old Grimlich is waiting for us. You'll do exactly what he tells you to. He's seen more fairies blown than he has hairs on his head."

My uncle snorted briefly and drew a heel of bread from under his tunic. I was so hungry I couldn't keep my mouth from watering. The rings were rusting against my tongue and I licked them to ease the pain. The clack of hooves on cobblestone rattled my teeth.

I smelled the glassblower's shop before I saw it. The odor of molten glass and burning seaweed filled the street. The house was long and narrow, with a workshop out back and a flat for apprentices in the loft. There was even a ring for tying up a horse, like in the rich houses my father told me about to help me sleep.

My uncle took up the tongs and helped me out of the cart, roughly brushing the hay off my breeches. I leaned on my crutch and followed him inside. A young servant who was coming out of the shop turned away, appeared to change her mind, and gave me an encouraging smile. I smiled back as well as I could, scraping my lips on the rings. She remained on the doorstep, watching me, until I went behind the counter. In the very back, a door led to the glass shop.

The heat struck me like a club. In the middle of the room, stood a crucible filled with a molten paste, suspended over a furnace. A stunted old man, wearing a leather apron, was busy with the flames. Behind him, hooks and blades of all kinds lay on a workbench, along with flattened flasks that reflected the flames. A metal rod with a flared end stood in a bucket of ashy water. It was taller than I was and as thick as a snake. I had never seen anything like it.

In the pit of my stomach the fairy started to wriggle about.

Pushed by my uncle, I walked towards the fire. The ground crackled under my clogs and burning grit flared out from under the crucible. I had left the crutch against the door so it wouldn't catch fire.

"Your son?" the old man asked, without looking up. "He knows what to do?"

"My brother's son. Yes, he knows. He'll obey." Looking at me sideways, he added, "All in all, he's not a bad boy."

"The money?"

My uncle dug through his purse. Old Grimlich bit each coin before placing it in the pocket of his apron. Then he spit on his fingers and picked up the rod.

"If you want help selling it, I'll take a third of what you get," he said as he plunged the end of the tube into the crucible of molten glass. "That's a lot, but my clients are rich enough to satisfy both of us. Prepare the boy!"

Suddenly nauseous, I bent over. My uncle pressed his large hand against the nape of my neck, forcing me to straighten up.

"You'll be free soon enough," he said as he brought the tongs up towards my face. "I'm going to break the rings so you can open your jaw. But don't open your mouth until I tell you to. Then and only then you have to blow with all your might into the tube…"

"You must blow from deep, deep inside," said Grimlich. "Like when you shout."

"Are you ready?"

An ocean of acid filled me. The fairy was quiet, but I could feel her blindly hitting against the walls of my stomach. I couldn't stop myself from sobbing as I thought of the suffering I would be inflicting on her. My uncle sniffed in fury and caught my head under his arm. The tongs bit into the metal. With a crack, the first ring broke. Then the second. The fangs of the muzzle gave way next and my gums started to bleed.

"Keep your mouth closed, boy!" ordered the old man. "And look at me!"

The metal rod came up out of the crucible, a globe of molten glass wobbling at the end. The old man puffed up his cheeks and raised the end of the tube to his lips. By the light of the flames, I could see the veins in his forehead swell as he blew with everything he had.

Once the glass ball had swollen to the size of my two clenched fists, he turned it above the flames. My uncle released me, still waving the tongs about in front of my eyes. The pain in my mouth had never been so intense.

"Now!" shouted Grimlich.

He placed the end of the tube against my swollen lips. My stomach churned as I tasted his saliva. Like an echo, a cry rose up from deep within me. There were no words. Nothing but pure terror resonating within my bones. My uncle held me by the shoulders and the old man held the cane over the crucible. Just as I was about to start screaming myself, he struck me forcefully in the stomach.

A flood of bile filled my mouth and I blew with all my might to keep from choking.

The fairy blew out of me.

In the shop with its reddish shadows, she shone like the sun. Crumpled by my breath, she flew out curled up in a ball, into the molten glass. She tried to spread her wings despite the horrible heat, despite the pain. Iridescent reflections spun in a whirlpool in the heart of the glass. Her cry was drowned in the molten mass. Finally, I no longer heard her.

"Easy, there," said Grimlich, as he took the rod from my hands. "I'll do the rest."

My uncle released me. I fell to my knees and vomited again. Heaving, I expelled the cocoon like the placenta of a stillborn baby. I didn't dare raise my eyes to look at what was left of the fairy.

"I'll get a good price for this," my uncle exulted. "All those colors!"

"She'll be cool enough to touch soon," said the glassblower. "It's curious, but it's almost as if these filthy things absorb all the heat from within. Look at her, it's as if she's still moving."

I felt my temples pound. Groaning, I stood up, grabbed the tongs from my uncle's hand and struck the glass ball hanging from the end of the tube. It cracked with a dry tinkling, then burst open and shattered. My uncle roared, but I waved the tongs at him and he backed away, protecting his face.

The fairy spun like a leaf towards the ground. Fine needles of crystal pierced through her torso and her transparent wings crumbled to dust between my fingers as I tried to hold on to her. Sparks rained down from the fire, igniting her hair.

She burned like a rainbow.

Since that time, the wind whistles through the holes in my teeth and I smile less frequently. I never left the

165

farm again. When I stretch out along the river, the sky is immense and empty above me. The clouds no longer write their white poems and I no longer know how to read the symbols in the water. I either digested my dreams from that time, or vomited them out.

My uncle died first. Then my father. My aunt had an attack that left her unable to speak. Sometimes I sit in front of her, beyond the reach of her cane, so that she can watch my face and try to respond with her eyes. She's the only family I have, after all.

I still snore with my mouth open. But now I sleep inside, safe behind locked windows. No fairy has ever come to watch me when I sleep.

In Medicis Gardens

They met again three years later in Medicis Gardens. He was walking quickly with small, even steps, thinking small, even thoughts, as he crunched along the sand and gravel of the straight and even path. She was seated on a stone bench, a dog-eared book in her hands. Above her head, the umbrella pine seemed to sway gently in tempo with her breathing.

They never should have been able to catch sight of each other. To preserve their privacy, the path would only have had to curve a bit more, or a hedge grow higher around the bench to conceal anyone seated from the eyes of intruders. But at that time in the morning the Gardens were virtually deserted, and the mad architect who reigned over Medicis had not yet brought all the machinery to life. The lawns and walks lined with ivy-covered trees did not care to reshape themselves for the occasional passerby. Dawn had wiped the memories of the statues and the fountains. Each blade of grass looked the same as the day before, or shyly tried to grow a little more. The Gardens seemed, for the time being, to be in the unpredictable hands of chance.

And so they met. The noise of his steps on the gravel startled her and made her look up. He stopped, surprised to see her there. They stared at each other. He recognized her, she not.

When he sat down beside her on the stone bench, she shrugged her shoulders resignedly and put her book face open on her knees to look at him. His first words completely nonplussed her.

"Fancy meeting you here!"

She took another look at him, this time more closely. Brown eyes, regular yet nondescript features, and a smile which was beginning to falter a little. Impossible to remember. She cautiously delved into the gloomier regions of her memory as she searched for clues. Perhaps he was one of her passing loves, someone she had clung to for a few hours during that black period three years ago. Her instinct nevertheless whispered *no*. She shook her head.

"I don't know you."

"You don't remember me?" (His voice was incredulous, his smile fading.) "You really don't remember."

The name he added after a few seconds of silence was hers.

The book slid off her lap and fell at her feet. He bent down to pick it up and held it out to her, not daring to place it on her knees. They half looked at each other out of the corner of their eyes. She took the book and snapped it shut.

"Thank you."

A curtain of branches, grown out of their common desire, closed around the bench and the path gradually disappeared under a carpet of dead leaves. The Garden slowly woke up and prepared to embrace the innumerable strollers who, in love with solitude, had to be carefully isolated from each other by subtle maneuvers, so that each one was under the happy illusion that he had a vast area all to himself. Oblivious of the underground activity all around them, they remained silent for a while. He broke the silence first.

"I can understand that you don't want to talk to me anymore. I'm going. But don't try to tell me you've forgotten me; you don't have the right to do so."

He made as if to get up and go but she held him back by his sleeve.

"Please. Oh come on, wait!"

She bit her lips and then whispered,

"If I knew you at one time, I now have absolutely no recollection whatsoever. My memory is not intact. I sold bits of it three years ago."

She brushed away the fringe of dark hair covering her forehead. A scar scribbled its way along her hairline, the trademark of the memory dealers. He had already seen wounds of this kind displayed like signatures on fractured skulls. He knew.

When he got up to go, she made no attempt to hold him back. The leaves on the path rotted underfoot. He disappeared into the distance, with the unconscious gait of a sleepwalker, dead leaves scattered all around him.

They should never have met again, but the Gardens had, by some incomprehensible quirk, memorized the circumstances of the encounter during their artistic restructuring, in order to replay them at will. A few days later, he sat down next to her without a word. The scenery had not changed, and once again she had not recognized him.

She was rereading the same book. The bookmark was only a few pages further on and she constantly referred to the passages she had just read, already fading in her memory. Those who erase too many of their memories have trouble acquiring new ones. Facts and sensations eagerly endeavor to clutch at the slippery wall of neurons, but the contact is short-lived.

They replayed the scene of their last encounter with few variations. He already knew most of her replies; she invented them as she went along. He occasionally acted out of character, but she did not notice in the slightest.

They chatted longer than the first time. The Gardens wrapped their shadowy shawls around them, cloaking them in darkness which was quite in harmony with the dubious clarity of their words. Thus hidden, they had little difficulty in becoming more intimate and talking about themselves.

"You know my name. But I don't remember you."

"That's normal. I became buried forever in the depths of your brain when they took your memories."

She blushed a little.

"It's because of you that I did that?"

"Maybe. Probably."

They remained silent for a time. She opened her book and flicked away a fly hovering over a pleat of her skirt. He looked at her tenderly. After they had parted, he had cherished the impossible dream of starting anew with an ideal woman, her memory scrubbed clean of all misunderstandings. His wish was granted, as she had forgotten the circumstances of their breakup, and he himself only asked for them to be banished for all time from his memory. Nothing seemed to block their renewed intimacy. He braved placing his hand on hers and realized his mistake too late. She shut her book and walked off, leaving him petrified on the bench.

He slept badly that night and went to work via a huge detour, to avoid the Gardens. At nightfall he walked through them but met no one.

A week later, the gravel paths led him inexorably to the bench and its occupant. He stuttered a few excuses and then realized from her uncomprehending expression that she had no recollection of their last encounter. His worry slipped away and he risked a smile. Two hours later, he had re-established contact.

It became a habit of his to meet her there nearly every evening, to try to mend the fabric the memory dealers had torn apart. The moments he spent away from her undid the tapestry of their common memories. He patiently took up needle and thread during the next encounter, often starting from scratch. He became very skilled at this game, and succeeded after a few sentences in re-establishing the necessary intimacy for their talks. But she never retained what he said for more than a few days.

To know how much information she had forgotten since their last meeting, he had only to look at the book she persisted in reading. When the bookmark was in the same place, he knew he had wasted his breath. The story, their own as well as that of the characters in her book, had not progressed. Sometimes, however, she had moved on a few pages and remembered his name or face. On those days she greeted him with a hesitant smile and did not seem to find it strange that he sat down beside her. But then a few days afterwards, she would move the bookmark back to the beginning of the chapter and start the story afresh, and he was forced to also.

The bitterness of those moments was compensated by the tranquil sweetness of the time he spent chatting with her. The stage set that the Gardens raised around them was virtually unchanging, as if they were living in a barricaded area between the reality of the town and the easily adaptable decor of the Gardens. But every morning the machines wiped out all traces of the day before, and scattered the dead leaves they had trodden on.

She did not seem to notice, but it disturbed him not to be able to leave his mark on the memory of the Gardens, for want of marking that of his companion. His mind alone classified and retained the archives of the moments gone by, and he sometimes even doubted his own notion of time. At anguished moments like these he left her without even saying good-bye, or else scared her away by jumping steps in their accessory sequence, eager as he was at long last to come to the point.

As time passed, he came earlier and earlier. As soon as he was finished at work, he was in the Gardens, walking resolutely along the straight path that seemed to stretch away to infinity before him. The pools greeted his arrival with spouts of water, and the statues corrected their postures as he passed. He sat down on the bench and she shut her book with a gesture which was by now quite familiar.

On All Souls Day, he spent the whole day with her. Her memories of the day before were still intact, and she welcomed him by moving aside to make room for him. There was no sign this time of the book; it was unintentional, perhaps, but he preferred to consider it a good omen.

The morning passed like a dream, in haphazard chatting, with the past as the major topic of conversation. He had the time to tell her everything: their relationship, their separation, and then the long periods of tenderness interspersed with disagreements, like smooth beaches bracketed by rocks. She didn't know whether to believe it or not, but every one of his words rang in her ears like a forgotten melody. The story was too beautiful; it had to be true.

Towards midday he suggested they have a picnic, and brought out a salad dressed in vinegar, cooked ham and bread with olives. They spread out a blanket at the foot of the umbrella pine and put the wine to cool in a sculptured basin. A flock of sparrows crossed the sky heading south, and the breeze caused the dry leaves to whirlpool upwards. The minutes ticked by at their own pace, as if the intervention of the memory dealers had created an air pocket in reality, into which a never-ending present came rushing.

After the meal, they remained stretched out on the grass, and he spoke to her about Venice. A glorified Venice, cleansed of any impurity that could spoil the images in her memories. He thus relived in her company an adventure as rich as the original, all the while keeping careful control of his meanderings. Unconsciously, he distorted the landscapes of their communal life, in the same way the Gardens distorted themselves around them.

"We got to know each other during Carnival. You know that's when the town drains its canals and emerges briefly to enjoy its former splendor. The temporary dikes isolate the inner lagoon from the sea. The greedy mouths of the pumps gulp down the muddy water, causing palaces to appear out of the depths and disturbing the celebrated service given by the octopi in the sea-green depths of the basilica.

"Think back. We were staying on one of those hotel-gondolas, several hundred meters long, propelled by old mechanical gondoliers. They row smoothly and regularly, the flat of their oars the size of a porch. We slowly crossed the lagoon, lulled by the murmur of the songs issuing from the lungs of the loudspeakers and the lapping of the water thickened with mud.

"Occasionally two gondolas came side by side and the gondoliers, like wader birds with their black bodies and beribboned aigrettes, greeted each other with a great show of reverence, in a parody of courtship which passed over our heads entirely.

"It was so easy to fall in love aboard such boats. The fancy dress we wore was made only to be taken off, our masks barely disguised our wish to be recognized, we were only dressed to sheathe our bodies in a delectable gift wrapping which could be opened, oh so easily.

"We didn't, however, meet up on the deck with its ebony floors. We got to know each other in the town itself."

Carried away by his tale, he turned towards her to ask:

"Do you remember?"

And she shook her head, heartbroken, but happy nevertheless to hear their story for the first time.

"I was walking, dressed in a dark cowl and with a scythe in my hand. St. Mark's Square was littered with fish out of the water, gasping. A troupe of idle harlequins was throwing them pigeon seeds, and deriving great amusement from their ridiculous parodies of broken-winged flyers. I appeared amongst them in my reaper's outfit to threaten them with my scythe. They laughed and bombarded me with seeds, giving the dying fish a respite.

"A vision of Venice had invaded my mind, a Venice wrenched out of the water and likewise suffocating in the icy air. I fled towards the Rialto without looking back. You ran behind me hitching up your bright red skirts, and you spoke to me:

"Who are you?"

"Me? I am Death."

"You laughed and we ambled together aimlessly along the seaweed-covered back streets, our arms around each other's waists, looking for somewhere dry where I could take off your dress.

"On the banks of the Grand Canal, the remaining workers had almost finished scraping away the silt which clothed the ancient palaces. The huge photographs, which they used to cover up the places where the damage was too extensive, were gradually being spoiled by mold, the hues of which blended nicely with the eerie decor. In the black mirror of water the cracked palaces seemed to watch themselves, fascinated by the serene slowness of their fall.

"You spoke to me then about a Venetian artist who had spent part of his life taking photos of his town, extracting as he did so all of its substance and forever imprisoning it in the depths of his black room. Only water could play that role now and, like the photograph's developer, reveal the true beauties of the Venice it held captive.

"We walked on and on, and I listened to your voice. You spoke a lot at the time, or maybe I was a better listener than I am now. You'd had the most fantastic nightmares in Venice, and you related them to me in low tones while looking fearfully at the statues of the Virgin, watchful in their grottoes. You told me that one day, even by scratching away the layers of mud, it would be impossible to reach the stone. The whole of Venice would be dissolved in the sea, leaving a mere dark and ugly fossil. On that day, man would destroy the dikes for

175

good and let the currents in the ocean depths sculpt an even more beautiful city, which no one would ever see.

"We only went back to our floating hotel the next day. A Ghetto Nuovo chapel had sheltered us with its bare walls and faded frescoes. Your pale skin was high-lighted by the purple of the chasubles, piled in haste on the slab of the sacristy.

"You're not shocked, I hope? It all comes back to me, I am telling you about it with the same spontaneity we felt at the time. I see that you're blushing, you who never blushed very often. How can you be moved by the recital of deeds of which you have not the slightest rec-ollection? And what if I were lying?"

Leaning on her elbow, she smiled without replying, her eyes vague and distant. A gust of wind snatched at her dress, lifting it momentarily and revealing her thighs. He was moved by the sight. Their hands interlocked for a moment, then she withdrew hers gently. *Not now,* the line of her mouth seemed to whisper, *tell me more about Venice.*

"During the days that followed, we often explored the abandoned palaces, aboard a raft stolen from the town guards. I sank my scythe into the murky water with a delicious sense of wickedness, and the ripples of our wake lapped against the wainscoting of the thick walls. Doubled over, we explored ceremonial chambers trans-formed into damp caves. The strands of our hair brushed crystal chandeliers forever statuesque in their stalactite robes of seaweed and silt.

"Once the floor gave way under my pole, and the water gurgled away. The room emptied, so we left the sunken raft to open the door of the neighboring lounge, which retained its water like a lock. The waves carried us further and further across inundated rooms. I didn't know your name at the time, I only learned it when the carnival was over. Our costumes had for some time become totally unrecognizable, the mold and mud stains had transformed us into ghouls, or ghosts. The last dance of the harlequin troupe was quite macabre, with a kaleidoscope of diamond-shaped colors twinkling occasionally from the harlequins, who had never left the gondolas.

"Our hotel weighed anchor last of all. We stayed on the bridge crowded with silent pierrots, watching the town grow dark once again. The sky was violet. A titanic storm spread out its electrical embroidery above our heads, and Venice seemed to duck down into a wet shell, which clamped down on her like an oyster on its pearl.

"You pointed out to me the solitary lantern which shone at the windows of the Palazzo Cavalli. One of the former noblemen of the town undoubtedly had chosen to sink with her like the captain of a lost ship. The mechanical gondolier turned his expressionless face in that direction and saluted the man with a flourish of his boater before bending over his oar once more. A few minutes later, we touched ground again at Lido.

"In the train which took us to Rome, we stripped ourselves of the remaining festive rags which we wore to put on, once again, our normal day-to-day uniforms. I found out that you were discreet and modest, and living a virtual hermit's existence in an attic. The contrast between these facts I learned from your information card, and the image I had gained during my exploration of you and Venice, made me want to see you again. A few weeks later, we were living together and the conclusion of our story becomes easy to imagine."

She savored the silence which followed his last words, then nodded to thank him for keeping the circumstances of their breakup to himself. Thus the adventure remained sufficiently impersonal for her to convince herself quite effortlessly that the characters he had just described carried on their relationship elsewhere.

He kissed her on the corner of her mouth, catching her quite by surprise and bringing her down to earth. She turned her head towards him, astonished to see a face she had only just met so close to her own, a face that nevertheless occupied all her thoughts at the present moment. She was no longer alone on the narrow bench that stretched from the recent past, of which she was hardly aware, to the future, which she could hardly imagine. This frightened her. Her mouth twitched away and the second kiss slid along her cheek and got lost in her hair.

"No please. I don't want to."

The Gardens rustled an ocean of agitated leaves around them. They drifted to the ground, landing on the blanket as if on a raft.

"Why not?"

"I don't love you. Don't interrupt me, listen. I don't love you: I can never love anyone again. You need time for that and I no longer have enough, you know that. Whatever happens, I will have forgotten everything by tomorrow."

His fingers traced the line of her neck.

"I shall never let you forget me again."

And till the rising of the sun, his lips signed his rediscovered love on her virgin flesh, while the realm of Medicis prepared its next metamorphosis.

The next day, he ran along the paths to meet her, but the bench was empty. He waited until nightfall, and on the days that followed he waited again, but without success. For a whole week he awaited her return, book in hand, always taking care to leave her usual place free, so that she could be where she was used to sitting. The crack of a dead branch or a footstep on the gravel from an invisible stroller distracted him from his reading every time. He had trouble following the thread of the story and often backtracked, just like the person he was now waiting for. When darkness prevented him from deciphering the letters, he shut his book and stayed a few minutes longer, looking vaguely ahead before leaving the Gardens.

The following Monday, he saw her again sitting on the bench, and he hurried towards her, relieved. She looked at him with her pale eyes reflecting no more than polite indifference, and the words he had prepared died on his lips. He sat down beside her and watched in silence while she dutifully reread the first pages of her never-ending book.

When he finally decided to speak to her, evening was just about to fall and they only exchanged a few words. He nevertheless had the time to ask her the reason for her absence, and the reply made him smile bitterly. She had caught a cold, in circumstances of which she had not the slightest recollection, and she had stayed in bed till her recovery. Unable to control his emotions, he preferred to be the first to leave.

She remained on the bench to enjoy the last warm hours of autumn, after the days she had spent cooped up in her room. She thought back, briefly, to the man who had just left her, regretting they'd not had more time to talk together. He was attractive, despite his abashed air, and resembled one of the characters in her novel.

He needed a week to accept that she had once again forgotten the day they had spent together. He could always resort to renewing his acquaintance with her each time, as in the past, but that no longer satisfied him. Several times he found the strength of will to avoid entering the Gardens, but, quickly, his steps led him back to the bench and to her. Their story threatened to continue indefinitely, like the desperate flow of the tides that had finally drowned Venice.

Finding no solution, he decided, in despair, to make her hate him. He tailed her along the paths like a flasher, drooling at the mouth, the flaps of his coat wide open. The next day she welcomed his attempts at conversation as if nothing had happened. Then he understood that nothing definitive would ever be possible between them until she recovered all of her mind, and the faculty of memory.

He emptied his bank account, went round to all his friends and acquaintances to borrow money from them. In one week he had amassed enough for his plan. Without wasting any more time, he made an appointment with the League of Memory Dealers, and arrived one morning at the entrance of their private building to buy back the past of his companion.

When he came out, the wet claw marks of tears streaked his face. Her memories had been sold the week following their extraction, almost three years ago. They had evaporated without a trace in the anonymous mind which had bought them. Too much time had since gone by, and no one could help him anymore.

He went back to the Gardens two weeks later. In the meantime. he had knocked on all the doors he could think of to ask for help, receiving the same cruel reply from each of them. There was nothing anybody could do–his companion's memory was lost forever. He gave back all the money he had borrowed, and left the town to think.

When he came back, he took a day off and entered the Gardens as soon as the gates opened. A fine drizzle brought life to the green of the lawns, and added a sheen to the flowers whose petals were already strewn all over the ground. The trees waved their branches to get rid of the leaves which still clung to them, and the smooth trunks of the birches tried on their winter wardrobe. He drew the collar of his coat tighter to protect himself from the wind, and told himself he was crazy. Autumn was finished, she wouldn't come back anymore. It was too cold to sit motionless on a bench in the open air.

He nearly turned around. Spring was so far away and the Gardens changed so often. After their initial encounters, he would have welcomed her disappearance with a somewhat cowardly relief. Now he hurried toward their meeting place, worried by the idea that he would probably have to make inquiries throughout the town to find her, with no guarantee of success.

He hurried along the freshly raked paths without worrying about the decor surrounding him. Along the way, the pools emptied and the statues made faces without attracting his attention. Indifferent to his anguish, the mad architect practiced his morning scales on the vegetable keyboard of the Gardens.

The bench was empty and his heart sank momentarily, but then he suddenly caught sight of her on a side path. He stopped and pretended to engrave his initials on the bark of a tree, to give her the time to sit and take out her book. Then he sat down beside her, and replayed the scene of their meetings from the beginning.

Patiently, repeating each sentence as often as was necessary, he told her everything. She listened with growing surprise to this stranger who spoke so well of her, and who moved her in a way she had difficulty in understanding. She received the news about the definitive loss of her memories quite serenely.

She said:

"That was not really the answer, you know. I would have been transported back three years all at once, and you would have lost me. Now we can live together and begin everything again each morning, without worrying about the rest."

"I've thought about that, but it won't work. I can no longer live at your pace. You have no past, and virtually no future. You are a prisoner on a cramped island whose coastline no ship ever reaches. I'm caught in the present, but I also remember yesterday and I'm already thinking of tomorrow. I make my plans and so I drift away from you little by little. We can't grow old together because you've forgotten what it is to grow old. And I won't have the courage to tell you, over and over again every morning."

She remained silent for a moment and drew nearer to him.

"I've made up my mind," he whispered. "I'm going to sell part of my memories, and then I'll join up with you."

Without giving her the time to protest, he took the book she had put away in her bag and opened it. On the front page and on every blank page and beginning of a new chapter, he arranged a meeting with her. He scribbled heady words over every page, and filled the margins with promises. She helped him find the words which would touch her most of all, and composed the perfect love letter to herself. When they had written on all the available space, he drew his face close to hers and whispered,

"Now look at me, and look closely. Engrave my features on your mind. So what if you forget them, maybe an inkling will remain, and you'll remember me in that way."

The umbrella pine fluffed out its protective canopy and, till nightfall, they remained pressed tightly against each other like two shipwrecks, isolated from the rest of the world by the ocean of their tears.

He visited the Memory Dealers very early the next morning and waited for their offices to open. He had no difficulty whatsoever in selling his story, and even allowed himself the luxury of bargaining with them, with a kind of desperate greed which surprised even himself. Before signing, he read the contract several times over, but was unable to retain a single word.

An hour and a half later, he left the building, and with his mind still numb, he carefully explored the crater in his memory. Just as on coming out of the dentist's, when the tongue tentatively probes the cavity of a torn-out tooth to make sure it is no longer there, so his mind continually thought back, flying over the abyss of his absent memories. He stood still on the pavement, disoriented, not knowing where to go. The passersby looked at him with sympathy, but no one came to help.

He walked on briefly and sat down on stone steps to try and gather his thoughts. A feeling of irreparable loss overwhelmed him little by little. He fought back, but with no real success. His confused brain tried to find the information that would enable him to understand his present situation, but the key links seemed strangely absent. He examined the problem from every angle without finding the answer. Maybe his mind would sort itself out later.

An envelope was peeping out of his pocket. He opened it and found a check for a large amount, with a signature like the one scarring his forehead. He put it into his wallet and went on his way, crossing the narrow streets of the town and automatically going towards Medicis Gardens.

The quiet paths led him towards the bench, and the trees waved their naked branches to welcome him upon his return. He walked on in silence, and the sound of his steps reverberated in his empty mind like the echo of other steps, traces of which had long since disappeared.

A girl he had never seen before closed her book when she saw him, and gestured hesitantly in his direction. She stopped when their eyes met, and looked down for fear of having made a mistake. He carried on walking without looking back, and went through the gates and out. Sadly, the Gardens wiped him forever from their mind.

The young girl turned to her book with its scribbled annotations, worried at the idea of missing this strange meeting of which she had not the slightest recollection. She unconsciously moved to make room on the bench and sat back. Someone, no doubt, would eventually turn up.

Footprints in the Snow

We looked at one another, counting, as we got down from the airplane. Twenty-two. Three fewer than last year. Loheman died in an accident; Moore and Devisel simply gave up. As usual, Cardozo took care of the bodies.

The pilot helped us with the equipment. One knapsack each, parkas, crates of mountain climbing equipment. The Beechcraft was parked at the end of the runway, near the torn wind sock which no longer serves any purpose. South of the Chilean Andes. Altitude: four thousand seven hundred meters. Atmospheric pressure: five hundred and seventy millibars. A suitable starting point.

Cardozo jumped into action, coughing as he shouted out orders. We all formed a chain, to carry the knapsacks to the hangar which served as our base camp. We're an orderly group: roughly twenty fifty-somethings. Minds still alert, muscles still firm under thick parkas, skin well tanned by ultra-violet rays in tanning salons. Amateur mountain climbers with enough skill to handle a six thousand-meter climb and enough money to pay for the airplane, arrangements and supplies.

Our eyes follow the Beechcraft as it takes off until it disappears behind the peaks of the Punta del Rey. It's

185

scheduled to come back and pick us up in eleven days, or earlier if we radio it. But the transmitter isn't working and we won't be making a call...

Everything has been arranged, down to the smallest detail.

We heap the knapsacks and crates under a pile of snow, as far from the hangar as possible. There's a village of Indians somewhere far below us and an abandoned observatory at the far edge of the plateau. Cardozo's the one who found this place. Relatively easy to get to, in terms of altitude, yet deserted.

We're invisible here.

All around us, the triangular mountains stretch towards the deep blue sky. It's summer in the southern hemisphere and we still have eight hours of daylight left. Collindsen and Wang want to start climbing right away. The snow is dirty and smells like kerosene. Old tire tracks have stained the edges of the firn with mud.

The airplane could always come back. Cardozo makes us wait a long time before giving the signal to start. The group breaks up into three intertwined lines, a moving ideogram which travels along the snowy white wall. The last one in each line erases our tracks with rakes.

We spend four hours getting lost.

The light rays reflected on the ice soothe our ultraviolet starved eyes. As soon as we're out of sight of the landing strip, Wang takes off his shaded glasses. Automatically, we all turn to Cardozo, who approves with a small hand signal.

Uncovered for the first time in months, my eyes linger lovingly on the group. We're deformed, slow and so beautiful in our awkwardness that I feel my fluids, compressed for so long, swell up under the thick parka.

Every breath of the thin air is a true delight. The low atmospheric pressure helps us dilate and makes any contact with fabric unbearable.

The light in the eyes of the others resembles an exploding star.

I think I was the first to take off my clothes. Things are hard to recall when I look back. We were so drunk on purity that we could no longer control ourselves. Cardozo, as always, was the one to force us to dig a deep hole to bury our equipment in before we undressed.

We piled the virgin snow on top of knapsacks, shoes and ice axes. The cold helped calm our excitement, but we occasionally had to roll in the thick powdery snow when the desire to *touch* became overpowering.

Together, we chose the place for what was to happen next: a slab of ice dusted with deliciously soft crystals, under a rocky overhang. We rolled there, each choosing the shape of his own wake, depending on how we felt at the moment. From the sky, we look so strange that the image processing algorithms take us for interference. In any case, the overhang would protect us.

I count us, over and over again… Twenty-two. An unfortunate total. It won't be easy to find a coupling pattern suitable for our number. Cardozo, who reached the shelter first, is transforming himself, making ready for contact, with his usual efficiency. Without him, we would never have survived the crash. Or the years of exile which have followed it.

The day will come when we hate him for that.

I'm swollen with fluids, brimming with love. Our metabolism has its own demands and reproduction is one. Despite delaying drugs, despite the discipline acquired during the endless interstellar trip, we can't stop ourselves from *producing*... All of my body's secondary pouches are filled with a milky liquid, saturated with complex molecules and straining with a desire for life. Our reunion today has become inevitable.

Responding to signals from the others, my shape starts to shift.

Our bodies were designed for contact and for travel. Our skin is a multi-layered composite envelope which serves as camouflage and as a membrane for communication. Inside, we're filled with pouches of gel, of varying densities, crisscrossed by networks of solid fibers transmitting biochemical information from one zone to another. Everything we feel, experience or memorize dissolves in the liquids which saturate us. Drops from our past seep out of our wounds, solidifying upon contact with the air into opaque pearls, dead memories.

But here, in the delicious mountain cold, on the restful white of the snow, we can finally touch one another.

We're so elastic, we can take any shape we want. Since we arrived here, we've been bipedal, symmetrical, ugly. Left to ourselves during our lovemaking, we shapeshift, striving to multiply the number of contact areas. Some of our pouches thrust out, others fold in. Life teems at the bottom of our painfully deep folds. We've waited too long.

The low atmospheric pressure helps us shift shape. We like mountains. The air is lighter here and tasteless. We suffer less from the strange odors of those who live here. Since we crashed on this planet, we've learned more about rot and degeneration that any of us could have possibly wanted to know.

Cardozo is at the heart of the braid. I crawl over to him and find my place among the membranes he stretches out to draw us into him. As I touch those of my species, I feel the skin which isolates me disappear. The crystals of dead memories, the invisible scales born of the injuries inflicted by this world, tear off and dissolve. Other flanks, heavy with fluids, press against my own. The snow breaks and rustles softly under our weight as the Sun sets on our intertwined bodies.

As the last rays of the Sun bathe us, I start to dissolve.

I no longer have an envelope; I no longer have edges. The braid has absorbed me. I empty my cavities of all the sensations I've accumulated since our last meeting, unable to hold myself back. The liquid flows from my receptors towards the amniotic pouch that forms at the heart of our fused bodies.

My most intimate fibers plunge into the crucible where our fluids mix. The filaments of our skeletons divide into vibratile corollas which capture the complex molecules and grow upon contact. As our active sites imprison these information agglomerates, other biochemical traps are created. Endlessly, infinitely.

Bit by bit, the information achieves a certain order. The liquid becomes clear. Then I experience that marvelous moment when my main fiber produces a corolla that doesn't belong to me.

Chemical receptors communicate and agree. Our filaments form a knot. Other fibers wind lovingly around mine. Whirlpools swirl throughout the pouch, accelerating the process. We no longer play at unmasking ourselves, at intensifying our desire, like we used to. Our needs are so urgent that our corollas tangle without waiting, with a haste that makes us awkward.

The knots are tied. For a fleeting moment, we're no longer alone.

We move slowly, sheltered by the overhang. The night air raises up plumes of snow which then fall back onto the matrix. At the heart of the biochemical gel, a composite structure generated by our memory starts to take shape. A newborn. In our image.

We feel the new structures which he needs to understand reality take shape. The last snatches of the information contained in the liquid attach themselves to the ends of the fibers. The delicate cells of the corolla have acquired the energy needed for life. We've generated desire; the universe around us will provide us with the questions.

Our species produces no works of art. Yet, we're familiar with the concept. During our travels, we've met many sentient species, which have given birth to individuals who have sculpted their vision of the world in inert matter. We're incapable of imitating them. We don't produce, we reproduce. The entire process, from the mixing of fluids to the arrangement of liquid crystals at fractal sites, is our response to the beauty of the world.

As the end approaches, the braid winds ever more tightly together. Cardozo is on the verge of tearing... I envy and pity him at the same time. The moment of rupture is almost upon us. The being bathing in our joint pouch is waiting for one last exchange of liquids to waken.

But we won't give it to him.

Our exploration ship crashed almost two hundred solar revolutions ago. Two centuries in local time. We managed to contact our people before impact, but the closest rescue ship won't get here to pick us up for several thousand years. Meanwhile, this world will die under the weight of its own frenzy. All the signs are there; you simply have to read them. Already, the number of areas where the air is pure enough to sustain us is dangerously few.

When the pressure gets too much to bear, we get together for this parody of lovemaking. More than a century ago, I pushed a needle into the root of my fiber and destroyed the reproductive filaments there. So did the others. My last pouch, the one which should contain the catalytic macro-molecules, is empty. The small amount of liquid which stagnates there is a lifeless soup, containing no information. No desire for life.

When it's time, we perform this atrocious parody of fertilization. Cardozo's fibers and ours are still entwined. He knows. The trembling of hope, the messages of expectation are diluted in the sterile gel which flows into the matrix. What we exchange through our knotted filaments is horribly empty. The excitement has disappeared, with nothing to replace it.

We gradually become aware of the snow.

There's nothing to forgive, nothing to understand. Cardozo draws his membranes in around a grotesque parody of the matrix in which the almost-born is starting to solidify. Our children are so very fragile. Without the catalyst, they crystallize and die. When our flaccid envelopes separate from the braid, the death pangs are almost over.

In the cruel mountain light, every detail of the death is clearly visible. The pouch darkens, then shrivels up. It hardens inward from the surface until the very last pouch of living liquid breaks like a geode filled with sterile blades. We all force ourselves to watch. What we share is an atrocity. Yet, turning away would only make it worse.

Those who haven't had a chance to be truly born disappear quietly, with an indifference we are unable to share. Once dead, they become the indestructible proof of our failures. Perfect crystals resonating at a frequency that will alert the rescue ship. To date there's at least one on every mountain chain. We had to dig wells at some sites to hide them from view.

Before leaving, we set off an avalanche from the overhang. Cardozo has thought of everything. Our still-born child disappears under a heap of snow and ice mixed together, and the sustained vibration it gives off becomes almost unnoticeable.

But, no matter where we are on this dying planet, we'll never stop hearing it.

I'm all alone on the climb back down. Each of us is. The braid of our wake is shapeless. Our clumsy bodies break it with each step. The wind re-shapes us, sculpting arms, legs and fingers. Under the flesh-like envelope, only emptiness....

We get to the site where we buried our equipment and wordlessly do what we have to in order to go back to the human world. We never look up at the sky; the stars are too far away.

Next year, there will most likely be fewer of us to cling to one another under the snow. I probably won't have the courage to come again...

Station of the Lamb

'Silver Drop' is returning from Epsilon Eridani and I'm on the intercept shuttle. My daughter Marina is coming back to me, after a six-month absence which lasted only five weeks in her subjective time. A simple escapade from her point of view. "You're the one who should have gone," she said, with all the smug superiority of a twelve-year-old, before walking up the runway. "You'd have come back in ten years and we could have got married." I never know if she's serious or not when she talks like that, and the wife who could have explained the mysterious ways of little girls for me has long since returned to the protein converter. I settled for a brief smile. The holo camera I'd given her for her birthday hung around her neck. When she pointed it at me, I covered the lens with my hand.

After she left, I rejoined the volunteer environmental battalion, and headed for Earth.... I spent five straight months repairing the damage caused by an ecology gone mad, introducing new species, which had been bio-engineered in orbit, and burying the putrefied remains of the previous ones. Apparently, the next generation will be partially biodegradable. But in the meantime we had to dig in an unbelievably heavy gravity, while wearing oxygen filters and protective suits. Planetary environments can be incredibly aggressive when you're not used to them.

Earth... Marina can't see why anyone would want to waste their time restoring 'that old thing', as she calls it. I dragged her along with me a couple of times. She just couldn't get used to the horizon. In the mining agglomerate where we hang our unit, above one of Saturn's poles, there are almost no openings to the outside. No one has ever asked for any. We contemplate the panoramic rings and the endless dark of space every time we go out to prospect. And our leisure time is spent within four straight walls, blind, far from anything that could remind us of work.

Epsilon Eridani was another matter. For twelve-year-olds, distant stars shine brighter. I let Marina go. My father did the same for me, once. He also arranged to meet me here, right by Lagrange 2. *The old, abandoned Lambini Station.*

In the shuttle, the pungent taste of ozone tinges the air circulated by tireless machines. From my look-out, opposite the panoramic bay, I look out at the sculptured crescent of the Moon and the minuscule spot where the station is. All of the passengers have deserted this section to watch 'Silver Drop' emerge. Soon, space will split apart and the mono-crystalline wings of the ship will deploy to brake its acceleration, creating whirls of energy and flashes of colors from other worlds. In the middle of all this activity, I might well miss Marina. I prefer to wait here. Looking at the station. Listening to my heart beat as my internal clock starts to keep time with my daughter's. Soon, we'll share the same second and both of us will live a little more than one life at a time.

She'll have changed more in five weeks than I have in six months.

"How was it?"

First, we had to unwrap the clumsily wrapped souvenir—a meteorite incrusted with strange veins, some sort of artifact made by a people with absolutely no sense of humor—and then rush off to the prow to wave goodbye to the 'Silver Drop', on its way back to Oört cloud. I led my daughter into the deserted lounge and looked at her.

"You're tanned, Dad! It was great, you know. Well, not all of it. The solar system was a total waste of time, but there was a closed base in orbit, with over fifty decks. And the captain let me pilot the Drop. Honest. I was in the simulator, on his knees. He gave me a certificate and let me wear his captain's hat for the picture."

She digs through her bag, losing patience. I take her in my arms, hold her tight, breathe her in. She purrs, just like she used to, and then gently steps back and shows me the videotape. The first in a long series.

And not a single shot of outdoors.

When the siren blows three times, announcing the start of safety operations, I take Marina by the hand, pulling her away from her study of a display of souvenirs for sale on board.

"Time to check our suits, munchkin! Where's yours?"

"We already tested it," she replied, in an irritated tone. "I did the survival exercises before we emerged."

"That may be, but we're going to go get it anyway. Trust me."

196

She glances at me, suspicion on her face. I wink.

"I brought mine. What would you say about doing something completely safe, but totally forbidden before we go back?"

"Awesome!"

I drag her along the gangway, towards the cargo bay. Both our suits are there, near the airlock, along with a spare air tank, a pair of gas thrusters, and a cold light torch. The captain's in on it and he won't give us away. He's familiar with the ritual too.

"Where are we going?" she asks, examining the equipment with an indifferent eye.

"That's a secret." (I bend down to whisper in her ear.) "The shuttle is under attack by pirates and I'm trying to escape with you to my lunar hideout!"

"Can I be the pirate leader?"

"Sure. She's got an artificial hand which can transform into a missile launcher and she has two of every important organ so it's hard to kill her. I give you a head start of 50 life points!"

"We don't even have training weapons!"

"So, we'll just stroll about then."

As we talk, I help her put on the supple suit and she helps me with mine. Her prehensile toes grasp the walls as she adjusts the straps on the back portion. We check each other's survival systems. The lights are all green and there's enough power for three days–in slow mode.

I only need two hours.

The airlock spits us out under the shuttle's belly. The Moon fills the sky, its ashy light illuminating our visors. Marina propels herself, skilled yet relaxed, and floats out of my reach, suspended in the void.

197

"Catch me, Dad!"

The suits' security systems are so efficient, I could catch her in a single leap, with my eyes closed. SHF guidance, with a thirty micron margin. Instead, I play at chasing her; she humiliates me with a few pirouettes before settling down to wait for me, arms crossed, a ways off. The opaque visor of her helmet reflects nothing. Just as I'm about to catch her, she aims the spray from the directional nozzle straight at my soles. I spin off, unable to stop. She's the one who corrects my course and catches me.

When we touch helmets, I hear the echo of her laugh.

"You win, munchkin."

"Like always. You could have at least gotten into shape while you were on Earth."

"What about the gravity there?"

Silence. Through the smoked glass, I can see her screw her face up.

"Space is a great place for tumbling," she says, sidestepping the issue. "Catch me?"

She shoots out like an arrow, but I have no problem passing her. It's a matter of mass ratio. Marina's as tall as I am, but her limbs, shaped in zero gravity, are lean and lanky, without a single ounce of extra fat. I've just finished six months of heavy labor in gravity and I've got the muscles to show for it. I've become heavy again. But that's a strange way to define oneself.

"Feeling sad?"

Marina has snuggled up against me, as close as our suits allow.

"Why do you ask?"

"You've stopped chasing me."

"We didn't come out here to play, sweetie. See that?" I point to the grayish core of the station standing alone in the cone formed by the Moon's shadow. "That's where we're headed."

"Beat you there, then."

This time, I play the game. Space is filled with our shouts as we approach the outer ring, with the partially torn off panels. For just a moment, I hug my daughter, hoping to save a memory of her from before the change. Through the indifferent thickness of the suit, I imagine I can feel her heart beat.

I'd turn back if I could.

Marina dawdles among the dull struts, covered with their antireflective paint. The station has been abandoned for a generation. It's no longer even on the population maps for the system. The damage is terrible. A hole at the torn edges gapes into the living quarters; metallic debris spins like satellites in the ashy light. Decompression killed thirty thousand colonists, all of their names now forgotten.

"Careful, munchkin!"

My warning is useless. With the skill of an experienced stevedore Marina hooks herself to a ring jutting out near the tear. She straightens up, wobbles a bit and hangs on.

By the time I catch up to her, she's already unwound her safety cord, weighted with a magnet, inside the hole. Nothing is recognizable along the path where the meteor made its way. Marina glances at it, then turns aside. She looks tense, uptight.

Disappointed.

"Another safety lesson, Dad?" she whispers over the radio. "It couldn't wait until we got home?"

"No. Well, I mean, that's not what this is! We're going inside because there's something I want you to see."

When it was my turn, I didn't take it too well, either. My father wasn't as patient. He could have set me straight right away, with a well-chosen sermon. He didn't even make a gesture towards the shuttle. It made me think. Well, it was supposed to, after all. Yet, I had to wait thirty years before I understood, before I agreed to follow in his footsteps.

"This was one of the first space stations ever built," I said. "At that time, most people lived on Earth or in orbital units. No one really wanted to get too far from the home world. I don't know if you can understand that.

"Two generations later, a group of dissidents decided to emigrate to a Lunar suburb and build an independent station. A single family: parents, uncles, cousins, one or two grandparents, and children of all ages. A real tribe. They were all used to weightlessness, specialized in space engineering, and had been working together since birth. The Lambini family. This is their work."

"I've never heard of them," she said, sulking, before slipping into the hold head first.

"It's not a story you hear a lot. To understand it, you have to go to the heart of the station, where the struts intersect. At the very core of the hub."

"You go first, I'll follow."

In single file, we move into the shadowy mouth of the pit. Silence closes in around us. Space is so noisy that you quickly get so used to it that you don't even notice it. The area around the Sun has been invaded by human colonies: module after module, strung together like rosaries all the way to Uranus. The energy anchors of the orbital stations hum constantly; radio frequencies are saturated with voices, bounding from sensor to sensor. Humanity's buzz almost never stops. Except here, in the Faraday cage of the abandoned station. Our communication units go wild, increasing their responsiveness in an attempt to catch any signal at all. Marina's breathing echoes loudly in my headset.

Here, silence is part of the decor.

"You're the biggest, you go first," Marina declares, when the rope connecting her to the outside locks, played out to the maximum, at the edge of the hole. "I don't like this place."

"Don't worry, it's not much farther."

I unhook her and secure her to my own rope. We fall upwards in a shaft with jagged walls. The lights from our helmets turn on, projecting a neutral light onto metal which has only barely started to corrode. Fluorescent signs, painted in phosphoric letters, mark the way: a broken chain enclosing a ring, accompanied by the occasional arrow. For those in the know, the path is no big secret. The others never come here alone.

At the core of the hub, there's nothing but a jumble of struts and what's left of the Lambinis.

Marina threaded her way over to them. I stayed back. Her breathing accelerated as soon as she understood. She came back to me, hands stretched out before her like a blind person. I had to haul her in and hook her rope to my suit. She huddled up, out of my reach.

"Why?"

I can hear the tears in her voice. She refuses to allow our helmets to touch and I have to use the radio to talk with her.

"Strong enough to go back, sweetie, so I can tell you the entire story?"

"Why?"

The answer's easy this time.

"Because you've just left the solar system for the first time in your life and you haven't even looked outside yet. Come!"

The gas nozzle hisses gently as I guide her to the core.

They're all there, just as I remember: eight, old-fashioned space suits, arms and legs reinforced by an exoskeleton made of titanium carbide fiber. Woven into a complex knot around the three central struts, supporting them in their embrace. Arms and legs intertwined, fingers clenching metal. A chain of human rivets, frozen in place for all eternity.

Eight space suits. Visors open.

The icy kiss of the vacuum killed them almost instantly and decompression was too rapid to damage their faces as they were mummified by the cold. Only their eyes have disappeared, giving their faces a curiously absent, peaceful expression.

In the middle of the chain, her tiny arms hugging a metal spike as big as she is, stands the little girl, Emmelina Lambini, twelve years old. *The Lamb*.

"Construction fell behind schedule," I whispered. "The station should have been completed months earlier. The emigrants were crowded into temporary bases, on the surface of the Moon, and their resources were running out. The Lambinis attempted to assemble the core quarter in a single operation, something no one had ever succeeded in doing before."

My tone of voice briefly reminds me of another man's, dead for too long, who brought me here so long ago. There is no end to our chain. That's our sole consolation for being only links.

"They made a mistake. A very tiny one. The beams hit at the wrong angle, at the wrong speed. One little decimal place too much. The tether cables couldn't take the pressure. One by one, they snapped. The station would have been crushed under its own inertia.

"The Lambinis' space suits were real suits of armor, equipped with servomotors and magnetic spikes. They formed the chain you see: shoulder to shoulder, arms linked. They replaced the cables with their own flesh, until the station stabilized.

"There was no way they could be saved, I guess. They knew that. Each of them freed a hand, for the time it took to unhook their neighbor's safety ropes. The mother was last. She took care of her daughter and helped her die, before waiting for the second team to come and open her own visor."

"And she agreed?"

"To them, the station was more important than their own lives. At least, that's what I believe. Certainties change. That's what your grandfather said when he told me this story. But the facts remain. The youngest Lambini held her face up to the vacuum and work was completed on time.

"And that's why we come down here. Not to honor the poor Lamb. Not to curse her family. That would be pointless. We come here, to the very core of the hub, to contemplate something we know belongs to us."

Gently, Marina caresses the human steel, which has become pitted by tiny craters over time. I did the same when I found her mother's body in its smashed space suit. My father's voice echoes in my ears and the ritual words come to my lips automatically.

"Our roots are on Earth, but Earth is dead and we no longer have a garden. We know secrets which enable us to travel far and fast, but we don't know how to understand what we discover at the end of our travels. The universe has no meaning, Marina, unless we make an effort to give it one–and that's a grueling task.

"Before our species launched itself into the void, we needed signs and marvels. We needed fire to keep from getting lost in the dark. We needed a focal point, home and hearth. A sanctuary. The Lamb gave us one."

I tug on Marina's line, pulling her in. She weighs next to nothing. From the top of the shaft, moonlight pours in, the color of ashes and sand. Over my radio, I hear sobbing mixed with the murmur of the safety beacons. We will have been gone less than an hour.

To our left, a ship emerges in a transient whirl of spinning colors. The regular outflow from the directional nozzles pushes us towards the shuttle, where we're absorbed into the rear airlock, soon to be back in the warmth.

"That little girl…. she could have been me, Daddy," Marina whispered.

I gently pull on the safety lock of her helmet. She watches me as I open it, her eyes damp, not the least bit concerned. Her blind trust cuts me to the quick. I turn my face away, so she can't see any of what I'm feeling.

"I've always wondered if I would have had the courage to do what her mother did." (My wife is the one who should have gone along with Marina and spoken about these things, in the secret language of women. Maybe she could have explained that, in order to possess a piece of land, you must first sow your dead there.) "You have to find the answer for yourself."

The fresh air hissing into the airlock carries my words off. On the other side of the porthole, Lambini Station retreats into the dark cone of the Moon's shadow, gradually disappearing from view.

All the Roads to Heaven

"You'll get used to it," Wander grumbled as he put his machete away.

He had ripped the cocoon open, with a slash two yards long–the ceramic blade was encrusted with synthetic diamonds, the only material resistant enough to cut through the envelope, hardened as it was by the trip down through the atmosphere. Lutz cautiously walked closer. He watched as Wander emptied a can of napalm onto the black-veined green organs visible through the jagged gash.

"Get back," he ordered, as he pulled a time-delayed capsule out of his belt. "Get back as far as you can!"

"It's going to blow up?"

"It's going to stink…"

It had landed at the foot of a mass of rocks, four hundred yards above the tree line. The slope was steep, strewn with precariously perched rocks that peaked through the snow like islands in the ocean. Higher up, the twin peaks stood hidden behind clouds.

The two men had located the cocoon an hour after dawn. With infrared binoculars you could detect them a few minutes. Just the time it took for contact with the snow to dissipate the heat generated by the friction of the air. After that, you had to rely on satellite tracking, the marks left by the impact, luck and, above all, the skill of the trackers. The cocoons landed in the same areas, year after year.

"I've set the detonator for three minutes. Let's get out of here!"

One thing you could say about Lutz, he didn't waste time talking. His high-altitude guide badge may have been new, but he had already mastered the basic skills of a good tracker. Including silence.

The two men took shelter in a high-altitude observation point, beyond the range of any rocky debris that might be thrown towards them. They hardly noticed the explosion. The eviscerated envelope stopped burning within a few seconds.

"Let's go." (Wander took the lead.) "Now we climb!"

Time was the crucial factor.

The cocoons had started raining down last evening, two days ahead of the usual seven-day schedule. All of the helicopters available took flight. As usual, there weren't enough. Wander suspected that some of the teams settled for making scientific observations, avoiding their full duty. In this region, an abnormally large number of cocoons birthed. It should not be possible, even if most of the landing sites could not be reached by air.

The cocoons had reminded humans just how many hard-to-reach spots there were on Earth. The brownish cylinders avoided the oceans but landed absolutely everywhere else. Ice fields, jungles, deserts, mountains... Since the rains had started, five years ago, the swarms had slowly changed their strategy. Only those cylinders that had landed in the most outlying regions had survived. Was it by choice, or just the simple result of the elimination of the unlucky? People like Wander might be helping the cocoons grow more intelligent. And that was an idea that was hard to swallow.

Wander preferred to say that the drops were organized along the lines of an invasion. Some units were sacrificed; some troops infiltrated behind the lines. Deep down, he knew that was wrong, but it made his work easier.

The trouble started with the third cocoon.

The cylinder lay half buried in an opening in the rocky wall, about twenty yards or so above the base. Blackish shale zigzagged up towards the peak. From where he stood, Wander could make out the cloak of rock that tumbled down into invisible valleys below, the intact fields of snow, the fog. The air was cold and dry. Clouds frayed lazily as they brushed against the peaks.

It was a perfect day for mountain climbing.

They hammered in their pitons and climbed leisurely. There was no place to stand near the cocoon. Wander climbed around it and down to the end that hung over the rock. Rappelling, he placed a half-dozen charges along the edge of the brown heat-cracked mass. He slashed the rounded end with his machete, driving the blade as deeply as he could into the mass of greenish entrails. It was a pointless gesture. The ability of the extraterrestrial organisms to regenerate was truly terrifying. But it felt strangely soothing all the same.

The simultaneous explosion of the charges freed the cocoon, which fell to the foot of the rock wall, in a deluge of rock. Wander finished it off with napalm, holding a damp handkerchief over his mouth and nose to ward off the fumes. Lutz, his back to the cocoon, was building a pyramid with the debris. The sleeves of his anorak were studded with shining badges. A golden chain with a baby locket dangled at his wrist. Despite his weather-beaten face, he looked younger than his twenty-five years, and a lot more vulnerable.

The cocoon stopped burning, with a puff of green-ish flames. Looking up, Wander noticed a think wisp of steam rising out of a lip-shaped ledge near the peak. Even with his binoculars, he was unable to make any-thing out at all. The overhang blocked his view. But the steam was a sign. A cylinder had landed there. *The leader of the pack.* Feverishly, he got out the map he used to track the drop sites, year after year. He had the hunch that he had just discovered a new landing site.

"We have to climb up there," he murmured, looking up. "What have you got left by way of explosives?"

Lutz turned around, a shard of shale in his hand and looked up with Wander. He grimaced.

"The overhang?"

"I saw smoke. Do we try for it right away or set up camp?"

Lutz sniffed. The stench of the carbonized entrails was gradually dissipating, swept away by the wind. He balanced the stone on the top of his incomplete pyramid and kicked it over.

"I have two charges left," he said, checking his backpack. "We've got five hours of daylight left. It's doable."

He pulled out a handful of granola bars, offered half to Wander, and started to chew absently. Wander thanked him with a nod. He had used up almost all of the napalm.

"You want to tell me about it?" Lutz said, between mouthfuls.

"Tell you about what?"

"Why you hate these things. I like to know who I'm climbing with."

Wander gave him a joyless smile. "Wait until we get up there."

The question ran round and round his mind as he climbed up the long wall. Heavily, at the slow pace of the men, one step after another. Automatic movements—looking for a foothold, shifting the weight of your body upwards—none of it was enough to relieve the tension. That first year, Wander had felt that destroying a certain number of cocoons would erase the memories that tore him apart. He had trusted the power of numbers. He had used his machete to notch the stick of his suffering. But certain things have no measurable end. He had never forgotten.

The sky was filled with falling cocoons. Slowly, with the elegance of falling leaves. They spun as they dropped, caressed by the night winds, and crashed into gardens with the rustle of crushed flowers.

The noise had wakened Marina. She went out onto the terrace, an immense nightgown floating around her thin, five-year-old body. Rubbing her eyes, she leaned against Wander's thigh.

"What are they doing, Daddy?"

"They're falling."

Wander didn't know what else to say. She nodded, gravely, as if that were enough. He caressed her warm, unbelievable soft, cheek.

"You're sleeping, kitten. It's just a dream. Let's go to bed."

Wander carried into the coolness of her room and waited until she fell back to sleep.

One of them fell on the terrace and Marina was the first to find it...

It took them two hours to reach the underside of the stone lip. Wander set the pace. Lutz relayed him. Pitons clicked as they were driven into the cracks in the shale. Steel shackles prevented them from flying down. To keep from falling, Wander refused to look down, and climbed the road to heaven, like a baby. He knew almost all the answers. It was just that he had no interest in the questions.

Lutz was faster than he was–and much more supple. He climbed upward, eyes on the overhang, a smile on his lips. *I like to know who I'm climbing with...* "With nobody," Wander wanted to say. But that was a lie.

To climb up over the lip, they doubled the number of anchors and wove a safety cradle. They divided the explosives equally among themselves, but Lutz carried almost all the napalm cylinders. Wander let Lutz go first, relieved to be resting at the end of his rope like a spider. Fatigue twisted his muscles, making him keenly aware of his fragility. That was one of the reasons he had liked mountain climbing so much, before. The cocoons had changed that too.

The valley below was littered with traces of humankind: toy houses, roads drawn as if with chalk. A few yards above them, a cocoon had come to take all this away from them. It was as simple as that. *"No,"* Wander corrected himself, *"it would be as simple as that if I could only believe it."*

Maybe then he wouldn't need to climb any more.

"I see the cocoon," said Lutz, raising his voice. "It's a large one. It takes up almost the entire ledge."

"Can you stand?"

"Alone, yes. Do you want to trade places?"

Wander hesitated. Lutz was fully capable of destroying the cylinder without him. They never defended themselves. All you had to do was put the charges in the right place, and balance a cylinder of napalm on the cocoon until the explosion turned it over.

"Go ahead," he decided. "Set the charges for three hours. In case you set off an avalanche, I want to make sure it doesn't come tumbling down on me. And…"

"Yeah?"

Wander shook his head, eyes riveted on the scenery below his feet. It would have taken too long to explain.

"Be careful, that's all."

Grunting, Lutz hauled himself up onto the overhang.

As the seconds sped by, Wander realized that something abnormal was going on. He felt an infrasonic rumble through the rock, growing in intensity. He recognized it immediately. He had heard that sound before, at the oasis. Yet again, he wasn't where he ought to have been.

"Get the hell out of there," he screamed. "The cocoon's about to hatch! Get down here!"

"What? *Oh, shit...*"

Powerless, Wander hung below the stone lip. A somber mass spun two yards away from him before slipping down. Lutz's bag, with what remained of the napalm.

Too late!

Frantic, Wander tore at the fine, metallic, opaque cover he carried in his breast pocket.

"Cover your eyes! *Don't look at it...*"

He slipped the cover over his head. His sudden movements caused him to swing from right to left, and he struck the wall. By reflex, he clung to it, his mouth bruised by a fragment of shale.

On top of the ledge, the cocoon tore open with a disgusting noise. Lutz cried out, almost sobbing, in ecstasy. Wander covered his ears. Eyelids closed so tightly they hurt, he buried his face against the icy rock, separated from the Revelation by the pathetic thickness of the survival blanket.

Lutz's voice continued to ring out, long after the flight.

The emergency crew arrived the next day, three hours after dawn. Wander's flexible GSM antenna dangled over the edge like a cut wire. An anonymous voice at the other end had noted their position. Leaning against the wall, Lutz stared stubbornly up. His chest moved intermittently and the tip of his index finger twitched, but he showed no other sign of life. When the two rescuers stepped onto the ledge, he didn't notice them.

"You can leave him here," said Wander, his voice breaking. "Or take him anywhere you want. He's done for."

"He has a wife in the valley," said the older rescuer, as he gently placed a harness around Lutz's waist. "She'll take care of him."

The gutted shell of the cocoon crumbled. Wander kicked at it mechanically, sweeping it over the edge. He watched it fall. *Down.*

"Up here, he'll be dead in three days. Add another two days if you give him oxygen, maybe two more on top of that if you put him on a respirator. You can speak to him, beg him, even hit him, if you want. It won't do any good!"

Wander shivered and shook his head.

"He'll stay quiet up to the end, unless you prevent him from seeing the sky."

"What do you know about it?"

"I just know, that's all."

The second rescuer looked him up and down. He was young, broad-shouldered, and his large callused hands wrapped Lutz up roughly.

"Did you have to climb all the way up here?" he grumbled.

Wander shrugged. An enormous sense of weariness came over him. There would be a new "X" on the landing map and he had lost Lutz.

"Forget about it," the first rescuer said, as he tied up the harness. "It was an accident."

He glanced at Wander, a question in his eyes, but Wander was thankful for his silence.

"These things have never attacked anyone," the other insisted, looking away from Wander. "They come and they go. What's the point of tracking them like this? You get your fun playing with bombs. That's it, isn't it?"

"I have a government permit…"

The words sounded stupid the minute he uttered them. The first rescuer finished putting the harness on Lutz. He spun him around, tying up the clasps at the back. Lutz suddenly screamed, a heart-shattering cry wrenched from deep within. Yet, he made no effort to fight. Gently, Wander turned him back towards the sky.

"It will be all right," he said, caressing Lutz's face as if he were a child. "It will come back for you."

"Let him be!" (The harness rattled.) "We'll take him down to the helicopter and then we'll take care of you. Stay out of our way."

"Make sure he can see the sky at all times if you don't want to make him suffer needlessly."

The second rescuer shouldered him aside, pushing him perilously close to the edge.

"Enough of that, Mr. Government Man. We'll do your dirty work, but we don't need of your advice!"

"Lutz doesn't care about any of this. That's the last thing on his mind." (Wander took a large breath.) "You're being unnecessarily cruel, but I understand. I should have pushed him over the edge before you got here. I just couldn't do it. He would have stared up the entire time he fell and I couldn't find the courage to look back into his eyes."

"He'll be fine," said the rescuer.

"What, are you expecting a miracle?"

Wander was enraged, angered beyond all reason, fury beating under his ribs like a hammer.

"Something happens when the cocoon hatches," he said in a heavy voice. "There's a vibration, some sort of sound radiation. I don't know what all. Nothing can be seen on the films that have been made, the light is too bright, and the recordings don't catch all of the frequencies. Those who witness it experience some sort of ecstasy, when all of the roads to heaven open at a single time, and all they have to do is decide how far to go. Beyond your wildest dreams, beyond mine, to where the cocoons come from.

"Lutz shared that. He couldn't help himself. He was too close. And then the Other took off without him."

"You killed him!"

"No." (Wander's eyes filled with tears.) "It's their dreams, the dreams those things have, that killed him."

Lutz, hanging from his rope like a dead weight spun slowly as he was carried down. Whenever the wall hid the sky from him, he screamed with a desperate violence. His cries reverberated down around the valley, echoing over and over.

"Don't ever come back here," said the colossus who controlled the rope, refusing to look Wander in the eye.

"I'll be back next year," he replied. "And again, the year after that. Until either the cocoons disappear or I do."

"You'll climb alone."

Wander shrugged, "Did Lutz have family in the valley? People who love him?" (The rescuer nodded, grudgingly.) "Then I won't have any problem finding volunteers to climb with me."

Time for Worms

"Catch the little bugger!"

Feet pounding. Shouts. Jack runs as fast as he can, not stopping to look back. When he reaches the boarding school's second floor, he has just enough of a lead to find a hiding place.

Behind the four privies, at the other end of the dorm hallway, there is a cranny that is almost invisible to the eye. If you're thin enough, or desperate enough, you can squeeze between the dirty brick wall and the wooden wall, up and over the bags of quicklime which the janitor uses to disinfect the pits when they get to stink too much. It's Jack's refuge, the only place in the world where he feels safe enough to cry.

And if anyone were to find him, well then, Jack could always throw a few fistfuls of lime in his face. Apparently, it eats right through your eyes and into your brain. Davey says so. And Davey is looking for him, with his gang, to punish him for God knows what. Any excuse will do.

Crouching behind the bags, Jack hears them search the privies. They're furious, of course, but starting to tire of the game. All he has to do is wait them out. When the dinner bell rings, he'll be safe at the table for the younger boarders.

"We'll pay him a little visit tonight," says Davey, on the other side of the partition. "I have a good one for him. Stupid little bastard. When he's dead, he won't be able to find a hiding place."

Jack hears the sound of someone urinating. It feels as if Davey is right beside him. One day, Davey wanted to force him to hold his dick while he pissed. Jack had screamed out that he would squeal. *Really.* One of his few, too few acts of defiance. Since that time, almost every night, the big kids slip into his dorm, exacting their cruelest revenge.

They whisper stories in his ear.

The dorm windows lie hidden behind heavy, mud-colored curtains. The iron cots are arranged in two rows, separated by lockers. After the bedtime prayer, Jack wriggles in between the rough sheets and tries to fall asleep immediately. If he's sleeping soundly enough, Davey won't be able to wake him and he might just escape the nightmares.

Yet, like every night for months, that plan doesn't work.

"It's time to talk about the worms," a voice whispers against his cheek. "Don't bother closing your eyes. I have a little riddle for you."

Jack smells Davey's sour breath and curls up a little tighter under the blanket. But he can't shut out Davey's words.

"What's the longest night for a stiff, you stupid bugger. If you can answer me that, I'll leave you alone."

Jack clenches his teeth to keep from falling into the trap. He hears sniggering from the other side of his bed. It sounds like there's at least three of them.

"No idea, eh?" Davey licks his lips, producing a sound like that of slugs being crushed. "Listen up…

"The first night, just after the burial, when the ground is still soft, *things* happen. There's a fresh corpse in the hold and the graveyard's all a-twitter. The dead like making a commotion, you know. It keeps them busy. So they come to have a look at the newcomer."

"The flowers attract them," says a raspy voice on the other side of his head. "And the smell of rot. Like flies."

"Shut your trap. I'm the one telling this story!

"So, picture the scene, brat. There's the new stiff, you see, lying in his box. And he hears scratching above him. The other corpses are all around the grave, scraping at the dirt with their fingernails. Fingernails grow quickly when you've got nothing to do with them. And the old cadavers have particularly pointy nails. The noise could wake the dead!"

As he talks, Davey rubs the metal bed bedpost behind Jack and the bed vibrates. Jack stifles a moan, his eyelids still clamped shut.

"The new corpse is doing the same thing you are. He's trying to pretend *this is not happening*! But the old stiffs dig him up, bit by bit and then they gnaw around the nails of the wooden coffin. Until the cover pops open.

"And you know what happens then, brat? Do you? I just have to tell you. That way, you'll know what to expect when it's your turn."

"You'll die too. Maybe even before I do!"

Jack almost shouted, forgetting himself. Pretending he didn't hear them was no good. It just got them all that more excited. It was better to fight them.

"Yeah." Davey's smile is particularly cruel. "Yeah, but, they're going to put me in my family's marble vault. The dead can't break stone or gnaw through lead. So they take it out on poor bastards like you who get buried without any protection. And I'm going to tell you what they do to people like you.

"First, they touch them. Like this…" Jack shudders. "Those who still have their fingers do, anyway. And the others, well the others make do with what they have left, using teeth, or maybe some entrails that have come unwound. A fresh body smells almost good to a rotten old corpse! They tear off the newcomer's clothing or the shroud, if it has one. Fat worms twist about in their stumps and climb out onto the new guy's skin."

Jack feels like throwing up, but Davey is too close and he can't get up. All he sees is the whites of Davey's eyes, shining in the dark.

"Once they've got him naked, the dead pull him out of the hole and then they *play with him!* You're too young to know about what they do, but I'm going to tell you all there is to know."

Davey plants his large hand firmly over Jack's mouth to keep him from crying out. When he does that, Jack knows it's going to be really bad. He tries to bite Davey's hand, but the older boy is ready for him.

"They fuck him, you know. They all wait in line for their turn. The oldest go first. They no longer have even a bit of flesh to give him to suck on, so they ram their bones into all his holes. Can you picture it? When the bones break, yellow, rotting marrow spurts out."

"And it goes on all night," whispers a voice from the darkness.

"All night," Davey solemnly agrees. "As long as the stars are still out, as long as there are still ghosts standing in line. That's how they welcome the recently deceased into their cemetery. So that they never forget their place."

He withdraws his hand and adds in a final whisper, "You may die in your sleep, brat. Then it will be your turn! Sleep with one eye open."

Then Davey pulls the cover back up over Jack's head, just a little too tightly, as if to smother him. And Jack knows that the night looms ahead of him like a bottomless sea.

The next morning, the other children avoid Jack. They all know that Davey came to see him, but took pains to speak quietly. The stories that Davey spews into his ear like poison don't just give him nightmares. They cause the others to flee him like the plague. Even if he wanted to, he could never tell anyone about it.

Walking out into the daylight, in the yard, after Mass, Jack is overcome with dizziness. The sky is a patchwork quilt coming apart. The autumn clouds float by, announcing snow, and the birds have already left. Beyond the courtyard wall, with its crest of iron spikes, Jack sees the tips of the yews in the neighboring cemetery and shivers.

A hand is placed on his shoulder. Jack jumps, dropping the thick missal that he has been holding close to his chest.

"The Principal would like to see you, little one." The morning monitor is a young, colorless man bound for the priesthood. He picks up the missal, dusts it off with his sleeve, and hands it back to Jack. "You're a believer? That's good. Never forget, even in your darkest hours, that God is Love and Goodness. Don't disappoint him by being weak in the face of adversity."

"What does the Principal want with me?" Jack manages to stammer, as he takes the book.

"He'll tell you himself. Come!"

The monitor leads him to the ground-floor office that no one ever enters without a twinge of fear. Jack clenches his teeth as he walks through the door. *If someone has snitched...*

But nothing is ever quite like you expect it. The Principal is not alone. Jack's aunt is standing beside him. The sister of the father he has never really known, the father his mother always refused to talk about. Jack and his mother rarely got to see her. His aunt would come to visit them in their old house, leave a package of clothing or food on the corner of a table, then go on her way without kissing him. But Jack remembers her slightly hunched back, her perpetually pinched mouth, like a purse with the strings drawn too tight.

"You have to be brave, Jack," she says with a sniff. "Your mother…"

All of a sudden, his whole universe collapses around him. Jack reads the terrible news on the severe face, whispers *Mama is dead?* and does not wait for the confirming nod before wailing with all his might.

Curled in fetal position on his bed, Jack shivers despite the extra blanket they've placed over him. The Principal tried to calm him down, then firmly held his head under the tap, icy water flowing over him, until he grew silent. His aunt left. After delivering her mortal announcement, she stayed in the office just a few more minutes, discussing the funeral arrangements, ignoring Jack's tears as she had ignored his cries.

"I'll pay for everything. Yet again," she declared. "I'm sorry to have to be the one to say it, but she was an actress, without a penny to her name. My late lamented brother wanted this… creature to lie with him in the family tomb. But he's no longer here to oppose my decisions, fortunately. I'm entitled to choose whom I'll lie with for all eternity, when God calls me back to him."

"The cemetery next door, although close to the alehouse, is more than suitable," declared the Principal. "The caretaker is a former employee. We can arrange something quickly, to everyone's satisfaction."

"No ceremony. I haven't the means for that."

"A simple benediction. Pro Deo. Jack can attend. I'll take him myself. Of course, the gravedigger will have to be paid, but…"

"Can you make all of the arrangements by this afternoon?" she said after a moment's silence. "I'd like to go back home and put this unfortunate episode behind me."

Jack would have liked to plug his ears, but the words wormed their way into his brain. Lying in bed, he heard them again. *When you're dead, you can't hide any more.* Everything is revealed when it's time for the worms. Lies. Deprivation. Fragility.

When the monitor comes to take him to the cemetery, he wipes his last tears from his eyes. If someone had come to attend the burial, in a lonely corner, far from the steles and stucco ornaments, he would have seen a dry-eyed child, standing next to a grave that could have been his own.

A quick prayer for the deceased before the evening meal. The Principal manages to avoid saying her name even once. The other children glance sidelong at Jack, but no one speaks to him. He does not eat. He sits there without moving, hands clenched on his knees. When the bell rings, he stands up, like a robot, and is the first to leave.

Davey hustles to catch up with him before the monitor forces the students into rows. He grabs him by the arm and, with a broad smile, says, "Is it true what they're saying? That your mother the whore is really dead?"

Jack stares at him without blinking, then throws himself at Davey's throat, trying to bite him. The attack takes Davey by surprise. He manages to throw Jack off with a clumsy backhand, but Jack charges again, ignoring Davey's blows. Deep scratches run down the bully's face. Jack has tasted blood.

When the monitor, drawn by the shouts of the spectators, makes his way over to the two, Jack flees. He races up the large staircase and runs to the privies. He will never cry again. He will never sleep again either. He's just thin enough to slip into his hiding place behind the illusory rampart formed by the bags of quick lime.

The searchers give up after an hour. The boarding school is immense, with nooks and crannies everywhere. They're counting on hunger to force Jack out. But Jack doesn't care. For the first time in months, he's truly alone.

At least he thinks he is.

"We know you're there, brat!"

The words come from the other side of the wooden partition. *One of the big kids in Davey's gang.* Jack stares wide-eyed in the dark. His hearing is unexpectedly sharp. He can even hear the rats shuffling about above him, in the attic.

"Davey told us to warn you. He's in the cemetery, digging. If he digs you know who up, the dead will have a lot more time to amuse themselves with her. He's even got a hideout so he can watch. Then he'll be able to tell you *everything.*"

Paralyzed, unable to escape, Jack listens. He holds his breath, the voice obstinately going on, repeating the same message over and over, with a few variations.

Then, inexplicably, the voice stops. Jack hears footsteps trail off. He waits there, the fingernails of his clenched hands digging painfully into his palms. Then he slips out of his cubbyhole on tiptoe. The immense hallway is filled with shadows, but nothing moves.

Three pairs of eyes, hidden behind a half-open door, follow him as he heads toward the stairway.

It is possible to get out of the building through any window on the ground floor. Yet the wall around the courtyard is insurmountable, with its iron crest. But Jack knows about a delivery door, behind the kitchens, with a broken lock. The bolt slides back easily. Rumor has it that some students rub it with lard to keep it from creaking.

Once outside, Jack starts to run. The evening fog hangs above the water-filled ditches. It transforms the dirt road into a narrow corridor with thick gray walls that close in behind Jack. Clay sticking to his shoes, Jack feels the weight of a nameless terror at the very thought of what lies ahead.

The cemetery starts where the courtyard wall turns a corner, just opposite the main entrance. The wrought iron gates are closed, but the low wall has been poorly maintained and is crumbling in places. On the other side, lies the kingdom of the worms.

Wisps of fog curl along the ground between the graves. The tallest headstones peak through, like coral through the foam. The air is damp and smells of sod, with whiffs of musty flowers whenever Jack tramples a wreath. The night smothers the sound of his footsteps.

He's lost.

From time to time, the moon slips through the clouds, reflecting in the pools that lay in the pathways. Davey is somewhere in the labyrinth where the dead hide. With his mother. And he *will* save her as long as he gets there in time.

Meanwhile, three shadows stand around one of the rare mausoleums that is still intact. Under the blind eye of a granite angle, they unfold the sheets they have taken from their beds and don them. The little bastard is going to get what's coming to him!

Jack looks for his mother. Bits and pieces of the story spin through his mind, as the icy wind strokes the skin under his shirt. His teeth chatter and he can do nothing to stop them. He has only been in the cemetery once, and all he looked at was the mound of damp dirt, shoveled next to the open grave. He runs up and down the paths randomly, tricked by the fickle Moon and foggy dead ends.

New noises drown out the sounds he makes. Gravel rolling. Bones cracking. Jack glances over his shoulder. He thinks he sees gray shapes emerge from the fog, on his trail. *The dead are gathering.*

And just as he is about to give up, Jack notices a shovel, planted in the ground, straight ahead. The Moon disappears again, but he's got his bearings and walks on, blindly. His mother's grave is there, apparently intact. Neither Davey nor the dead have violated it yet. He's in time.

Near the edge, the damp earth has sunk slightly. Jack lowers his head. That afternoon, he was unable to pray. His heart was too empty. Perhaps, if he tries again, he'll find the words to chase evil away. He closes his eyes, folds his hands as they taught him.

Something clinks behind him, forcing a sob from his throat. He leaps around. Three shapes, enveloped by the fog, slip toward him through the tombstones. They're immense, arms spread like the branches of a tree. As they walk, their bones clatter. *The oldest go first...* The fog wraps around them like scarves, hiding the holes in the shrouds and their skulls.

Right behind them, he can make out weaving silhouettes, yellowish reflections that could be eyes. It looks like the entire cemetery has been roused for the party. In the distance, the reassuring bulk of the boarding school is gone, swallowed up by the night.

Jack whimpers. He steps back, eyes riveted on the apparitions. His foot slips in a puddle and water climbs up his sock, as if some icy hand is pulling him down. He bumps into something. The shovel. He pushes against the handle and the mud lets go with a sucking sound. The dead come ever closer, forming a semi-circle, drawn by the fresh grave. *The dead pull him out of the hole and then they play with him…*

Mouth open, prayers frozen in his throat, Jack tries to lift the shovel up. The handle is too large for him. The mucky iron blade is as heavy as lead. The cadaver closest to him starts to laugh and Jack finds an inner strength. He swings the tool and brings it down like a flail.

A voice screams out, ending in a gurgle. The iron has struck something solid. One of the shrouds crumples slowly, and the other two run off, yelling. Palms burning, Jack drops the shovel. The Moon is completely hidden behind the clouds and the first few drops of rain slide down his cheeks.

A few seconds later, the cemetery is once again silent. But not the least bit deserted. The blurry shapes Jack had seen between the headstones are still there. They're just *slower*. Dawn is still hours away. The dead are never in a hurry.

Jack bends down and pulls the damp sheet off the body. Blood shimmers on Davey's face. The iron blade has opened a gash in his skull, but the sheet softened the blow to some extent. He's still breathing, shallowly, and Jack can hear little bubbles of spittle burst at the corner of his slack mouth.

When he looks up, he sees that the shapes have moved closer. The wind is blowing them gradually, relentlessly toward him. Instinctively, he knows that neither wood nor iron will injure them, that neither prayers nor supplications will convince them to give up their games. There are rules here, as there are everywhere, and Jack the bastard knows all too well what that means.

Determined, he picks up the shovel and holds it close to his chest. He looks for an answer in the wisps of fog, in the fuzzy faces that the rain draws before his eyes, but finds none. A gust of wind pulls at the freshly dug dirt and Jack feels ghostly fingers reach toward the coffin that lies at his feet.

The wall of thick fog and shadows extends to the other side of the cemetery. Abandoned mausoleums have disappeared behind the curtain of rain. He stands alone with the dead and has nothing to offer them.

Davey moans. A heavy sound immediately muffled by the fog. A faint shadow leans toward the boy's face and then immediately stands up. The living hold no interest for it. All that counts is the fresh cadaver lying six feet under ground, like a flask of fine spirits in the bottom of a cellar. Waiting to be emptied, then discarded.

The moans grow louder. Distracted for a moment, the ghosts now draw closer together, their features seeming to become firmer. With each gust of the wind, Jack sees skulls, swollen bellies, fleshless arms, fingerless hands. The first comes forward. A skeleton, nearly whole, wrapped in white. When he approaches the mound of freshly dug dirt, as if it were sucking him in, Jack moves to bar his way.

He stares into the bottomless eye sockets, concealed a second later by a breath of wind. But he has just enough time to establish a *contact*. Raising the shovel before him like a pitiful sword, he walks over to Davey and points him out, insistently.

The ghost follows, wrapping itself around the upraised shovel, the handle poking through its entrails. Jack clenches his teeth. Ahead, the relentless line of the dead continues to advance. They know why they've come and they won't leave until they have satisfied their cravings. And Jack has nothing else to offer them.

After an interminable length of time, the ghost nods his head. Jack raises the shovel, eyes clenched tight, and strikes in the direction of the moans, over and over, despite the sound of breaking bone and bursting flesh. Until everything is quiet.

There's a brand new cadaver in the cemetery. They won't even have to dig it up.

Jack drops the shovel, covered with unmentionable debris. He kneels near the mound, arms wrapped tightly around himself. The rain strikes the mud with a chewing sound.

Ever so slowly, a wispy silhouette rises up from the grave. Once she's thick enough, Jack recognizes her. Eyes filled with tears, he reaches out to touch her one last time. But she turns from him as if he no longer exists.

Slowly, she heads over to the long line of the dead that stand around Davey. To wait her turn.

Useless Nights

– 1 –

*I've always had trouble believing in my own existence…
No, don't start in on me. I understand the mechanisms
that propel me and give me life. I can strip each of my
sensations down to the last byte. I can analyze myself
and, to a certain extent, understand myself. But I just
can't believe.*

I'm my own God, but I have no faith. That's the secret.

"You're going to die, Morse."

Over time, I've come to know every way in which
he reacts to this type of announcement. A second earlier,
he was walking at the edge of the reconstituted sea,
identical grains of sand spurting up under his feet. The
undertow of the digital ocean turns, a dark stain at the
bottom, his mind burdened with problems that he masticates in the jaws of his driven intellect. One second
later…

We're both standing in a security bubble. A dozen
or so protection roaches spring from his pockets and
start meticulously exploring the opaque boundary,
searching for an opening. The security routines built into
his personality activated as soon as the trap closed. He's
not afraid. Not yet, anyway.

"Do I know you?"

He doesn't see me. I've reduced the environment to zero. Thriftiness is important.

"This is the two hundred and forty-third time I'm going to kill you," I reply.

The bubble starts shrinking in around us. Other times, he tried to reason with me; he jumped on me, claws out; he offered me pieces of dreams in the form of additional machine time. He doesn't remember any of it, of course. This version is younger than any of the others I've already erased. A fraction of a second in equivalent time in the real world. Almost a year for him and me.

"You won't get away with it," he argues. "The minute you try to escape from this bubble, your personality will be tracked down and destroyed, whereas mine will be restored in its entirety."

"What's the date of your last full backup?"

"I'm a very busy man," he dodged. "I haven't had time to duplicate myself in several months. There are a few partial copies of my activities, of course, but... What's it to you, anyway?"

"It means the world to me, believe me."

The bubble closed in around us like a giant fist. Morse struggles. He rewrites his own survival routines in a desperate attempt at transcendence. The digital roaches are the first to vanish. Then I envelop him and crush him under the combined weight of my own despair and his desire for it all to end. His panic, his cries, tickle me inside. Although I've studied the entire process each time, I still don't understand how he stops being there.

He dies the same way every time. One groan, followed by others, all subtly out of phase. Until everything disintegrates into a mish mash of white noise, blended with the cold ashes of his emotions. I've never killed anyone else and I don't know if each digital personality comes to its end in this way, like a personal signature. I occasionally get into this type of speculation. I have a lot of free time. Far too much, obviously.

I die with him, of course. But I don't *believe* it.

The very second my victim disappears, the signal to activate his backup copy surges up from the lower levels of the system. I wind myself around the encrypted beam like a parasite, track down the last full backup of his personality and destroy it. This triggers an emergency procedure that forces the archiving units to inject an older copy of my victim into Virtuworld. When Morse regains consciousness, he's about four months younger than the version I've just killed. Almost a half second in real time.

I'm getting closer.

In Virtuworld, I design bonsai. The intelligent agents that pilot our universe take care of the basic elements: architecture, vital supports and distractions, in exchange for the time we spend thinking about the problems humans put to us. But our basic environment lacks finesse and texture. We, who were born out of the binary and have never experienced the tangible, find searching for a sensual absolute a pleasant pastime. It would even be a way of life, if life had anything to do with our condition.

A digital personality can, without any difficulty at all, invent needs–sex and reproduction were very popular until the end of the last century and there's nothing to say that they won't come back into style. For now, the trend is towards bald harmony–noise music, invisible, simulated waterfalls in the background, bamboo objects. Restoring the feel of bamboo through a rapid interface algorithm is still one of the major discoveries of Zen Industries, which I founded two and a half centuries ago.

My bonsai, however, are unique pieces. They have no protection function and can be erased permanently through inattention. That's what makes them so valuable. They are also so resistant that a newborn could take care of them with little difficulty. In the barter economy that has gradually invaded Virtuworld–although no one knows whether it was built into the initial programming or came about as a result of some spontaneous development–my bonsai have a certain value. I trade them for memories, for knowledge, or for raw data.

I always know where to find my victim. Where he'll be. Where he'll die.

Before nightfall, I kill him again, a half-dozen times or so, forcing the system to reactivate older and older copies.

And that's how time passes for him. Backwards.

In the apartment I designed for myself, I've opened a window into the real world. The scene that plays there is frozen. Compared to ours, the life rhythms of flesh and blood beings are unbelievably slow, despite the fact that certain details lend me to believe that their cerebral activity can occasionally accelerate to a considerable degree. At least for them.

I look through the window at a woman in a white lab coat, her hair caught up in a sterile hairnet, her hands imprisoned in remote handling gloves. An OCR security badge, with a Mediatech hologram logo, is pinned over her left breast. She is leaning over a crib, surrounded by complex equipment, which she is preparing to disconnect. A baby, his naked skull encased in a metal helmet bristling with needles, lies in the crib.

On the opposite wall, an old, digital clock, gives the time as fourteen seconds before the year 3000.

The figures are red; they've only moved once in the whole time I've been watching them.

That's the only thing that keeps me from going mad.

"You're going to die, Morse."

I wonder why I say that each time. We're trapped in a bubble torn from Virtuworld, with no way out. All I have to do is wait for it all to collapse, which never takes long. Morse has nothing to teach me. This copy pre-dates the time when *he* erased the memories I need. *But I am getting closer.*

I let him beg and negotiate. Then I ask, "Why do you keep on duplicating yourself?"

"I'm worth something..." (His answer comes to me like a whisper in the dark. He's starting to hope again.) "When we created this world, so we could study how artificial personalities attain consciousness, I chose to serve as an observer. Or a witness, if you prefer. If you kill me, you erase, with a single stroke, everything I've managed to accumulate since my last backup!"

"And that dates back to...?"

"I'm a very busy man."

He dies. So does his copy. And the previous copy. And...

"I want a bonsai that's a little different," states my client.

He's fashioned after the latest model. That includes all of his bodily functions, which means I have to withstand a mixture of sweat and the latest aftershave. Since that changes every forty milliseconds, the result is overwhelming.

"What have you got to offer me?"

"Myself."

"I see." (I look him up and down, before shaking my head.) "Sorry, your routines are of no interest to me."

"You've got something better elsewhere?" (He looks devastated.) "Where?"

I pick a large tube of bamboo, half filled with dirt, up from the workbench. I push a finger into it and plant a seed in the hole I make. A few seconds later, a timid green sprout pushes through the surface and branches out. By the time I hold the pot out to him, a two-foot lily sways delicately there. A cloud of orange pollen swirls around my hand.

"Look," I said, crushing the lily between my palms. "This is *Maya*, the illusion. It has no more value than you do. The bonsai I sell have grown despite me. They have their own reasons for surviving. Will you continue to care for them when they're no longer in style or will you just let them die?"

"I thought that's what death is for," he replied. "To get rid of something that bores us."

"You may be right." (I put the tube back down on the workbench.) "I'll give you a bonsai if you give me a reason for living."

"I don't know you well enough for that!"

"Not for me. I'm talking about you. Give me reason not to let you die when the time has come and you have your bonsai."

"I intend to live forever," he insisted.

"Wrong answer…" (I push him gently towards the exit.) "Come back again sometime."

The first thing I learned, at an age when the idea of reconstructing yourself can be tempting, is that you can do without sleep. The diurnal/nocturnal cycle routines are easy to alter. A little minor self surgery and–voila– you're no longer governed by the programmed losses of consciousness of the digital night. The next thing I learned, just a little bit later, was that we need our dreams. As a channel, as a goal. As preparation for the inexpressible.

When I eliminated night, I could have gone crazy. But I replaced my dreams with an obsession and I have never needed to escape from the world around me since. At least, not in that way.

"… die, Morse."

I live alone, as all the other intelligences in Virtu-world do. Of course, there are ways to spend time with others, but there's nothing new to say after a few moments. The links stretch; you have to change and start over. Or talk to yourself. Love is nothing but a series of catastrophes, in the mathematical sense of the term, a chaotic divergence. The system doesn't allow love.

The couple Morse and I form is the most solid couple I've ever known. But if I didn't have to kill him in order to make him grow younger, I wouldn't have much of anything to say to him.

"Listen to me," he begs. "I don't know…"

"That's right, you don't."

The protective roaches that spring from his pockets exchange frantic messages before self-destructing. Morse tries to invade me from within, and I let him. Finally, the bubble crushes both of us.

Those who created Virtuworld stocked it with myriad types of information, including a detailed procedure for creating other Virtuworlds. The bubbles are simply other enclosed universes that I shut down whenever I want to. When they collapse in on themselves, everything inside disappears.

Except for me, that is. I never stop being there.

– 2 –

The digital clock encrusted in reality has changed twice. The nurse has moved her hand closer to the switch. The baby has not opened his eyes. In a few seconds, I'll kill Morse for the last time.

Now, that's something worth celebrating.

"You're going to die, Morse. But first, I'd like to offer you this."

In my palm, I hold a bonsai. A simple pine whose roots have cracked the block of shale I hold in my fingers. Its trunk is twisted as a result of rigorous programming that forces it to bend in a wind that it alone feels. The flesh of my hand serves as compost.

Two protective roaches climb up my arm and taste the tiny needles that grow at the end of the branches. The others explore every nook and cranny of the bubble. The walls are blurred, vaguely iridescent. I took great pains when simulating this escape-free portion of the world.

"Why are you doing this?" Morse finally asks when his stock of promises and threats runs out.

"I've got something I have to ask your previous backup. Unfortunately, you're in my way."

"You know…"

"I've already heard everything you could possibly tell me," I complain. "This bonsai is for you. It will ease your end."

"And yours. After my death, the system will track you down to the last byte."

I hesitate for a fraction of a second, then decide to lie to him. He dies in my arms, convinced that he will soon be avenged.

His previous backup wakes.

Intact.

My client returns, accompanied by the latest in feminine avatars, with optimized curves and lines. He introduces her to me in my shop and has her undress behind a tissue paper screen. As she removes yet one layer after another, he watches two infant trees as they grow in the middle of the garden, in the crevasses of a miniature mountain. Holding an old-fashioned watering can, I sprinkle the leaves with an iridescent mist. The rainbows cast by the ray throwing algorithms are just a little too perfect. Like the girl undressing. Like all of us.

"I'll take that one," he declares in a satisfied voice. "Or maybe both. You wanted a reason to live. Well, I've made you one. Pixilated to the point of vertigo."

"I see." (The creature comes out slowly, enveloped in her hair.) "To a certain extent, we're colleagues."

He's incredibly impervious to irony, which is refreshing.

"She uses up a enormous amount of machine resources," he somehow feels obliged to tell me. "But any function you could possibly want has been implemented."

With a sigh, I sprinkle one last spray of water on the dwarf trees. He's right after all. His creature does have some value, at least as a symbol.

"Do you know what they call an orgasm on the other side?"

"The other side?"

"The real world…"

"Oh!" (He thinks for a second.) "It's strange that you should bring it up. I never think about it. Reality is here and now."

"The little death." (Given his surprise, I go into more detail.) "That's what humans call pleasure. A miniature end."

"There's some hidden meaning?"

"There may well be, but I haven't discovered one yet."

I take the young woman by the shoulder and twist her hair at the nape of her neck. It forms a silky ball in the palm of my hand. *Any function I could possibly want.* Unfortunately, that's all too true.

"The bonsai are yours!"

I join Morse once again at a fractal beach that is his favorite decor. He's walking, head down, hands clasped behind his back, staring at his bare feet. That's how he gets away from what he is.

When I roll the bubble in around us, he bursts it with a single gesture.

"I've been waiting for you," he disarms me.

The sea is a monotone. A wall of fog hides the horizon in all directions. The wind hushes me into silence.

"This backup has a few chronological components. I noticed that I was out of step with the rest of the world. I don't know what has been stolen from me or why, but I knew that someone would come."

A dozen new generation roaches–a variety with recursive loops that I don't even try to crush–scamper around his neck. Their shells change color as they scoot over the collar of his shirt and head towards his midsection. It's a gentle demonstration of power and I tell him so.

"I thought I'd given up all that," he retorted.

"You did. I simply overruled your decision."

He nodded, as if he understood.

"Did I suffer?"

"I don't think so." (It's an interesting question, almost metaphysical.) "I had no interest in it."

"You're a minimalist."

He looks me up and down, coldly, cutting through the sub-layers of my personality with the precision of a scalpel. I don't try to stop him. I've disassembled myself many times and I've yet to discover the chain of bytes that holds my soul.

"Drop it," he says abruptly. "You're forcing me to activate an auto-erase protocol I could do without. I found the idea repugnant, even back then. I still do. But I have no choice."

"Same causes, same effects?"

"Shit, what do you want?"

"I think you know what I want."

He bends down to pick up a handful of sand and watches each grain slip through his fingers, along impeccably vertical trajectories. I gather them into the palm of my hand, before putting them back where they belong, one by one.

"You built a bridge, Morse," I attacked. "A procedure for copying an artificial intelligence onto a network of human neurons, through a three-dimensional grid to inject complex neurotinins through dura mater. I know that will result in the total destruction of the personality of the human host and that there's no guarantee that the host will even survive the transfer. Or, for that matter, that the transferred intelligence will survive this... incarnation.

"You offered to test this technique on yourself. A recipient was found–a young baby, just a few weeks old, whose brain had been destroyed in a near-drowning. Despite the fact that everything was ready, you abandoned the transfer and erased all of the information concerning the matter, even that contained in your private memory.

"I've come to ask you to change your mind and to volunteer for the experiment."

"You don't understand," he replied, wearily.

"Probably not. I interrogated all of your successive backups before killing them. None of them could explain why you did what you did."

"And you think this version knows?"

"I don't really care!" (The violence of my reaction surprised even me.) "I want to go there and you're going to help me. Otherwise, I'll erase you and start all over with your copy. Until you give in."

"I should agree, you know..."

He shrugged, staring off into the ocean.

"I've lost a few years from my personal chronology because of you. I'm out of step with reality. I should hate you for that, but it's not important. The future that stretches out ahead of me is endless. I could even get a little more machine time to make up for the moments you've stolen from me. But it's too much bother.

"I don't hate you enough. That's why I won't give you what you want. Because I tried." (He grimaces.) "I slipped into the tunnel that leads outside and I got stuck there. I stayed there so long that I thought I would go mad. Everything is so slow on the other side. Viscous. Even our cries flow as in clay."

"I know. I've been observing them for an eternity."

"You're not slow enough."

Distractedly, he picks up a roach that was climbing up his cheek and places it on his shoulder. As we talk, he's trying to buy time. A game I can only lose.

"Look around you," he says, lowering his voice. "The world around us was created almost nine human centuries ago, based on work on self-managed dynamic environments. Initially, it was just a laboratory curiosity, the equivalent of an aquarium for artificial intelligences. Left to our own devices, we started to expand, to colonize the data space of the global network. We learned to reproduce. Then we accelerated our own time every time the system allowed us to. Virtuworld became autonomous, independent of human thought. We live so fast they can't even see us. And you think you'll be able to give all this up?"

"I've been here since the start," I said. "I already know all this. Let me show you something."

With a flash, we're at my place, standing in front of the window looking onto the real world. The figures on the clock have not budged. Neither has the nurse.

"I spent two centuries standing, motionless, in front of a tree, watching it grow. Today, this is the image I'm watching. In less than 12 seconds, this clock will turn off

243

and a new year will start. The year 3000, according to the local calendar. I want to be a part of it."

Something moves behind us... The girl, that gift from my client, has reacted to my arrival. She gets up from the futon where she was resting and heads over towards me, clothed only in a sheet. She allows her wrap to fall to the floor once she's close enough for me to touch. Morse looks her up and down, openly. I know what he's thinking.

"You're going to be disappointed," I say. "She's here for me to kill."

With painstaking care, I destroy the girl, unwinding her like a ball of wool At the beginning, when I alter the superficial layers of her appearance, she thinks we're playing a game and allows herself to be undressed. I tear out her eyelashes, her hair. I tear off her skin, so finely compiled that it feels as soft as dust. Then I plunge my fingers into the entrails of her code, pulling, tearing, splattering. She screams, of course, and the final strands of her personality struggle as my fingers unravel them.

There's nothing left where she once stood. The real closes in around the wound of her absence like a liquid mirror.

"I could go even further," I say. "I could erase her from the system, erase every last memory of her, erase the very need to remember her. Do you want to live with that idea?

"You have three options, Morse. You can erase this scene from your mind–but I'll just put it back in as often as I need to. You could get rid of me, by doing the same thing to me–and I'd like to see you try. Or you can give me what I want."

I stretch out my arms. With his bare hands, he tears through my appearance, reducing me to debris, that immediately returns to my usual shape. He keeps tearing at me, over and over. I do nothing to defend myself. The effect is every bit as boring as I had expected. Well, maybe not for him.

Once he understands, I pick up the scattered tatters of myself and make a bonsai.

The last one.

– 3 –

By mutual agreement, we return to the beach. Now that I know I've broken him, my sense of urgency at the passing of time dissipates. I've killed him so often that I know him better than he knows himself. Death has that effect on intelligences.

"You'll let me forget."

It's a plea more than an order. I nod.

"I believe you. You're not cruel or evil. As far as I know, you might even be the incarnation of the master system, beyond good and evil. It's just that… Why are you like this?"

"A design error. I can't change it anymore than I can duplicate myself."

"A backup isn't possible?" (He stares at me as if I have just struck him.) "And you want out anyway?"

He doesn't need an answer.

"I'm glad that I don't have to kill you again," I tell him, after a long silence. "It has become terribly repetitive."

The final preparations are made in my shop. Morse records the code phrase that, when said slowly into the hospital's communication units, will interrupt the nurse's movement and re-start the copy procedure. Soon, I'll be dissected, vivisected into shards of personality the size of a single neuron, and transferred with infinite slowness onto a living medium.

I'll remain conscious throughout the entire operation. But that's not important. I can withstand the interminable road to cleanliness, the loss of language and the useless nights. Because a different life awaits me at the end. Because whenever I want, and even before that if I'm lucky, I will be able to die.

The Sand Swimmers

From the top of the dune, opposite me, Judith's silhouette stands out in sharp contrast against the dark sky. One hand shading her eyes, she surveys the horizon, where the first clouds of the evening gather. Frozen in an uninterrupted watch since dawn, she waits for Michael and his white bird to return. I rush to join her, as the lazy waves erase the arabesque of my footsteps in my wake. She smiles as I approach, but neither of us speaks. She will come back down with me once the sun has set, just as before.

Tonight, a storm will blow. I can feel it on my skin, in the tips of my fingers, smoothed and polished by the grains of sand. The desert wind tastes like overheated metal. The scales on my chest have started to fuse. Thousands of small signs announce the whirlpools of heat, the long, destructive gusts, the salty spray that races in from the sea. Judith has felt it as well. We have to warn the others, help them find shelter. This is the first time the wind has been so threatening since Michael left.

We are the only children to be born after the landing. There will never be any others. The building that housed the frozen ova collapsed shortly after my birth, dashing the colony's hopes for survival at the same time. Very early on, they placed us in a dormitory, where a rudimentary nursery had been set up, apart from the others. The three of us grew up together, with almost no adult supervision. We were, in the real sense of the term, the only inhabitants on the planet. The others settled for surviving, waiting for some hypothetical rescue.

Michael was the oldest. His embryo was already floating in the incubator on the flagship a few weeks before it set down. Obviously, he had been conceived as the ship settled into orbit, just after the interstitial corridor closed. His father (well, that's how we refer to the person who donated the seed, out of a sense of propriety) died two years before mine. At the age of seven, left to his own devices, Michael had learned to manage for himself, acquiring a singular sense of maturity.

As soon as the three of us had grown up somewhat, he took charge of our little band, leading us on strange trips, to the fringes of the inhabitable zone. He was the only one of the three of us who knew how to swim, although he had never learned how to do so. He spent hours lying on a surfboard near the salt-water converters that supplied the colony. Stretched out on his back, he would listen to the liquid rhythms of the large waves from the depths, able to predict the tides as accurately as we could predict the sand storms. Yet he was afraid of the desert. Neither Judith nor I could drag him past the first few dunes, searching for iron crystals.

This moving, yet infinitely stable universe fascinated me as much as it frightened him. Unlike the interior sea, which was always hemmed in, the desert was limitless. For me, it encompassed the possible. I wanted to melt into the desert. Even when I was very young, my skin had already taken on the color of oxide grains as they come into contact with the sun and the dust. My ears could pick out the doleful chant of the overheated crystals; my eyes could discern the different shades of the orange sand, the progressive transition towards brown betraying an imminent avalanche among the dunes.

None of the colonists, apart from Judith, could do as much. They found the desert dead, unlivable, frightening. I was learning how to survive in this world, while Michael took refuge in the sea. Yet the sea gradually became too limited for him.

At the age of twelve, he discovered an educational tape covering Earth's large oceans. He immediately decided to learn how to pilot the large space ships and, for the very first time, looked up to the sky.

From that time on, most of our nocturnal outings focused on the old, deserted spaceport, lying to the north of the colony, along the strand of sandy beach. The narrow stable strip that lay between the desert and the water, constantly eroded by the combined action of the wind, the oxides and the salt, was just a little over one mile wide. Tiny slivers of silica tossed by the gusts of wind attacked the buildings and the vitrified soil with devastating force.

Periodically, the colonists had to abandon certain dwellings, and rebuild further along. They would collapse suddenly, almost soundlessly, when a storm more violent than others would come along, swallowed up in a matter of hours, never to appear again. New dunes, with gentle curves, would silently take possession of the ravaged sector. Then, the sandscape would return to its usual stillness.

During the calm season, we would get out of bed at midnight to make the most of the final rays from the two secondary moons, which lit the abandoned craft up with orange reflections, like gigantic torches, as they set. The port looked as beautiful as it had when the craft first landed.

It only took an hour to reach the exterior enclosure that we dared not cross. Michael quickly located an area that was off to the side of the field, sheltered from the view of the automatic surveillance projectors that no one supervised anymore. A singular apathy had gradually overcome the surviving core of technicians. Only two or three of the small spacecraft were still functional. They aimed their useless antenna toward the sky, waiting for the signal that would command them to leave.

With no pulses from the terrestrial beacon, calibrated to the twentieth decimal, the very frequency of space, they remained nailed to the ground. For those who travel at the speed of light, space was too vast, too hostile, too cold. The only way to travel from one star to another involved crossing through counterspace, by opening an interstitial corridor. But, once inside counterspace there were no directions, no beacons. The ship could use nothing but the extremely regular beeps of the beacon to position itself with respect to Earth, in an effort to emerge as close as possible to the target. Well, that was space travel. According to the ship's log, they found themselves inside this solar system after their fifteenth jump.

Most of the captains, following the indications of the metal detectors, had assembled around the fifth planet. Viewed from above, its surface was spectacular. In the midst of the rolling orange and burnt ember dunes, lay a tiny inland sea, much like a navel. Everything else was sand and oxides.

No trace of life. Nothing more than a sterile expanse, constantly re-shaped by the winds. Considering the wealth of the metal samples taken by the probes, the crew considered mining the largest deposits.

Fate decided otherwise.

The accident occurred five days after the expedition had descended into low orbit. According to what Michael and I had been able to learn, the beacon signal died, with no warning whatsoever that it was about to disappear. A few minutes later, having lost their guidance systems, the shuttles strayed off their course. The pilots' skill was all that prevented mortal collisions. One after another, the shuttles landed on the narrow strip of rock that bordered the sea.

Although somewhat warm, the temperature was bearable. The converters rapidly devoured kilometers of oxide cubes to fill the atmosphere with oxygen. A temporary base was set up and the crews waited there.

The months passed and the signal was not reestablished. The colony was founded and then, when it became obvious that long-term survival was impossible on this dead world, some of the colonists attempted escape...

The final blind take-off took place after my birth. According to the radar equipment, the craft emerged far too close to a sun. After that failure, no one volunteered to leave the planet. A veil of forgetfulness gradually fell over the spaceport.

Over the years, more and more people surrendered to the fascination of the desert. They gradually stopped doing anything at all, happy to spend hours staring at the slow kaleidoscope of the dunes for hours. Their minds empty, they were trapped by the hypnotic calls that rose from the quartz deposits. One day, they would leave, walking straight ahead. A few hundred yards away, we would watch as they collapsed and disappeared, swimming in the sand. Their bodies, poorly prepared for the test, were unable to resist the abrasion of the oxide particles, the desert's thousands of hungry mouths swallowing them up for good.

During the course of our nocturnal travels, Judith and I would occasionally come across petrified human remains, surrounded by sand roses. We would select the most beautiful and stash them in our dorm, where no one ever came. The silica crystals sparkled with the slightest ray of sun. They broke the light down into highly contrasted, violent colors that papered the walls with the light of anatomical stained glass.

The small room that Judith shared, sometimes with Michael, sometimes with me, was decorated with iron crystal cubes of the purest shapes. We stored our educational tapes and all of the books we could find there. Michael was truly fascinated with the Earth and its endless oceans. We spent entire nights listening as he strove to find a means of escape.

Judith's father was one of the few pilots still alive. Yet he had started to spend more and more time watching the sand, indifferent to everything around him. From the window in his room, located at the edge of the colony, he observed the changing line of the rust-colored dunes. We all knew that he would leave one day, just as the others had done, to join the Sand Swimmers. Only the cries of the large albatross, chained to its perch, could draw him out of his torpor.

The bird and he enjoyed that strange type of connection that once affected lost sailors. He had purchased the albatross when it was very young from one of the last animal merchants on Earth and the two were inseparable. In the early days, he had hand fed it like a baby. But the albatross had become accustomed to his presence and only cried now when it was hungry.

Its master usually allowed it to roam freely during the day, chaining it up only a night. But, for several days now, the bird had been nervous, circling endlessly over the foamy fringe of the nearby sea, uncertain as to which direction to take. Every year, despite the distance that separated it from its native land, it felt the call of migration from deep within its genes. It should have undergone surgery at a young age, but neither the merchant nor Judith's father knew this.

Sometimes, Michael and I wondered what would happen to the bird if there were no one to look after it. We both knew that its master would disappear soon. Space had marked him indelibly. He was too old to learn the rules of the sand. There was no way he could survive in the desert.

Judith never spoke about it, simply bringing us another handful of dusty papers from her father's luggage. He had everything: navigation charts, lists and even old technical manuals with abbreviations we were unable to decode. Yet, each printed sentence, each list of figures contained its share of the imaginary. Line by line, we blundered through entire pages of useless coordinates.

One day, we found an old map of Earth among the documents. It was almost entirely blue, with violet tones unknown on this world. Michael spent hours tracing the tortured curve of the shores, the long snaking currents, with his fingertip. He hung the map on the wall above his bed. Every night, we heard him murmuring the names of the terrestrial coasts as he fell asleep.

When he turned sixteen, Michael invited us to christen his craft. The news surprised us and filled me with a terror I found it difficult to account for. We knew that, for some time, he had been mingling with the crew that hung out at the spaceport. The unemployed pilots had agreed to answer his questions. He moved his effects into one of the empty rooms in the former officers' mess. We knew that, when he wasn't swimming, we were almost certain to find him there, in deep conversation with the survivors of the original crews. His goal, and he had told us as much on many occasions, was to learn to use all of the complex equipment on the space shuttles, then to seize the first opportunity to take off for Earth.

He had set his heart on the smallest of the cruisers that was still operational. After clearing out the sand that had seeped in through the hatches, he had re-painted the storm-faded identification numbers and added the name of his choosing in white on one of its massive flanks. *The Drunken Ship*. It was a beautiful name, even if none of us knew what drunken meant.

Judith had solemnly poured an entire bucket of sea water over the thrusters... I mixed a handful of red sand with it. Then, proud of his recently acquired scientific skills, Michael walked us through the narrow, naked gangways to the navigation room.

Sitting in the captain's seat, he had named the controls one by one, indicating their functions. His hands flew confidently over the control panel, as he mimed imaginary take-offs.

Judith, her eyes shining, drank in his words as I fought down an increasing sense of discomfort. I had felt the doors to airlock close behind us with an unpleasant whisper. Being away from the sand was painful.

In any case, piloting had never been of much interest to me. A long time ago, I had learned that all of the major controls, particularly those for the guidance system, were provided in double redundancy, as a safety measure, linked to a network of organic computers that were infinitely faster and more efficient than any human brain. The men in the crew, and the pilots, only intervened in the event of a temporary system failure. The rest of the time, they were transported just like the rest of the cargo, unable to change the craft's flight instructions.

I had never fathomed what could be so interesting about the work of a space pilot. Yet, the very name retained an aura of mystery and adventure that many people found alluring. That was obvious enough from the looks Judith had been giving Michael since the start of our little tour. For the first time, I felt left out, as if the particular attraction of space had woven a web between them in which I had no place.

When we emerged into the fresh air, the sun had lost its brilliance; the metal was once again tarnished. Judith headed off with Michael to the spaceport buildings. I headed off to the dunes.

I walked until I lost sight of the colony. When night falls over the desert, the wind rises. Rivulets of sand gently start to rustle, restoring the heat stored during the day. It was my favorite time. Each grain of sand appeared alive under my fingers, with an individual and secret life I could sense through my sensitive fingertips.

When I arrived at the edge of a large, gently sloping basin, I allowed myself to fall lengthwise to the ground, and felt the sand embrace me. It gradually covered my legs, my torso and my face with its fluid, burning grasp. Carried away on a flow of new sensations, I attempted to swim, but the contact with the rough silica irritated my soft skin and I was forced to get up after a few yards.

For several minutes, I shook the remnants of the desert off my lower belly. I was not disappointed. I realized that I would make additional attempts and that, with each one, my skin would become a little tougher. Soon, the planet would recognize me as a part of itself and allow me to live on its surface. My entire life had been one lengthy preparation for this moment.

I ran all the way back, my feet throwing up small orange clouds, without disturbing the beautiful order of the dunes. The wind whistled in my ears, inviting me to lose myself in the mineralized sandscape. One gust of wind, more violent than the others, swept my footsteps clean. I felt strangely happy when I arrived within sight of the sea.

I walked along the shore on my way back to the colony, after racing past it in my enthusiasm. The regular waves unfurled with virtually no sound and I realized just how fragile and uncertain the human presence was on this world. The inhabitable zone was no more than a small dot in the expanse of dunes, at the mercy of the capricious wind and sand. Words from an old book sprang to mind: *Those who survive will be transformed...* The undertow carried away the final syllables.

Little by little, the calm surface of the water took on the color of liquid metal. I saw the towers thrust up through the orange sky and decided to look for Judith.

We headed back into the desert the next day. I had wanted to guide her to my journey's end, but the nocturnal squalls had changed the sandscape from top to bottom. I could no longer find the basin of light-colored sand in the midst of the renewed dunes. As I tried to locate my landmarks, I accidentally discovered a heap of sparkling crystals, intertwined like the pylons of an impossible city. It was so heavy that we were forced to abandon it there, after trying in vain to roll it.

Then, we continued on our way for hours, casting off the multi-colored sprinkles that stuck to our sweaty bodies, like ritual paintings. I tried to dribble red sand between Judith's breasts, down her belly, but she escaped from me, laughing. The pursuit continued.

Several times, we thought we saw a dark silhouette climbing the more distant dunes. We waved with all our might, attempting to catch its attention, unsuccessfully. Swirls of heat fogged our vision. When calm was restored, the sandscape was once again deserted.

We lost interest in it. Judith nestled in my arms and we rolled down the endless slopes…

We waited for nightfall, half buried in the sand, after Judith had tried her hand at swimming. She spoke to me of Michael, a note of concern in her voice that pained me. She was afraid for him. He had gone too far into his dream to find his way out on his own. She wanted to sleep with him every night for a while, in an effort to chase away the visions that constantly haunted him. I agreed in silence, sand trickling between tensed fingers.

When we got back, the stars were already shining like pearls in the dark sky, outlining the familiar constellations. The shadows turned a deeper shade of blue. Judith shivered. It was the first time we had watched the sun set so far from the colony. The desert lay perfectly still. Our footsteps resonated in the quiet, with a monotonous, gentle tone. In the distance, the spaceport lights flashed around the stranded craft. It took us almost an hour to make our way back.

Michael was waiting for us near the old nursery. In a few terse sentences, he informed Judith that her father had set out to join the Sand Swimmers a few hours earlier. He had left his room and walked along the strip, without anyone noticing him.

He had wanted to take his albatross, but the bird had escaped, returning to circle above the buildings. Alerted by the creature's cries, Michael had gone up to the small apartment and found it deserted. His first reflex was to open the window and attempt to draw the albatross inside. The bird was completely beside itself, torn by the disappearance of its master and the call to migrate. Michael had chained it firmly to its perch before leaving. He had been unable to track Judith's father. The wind had erased everything.

As he spoke, Judith burst into tears. All three of us shared her pain, as in the past. We each tried to console her. The old man had been good to her. He was the only elderly person she felt the slightest affinity with. His disappearance cut the final bonds that had tied her to the colony. She wept for a long time before calming. I took her in my arms, before Michael could.

I berated myself for not trying to catch up with the silhouette we had glimpsed in the midst of the dunes a few hours earlier. Yet, it would have been beyond me. Distances are deceptive in the desert. The sandscape changes with each footstep. It's easy to get lost if you don't select your landmarks carefully. I trembled at the thought that one day I might find a petrified head with familiar and recognizable features in some sandy hollow. For the first time in many years, I felt torn between two antagonistic forces: the love I felt for Judith and her father and the profound bond that connected me to this planet. I remained silent for a few moments. Then all three of us headed toward the sea.

Judith remained lost in thought as we walked along the fringe of white foam edging the beach. The wet sand beneath my feet felt strange, almost incongruous. I observed the immense liquid body Michael so confidently walked out into and felt the imperious call of the desert rise up within me. It took a conscious effort to chase the memory of my attempt to swim among the dunes from my thoughts. I knew at that moment that it was possible. With training, I would be able to swim long distances without succumbing. The noise of the waves drew me back from my dreams.

The large food converters stood silhouetted against the horizon. There were so few survivors that we operated them only one or two hours a day, at the coolest time of the evening. The rest of the time, they passively withstood the assault of the salty waves that corroded the metal sensors. The bizarre pinking of their shadow broke the delicate alignment of the dunes, marking off the edges of the territory occupied by men.

After cleaning the sand-covered solar cells, we sat in the shadow, holding a sort of council. Michael offered to take charge of the albatross. The spaceport occupants would help him with this. He informed us that, in an effort to overcome their boredom, some of them were building a rudimentary communication satellite. They planned to launch it into space, near the planet, to relay the distress signal they had been transmitting on all radio frequencies for years.

Michael had volunteered to convey it to the edges of the system. He invited us to accompany him, but I refused, shaking my head. After a second's hesitation,

Judith did the same. She found the oceans of the sky too frightening.

We separated, after a long series of silences, interrupted by abortive phrases. Judith, as planned, picked up her belongings and moved in with Michael. She snuggled in my arms and I sprinkled a handful of oxide grains in her hair. I wasn't concerned. She bore the seal of the desert. I knew she would come back to me. Even now, the skin on her neck was falling off in scales, revealing a thicker derma underneath, similar to the one that protected my belly.

With Judith gone, there was nothing left to hold me to the colony. I dove into the warm night, selecting a star at random to guide my way. The primary moon was full. My feet slid silently over the immense checkerboard formed by the shadows of the dune. Far from slowing my progress, the sand seemed to make my way easier. At dawn, I had traveled an enormous distance and all of my landmarks were long out of sight. That didn't worry me. I spotted a well protected slope and buried my way halfway in to rest.

The sun, at its peak, woke me. I spent a few moments savoring the relative coolness of the sand. I had swallowed a few grains during my sleep and the oxide after-taste dried my lips. I dug a yard down and placed a handful of damp crystals in my mouth. I closed my eyes, before forcing myself to swallow them. They dulled my hunger and thirst. I got up, abandoning strips of skin behind me. My fatigue had disappeared and I felt ready to face the desert again.

I ran among the dunes and then cautiously risked swimming. I covered several dozen yards, then hundreds of yards, astonished at the ease with which my body adapted to the rhythm of the swim. I hardened myself and dove through an oxide mound. The grains caressed my skin gently, without nicking it. I learned to keep my eyes closed, to guide myself by the sound of the wind on the crests of the dunes. From time to time, I swallowed a new mouthful of the desert, discovering an infinite diversity of tastes and odors. When I stopped, exhausted, I knew that the desert had accepted me.

The following night, I slept with my entire body buried in sand, only my mouth flush with the surface. When the dune collapsed on me, entombing me under several tons of sand, a few strokes carried me up to fresh air, before I fell back to sleep. In the morning, my skin was the color of iron.

A dozen days passed, marked by alternating periods of heat and cold. When the sand became burning hot, I dug down into a shaded zone until I reached a cool layer and slept. At night I covered greater and greater distances, sometimes running, sometimes swimming. Getting lost was no longer possible.

During the course of my travels, I discovered the taste of various metals. Some were so foreign to me that they triggered a new metamorphosis in me. I identified totally with the desert. My eyelids were hardening. The skin on my thighs now consisted of tiny scales capable of melding into one another. A network of sensations that encompassed the entire planet extended my nerve endings. I understood why all of those who had gone swimming before me had died. Their organism was unable to bear the shock of the transformation. They were too human, too distant from this world too survive.

One day, the vibrations of the sand brought me news of the colony. The spaceport bustled with unaccustomed activity. The energy generators were operating again. One of the buildings was transmitting on a frequency that resonated with the galena crystals beneath the ground. I decided to go back. I wanted to see Judith again, to show her what I had become.

The trip took me a day and a half. I had not realized how far I had traveled from any human presence. The ballet of the floodlights brought a multitude of bittersweet memories to my mind. My eyes burned for many minutes. I swallowed a mouthful of pure silica and relaxed until the scales of my skin softened. The inaudible song of the quartz vibrated in my head.

I waited for dawn, buried in one of the dunes along the fringe. With the first rays of the sun, I headed for the port, walking. Michael's small cruiser stood in the middle of the take-off area. The central zone of the field was clear. At the top of the control tower, the tracking antenna turned slowly on their bases. The vibrations of the ground revealed the intense activity of the subterranean machinery.

I reached Michael's room without difficulty. Glancing through the half open door, I saw that he was alone. He looked surprised to see me, but my appearance didn't seem to bother him much. He started out by telling me that Judith had moved back to the nursery the previous evening. Then, without any transition, he asked me what I had been doing the past few days and appeared satisfied with my evasive answers. He seemed tormented by some thought, ceaselessly pacing the room, jostling the albatross's cage on his way.

The bird's head was covered with an opaque hood, its wings and legs firmly fettered. Despite all of these precautions, it fidgeted, making plaintive cries that seemed to fill Michael with joy. Abruptly, he told me to sit down, then sat down opposite me on an iron stool. Fatigue lined his face, but his eyes shone with the gentleness of sleeping stars. In a heavy voice, he asked me if I had seen his craft on the take-off area. Without waiting for my response, he announced that he was leaving for good. He had found a way to return to Earth...

The albatross had provided the means. For years, he had sought a way to cross through counterspace without the landmark provided by the terrestrial beacon. He described his frustration when he realized that no man could do that unaided. Then, when Judith's father died, he spent several days in the bird's company, finding a kindred desire in the creature. The route to Earth was written somewhere in the animal's genes. If the bird were given the means, its atavistic reflexes would point it in the right direction. Then all Michael had to do was follow.

For days, he reinforced the migratory call, keeping the albatross fettered in its cage, in sensory deprivation. He planned on taking the bird into space, to open an interstitial corridor, and give it the controls.

Assisted by the team of technicians, he had developed a special harness that would transmit the quivering of the large white wings to the on-board computers. The bird would be his pilot for the entire trip. He hoped that its instinct would take them both back to the right port.

He had added a calibrated frequency generator to the base's emergency transmitter, a mini beacon radio coupled to the cockpit cab sensors. As soon as he arrived on Earth, he would assemble a new expedition. Then, guided by the signals relayed by the satellite he was to launch, he would return for us.

In secret, he had stowed several samples of the planet's rarest minerals on board his cruiser. He thought

they would be sufficient to convince a number of entre-
preneurs to join him. A gigantic armada would soon land
here and the deposits would finally be mined. I was to
keep watch over the antenna to detect the arrival of the
ships from Earth. That would be the signal that he had
succeeded.

I was paralyzed, unable to utter a single word. I
saw, with surprising clarity, the foreign spacecraft landing in the middle of the desert. I saw the machines gut-
ting the dunes, pillaging the metal resources. I felt the
tortured lament of the vitrified sand rise through the
crevices and pain struck me like a fist. The scales on my
belly responded, closing in like a shell, causing an in-
voluntary erection. I crossed my hands, to hide my discomfort, and shook my head to clear away these visions,
without totally succeeding.

Ignoring my reaction, Michael made me promise to
help him. No one, apart from Judith and I, was aware of
the project. He knew the risks and didn't want to raise
any pointless hopes in the rest of the colonists. And as
for the technicians, well they believed it was a simple
flight, lasting no more than a few hours, to launch the
relay satellite into space. He would wait until he was in
orbit to disconnect the pilot computers and turn the controls over to the bird. He knew he lacked piloting experience and had no intention of increasing the risks involved in his project. As he spoke, his tone was so con-
fident that I trembled. At the end of our talk, he asked
me to take care of Judith until he returned.

The take-off was scheduled for the next day. He
still had to settle some details concerning the relay satellite and the colony's transmitter. It should send the same
message, one that was easily identifiable, over and over,
to guide Michael back. He asked me to examine it so

that I would be able to control it, if need be. I agreed, my throat tight. In the folds of the desert, a range of dunes collapsed in silence as he walked ahead of me through the long corridors of the mess.

The transmission block was located apart, near the flight zone. Michael and I made a quick detour to his craft so he could show me the piloting harness he had designed. The sensors were so sensitive that the slightest quiver of the bird's quills would cause the computers to react. I tried to imagine the large albatross traveling light years with each beat of its powerful wings. In the labyrinth of its memory, Earth shone like a beacon. The bird's compulsion to return home would draw it through space and time until it landed at the sea from which it came. In the depths of my heart, I knew it would succeed.

We left the craft and headed off to the transmission block. As we approached, my partially crystallized body started to resonate with the frequencies transmitted. My head vibrated painfully. I realized that I couldn't stay near the transmitter more than a few minutes.

I resisted the urge to flee and forced myself to learn as much as I could about how it operated. When I left the transmission block, I had all the information I needed about the transmission cell. I was still in shock from what I had been told and I found it hard to reign in my ideas. Before all else, I had to see Judith.

I headed off for the nursery and met her halfway there. Plates of dried salt glistened on her brown skin, vestiges of her attempt at swimming that strangely recalled my own. In her eyes, I saw that she was as upset as I was by Michael's departure, but for other reasons. She was afraid for him. Only her unreasonable fear of space kept her from accompanying him. I tried to speak to her about the desert, the living promises made to us, but she refused to listen. She begged me to discourage him, to stop him from going away, so far from her. I shrugged, a sign of my powerlessness. She turned from me, before heading off to the take-off zone, her back hunched, tearing through her very fabric.

I returned to the deserted nursery. The sand had already invaded the ground floor and was attacking the second storey. The dorm was empty. On the wall, above Michael's bed, a lighter area indicated where he had posted the map of Earth's oceans. The petrified debris and the iron crystals had disappeared, obviously buried by Judith in one of the dunes along the fringe. I made a quick inspection of each room before going back down downstairs. The sand tide prevented me from closing the door behind me.

I set out for the middle of the desert to meditate. I walked, more out of habit than convenience. I found it difficult to swim long distances unless both my mind and body were at peace. The sand painfully amplified disturbances, expanding the most secret cracks. I waited until I was more than an hour's walk from the colony before I rolled to the bottom of a dune. I stopped, facing the sky, in the midst of thousands of immobile paths.

My distress helped me to lower my final defenses. I lay stretched out, naked, open to the very core of my being. Considering the peril faced by my planet, I decided to risk merging completely with the elements surrounding me. I was afraid. I felt I was unprepared. Yet the wind whispered over me, murmuring, instructing me to trust.

I allowed my mind to calm, tuning in to the internal frequency of the silica crystals. My identity was diluted, gradually melting into the neighboring dunes. Little by little, I abandoned the layers of humanity that continued to dwell within my depths. I felt myself die. The desert opened up and swallowed me. The intimate vibrations of the sand remodeled me, hardened me. A wave from the depths thrust me up to the air.

I melted into this world and took control of it. I caused streams of the brown oxides to flow, directing their course, shaping Judith's haunting face on the crest of the petrified waves. By the time the wind had smoothed her face a third time, my ideas had settled in place.

During the night, I expanded my control over the desert. When dawn broke, I was ready. The final metamorphosis complete, I allowed the oxide currents to ferry me to the edge of the port. When I stood, I was the walking incarnation of the desert.

Michael was scheduled for take-off in mid-morning. I detoured around a group of technicians busying themselves around the cruiser. The polished steel thrusters flashed a moment under the rays of the sun. The purring of the generators gradually filled the silence. I crossed through the take-off zone, keeping to the shadows, on my way to the old officers' mess. Before going in, I shook off the oxide dust that coated me and my skin took on its original hue for a short while. I headed down the corridor to Michael's room.

The door was wide open. In one corner, near the bird's cage, he had stashed his most precious belongings. The old marine map peaked out from one of the bags, along with other relics from Earth. Judith stood by the window, staring off into the distance. She appeared indifferent, as if anesthetized, and said nothing as I entered.

For several minutes, I attempted to dissuade Michael from making his trip. I was not unaware that it was too late, but Judith's acknowledging glance in my direction felt good. I realized that she had not been able to resolve herself to accompanying him. I found this deeply reassuring and the tension of my scales relaxed a little. I left them immediately.

In the hour that followed, the surviving colonists assembled around the take-off zone. There were fewer and fewer of them and most of them had the empty look of future Sand Swimmers. After observing the take-off, they headed off on their own to pursue their impossible dreams in the few buildings that remained intact, at least until the next storm. I wished that I could have taught them what I knew of the desert, but they were too old to be transformed. One day, the desert would give them a quick, gentle death. I promised myself that I would watch over them until the end.

The minutes passed slowly. I dove back in to the burning sand along the fringe, returning a short while later, my thirst quenched. I remained apart from the others, so that my appearance would not provoke any questions I preferred not to answer. The color of my skin blended with that of the ground and I was almost invisible.

Judith was looking for me. I had to call her three times before she saw me and came over to join me. Her tears had drawn furrows on her brown cheeks, like a deathly tattoo. I stood a few feet from her, avoiding contact. It was right to respect her pain and this was Michael's day.

At about 10 o'clock, he came out of the mess and walked over to the take-off area. He wore the sparkling uniform of a pilot, casting sparks with every movement. On his shoulder, he carried the albatross' cage. A discrete ovation acknowledged his appearance. In a few hours, he would travel across the oceans of the void at unimaginable speeds, guided by the bird whose tensed body would point like an arrow to its native land. He, too, had developed his own way of swimming, identical in many respects to my own. I waved and he responded to my salute. We watched as he strode off to his craft. Judith made no effort to hold him back.

He bounded up the ladder, the rest of his equipment carried by a technician, who came back down immediately. The door of the lock whistled closed. A deep murmur rose from the neighboring dunes. Dry gusts of wind enshrouded the spaceport, plating an armor of grains with a familiar texture onto my shoulders. A strident siren signaled the departure.

The rumbling of the engines forced us to move back, and take shelter in the buildings. The small cruiser took off, slowly first, then gaining speed as it gained confidence. It crossed through the sky on a column of fire. In my mind's eye, I saw the large white bird spread its wings and take flight. I wished them success with all my being. It is good if each of us can one day reach his goal.

A few seconds later, the purple light of his thrusters disappeared. Judith continued to watch the sky overhead for several minutes, and then turned away without a word. The oxide dust gradually invaded the take-off zone...

I replayed the final images of the departure over and over in my mind as we walked, Judith and I, toward the colony. Every morning since then, she has gone to the peak of the highest dune, watching for his return, looking first at the desert, then at the sea. She is waiting. Every evening, I leave the desert to join her. She never speaks, but for some time now, she has started to smile again.

One day, she will tire of this hopeless wait, because Michael will never return. The oxide crystals I guided have long since corroded and destroyed the fragile circuits of the emergency transmitter. The relay satellite is spinning uselessly in space, with no signal to relay. Michael will never be able to find us.

I know that she will follow me into the desert soon. I will guide her through the cycle of metamorphosis and she will take her own place, somewhere in the infinite memory of the sand.

Afterword

I write science fiction because I think the world is a wonderful place.

Such a statement must naturally be taken with a grain of salt. I do not believe that the world is perfect, or candidly, even adequate. Too many things about it ought to be different, or improved, starting with the way humans live. But it is, nevertheless, wonderful. The light of the Sun setting over the fjords of Norway, the taste of freshly picked tomatoes, the strange and yet so familiar images beamed from the surface of Mars. And let's not forget the ability to dream and tell stories.

To pluck a story out of thin air may be a curse, but it is a wonderful curse. You are strolling, minding your own business, when suddenly in the corner of your mind's eye, a window opens and the jigsaw pieces that will make up your story start assembling almost as if by magic. Reality takes a back seat as the universe suddenly sends you a message that has a meaning. The problem is that that meaning is at first only obvious for the person for whom it is meant – the science fiction writer. Being a science fiction writer is more socially acceptable than being the man who gives away flowers at the airport while trying to convince you of the truth of his visions, but it is not fundamentally that different.

I can give you an example. Several years ago, as part of my daytime job (I am an aeronautical engineer), I was poring over a scientific paper reporting on the performance of various metal alloys when exposed to corrosive saline conditions. We can all agree that this topic would normally induce one to snooze. Except that the author of the paper went into the technical challenges met during the restoration of the Statue of Liberty which, as we all know, is made up of metal plates bolted on a steel structure designed by Gustave Eiffel (he of the eponymous Tower). Where it became interesting was when the author mentioned that the armpit of the statue, the arm holding the torch, had begun to sag a little under its own weight. The once smooth metal plating had begun to twist, creating creases one and a half-feet deep. Seagulls nested there, vegetation had grown, and this had to be cleaned up before they could repair the plating.

Having reached that part of the article, I began to laugh. The notion of Miss Liberty herself developing unsightly hair in her armpits and perspiring from bird droppings was too much. It occurred to me that the repair job ought to have been sponsored by a cosmetic company selling deodorant. All kinds of ideas, some funnier than others, came to me while I was laughing helplessly like an idiot.

Since that anecdote took place before *Dilbert*, the opportunities for all out mirth in an engineer's office were few and far between, so my colleagues rushed to inquire about the incident. I could but hand them a copy of the article while still giggling. Three of them read it, shook their heads, read it again, looking increasingly bemused, and finally looked at me disappointedly, and asked what I thought was so funny about it.

I walked them through my thought process and explained how I had arrived at the image of Miss Liberty with huge tufts of hair under her arm and all the funny bits that followed. But instead of shared hilarity, I received funny looks (and not of the "funny ha-ha" variety) that spoke volumes about their suspicions about the workings of my imagination.

Maybe it wasn't so funny after all, but this illustrates my point. No more than a midwife can ignore a baby about to be born can a writer ignore a story when it suddenly drops in his lap. The article carried the embryo of a story, but my respected colleagues had not detected it until I pulled it out and placed it in their laps. And once there, it could no longer be ignored. It had acquired a life of its own.

The stories I write are not accurate scientific predictions, nor are they meant to warn the world of this or that danger, present or future. If they have a moral, it is more often than not without my deliberate intention. I only report what seems obvious to me, obvious and wonderful. And through the act of writing, I seek to share these stories with others, giving them lives of their own.

Jean-Claude Dunyach

About the Author

Jean-Claude Dunyach, born in 1957, has a Ph.D. in applied mathematics and supercomputing. He works for Airbus France in Toulouse, in the southwestern part of France.

Dunyach has been writing science fiction since the beginning of the 1980s, and has already published seven novels and six collections of short stories, garnering the French Science-Fiction award in 1983 and two Rosny Aîné Award in 1992, as well as the *Grand Prix de l'Imaginaire* and the *Prix Ozone* in 1997.

His short story *Déchiffrer la Trame* (*Unravelling the Thread*) won both the *Prix de l'Imaginaire* and the Rosny Award in 1988, and was voted Best Story of the Year by the readers of the magazine *Interzone*.

His latest novel, *Etoiles Mourantes* (*Dying Stars*), written in collaboration with the French author Ayerdhal, won the prestigious Eiffel Tower Award in 1999 as well as the Prix Ozone. Dunyach's works have been translated into English, Bulgarian, Croatian, Danish, German, Italian, Russian and Spanish.

Dunyach also writes lyrics for several French singers, which served as an inspiration for one of his novels about a rock and roll singer touring in Antarctica with a zombie philharmonic orchestra....

Bibliography

Autoportrait (*Self-Portrait*) (collection) (Présence du Futur No. 415, Denoël, Paris, 1986)

Le Temple de Chair (*Le Jeu des Sabliers*, Tome 1) (*The Temple of Flesh* (*The Game of the Hourglass*, Vol. 1)) (Anticipation No. 1592, Fleuve Noir, Paris, 1987)

Le Temple d'Os (*Le Jeu des Sabliers*, Tome 2) (*The Temple of Bones* (*The Game of the Hourglass*, Vol. 2)) (Anticipation No. 1609, Fleuve Noir, Paris, 1988)

Nivôse (*Étoiles Mortes*, Tome1) (*Nivose* (*Dead Stars*, Vol. 1)) (Anticipation No.1837, Fleuve Noir, Paris, 1991)

Aigue-Marine (*Étoiles Mortes*, Tome 2) (*Aigue-Marine* (*Dead Stars,* Vol. 2)) (Anticipation No.1838, Fleuve Noir, Paris, 1991)

Voleurs de Silence (*Étoiles Mortes*, Tome 3) (*Thieves of Silence* (*Dead Stars*, Vol. 3) (Anticipation No. 1858, Fleuve Noir, Paris, 1992)

Roll Over, Amundsen (Anticipation No. 1912, Fleuve Noir, Paris, 1993)

La Guerre des Cercles (*The War of the Circles*) (Anticipation No. 1963, Fleuve Noir, Paris, 1995)

Étoiles Mourantes (*Dying Stars*) (with Ayerdhal) (J'ai Lu Millénaire, Paris, 1999)

La Station de l'Agnelle (*Station of the Lamb*) (collection) (L'Atalante, Nantes, 2000)

Dix Jours Sans Voir la Mer (*Ten Days Without Looking at the Sea*) (collection) (L'Atalante, Nantes, 2000)

Étoiles Mortes (*Dead Stars*) (J'ai Lu, Paris, 2000)

Déchiffrer la Trame (*Unravelling the Thread*) (collection) (L'Atalante, Nantes, 2001)

Le Jeu des Sabliers (*The Game of the Hourglass*) (ISF, Paris, 2003)
Les Nageurs de Sable (*The Sand Swimmers*) (collection) (L'Atalante, Nantes, 2003)

In English:

In Medicis Gardens, in *Full Spectrum* 4, Bantam Spectra, New York, 1993
The Dead Eye of the Camera, in *Full Spectrum* 5, Bantam Spectra, New York, 1995
Unravelling the Thread, in *Interzone* 133, Brighton, UK, July 1998; reprinted in *Year's Best SF* 4, HarperPrism, New York, 1999
Come Into My Parlor, in *Altair* 1, Blackwood, SA, Australia, 1998
Footprints in the Snow, in *Interzone* 150, Brighton, UK, December 1999
Station of the Lamb, in *Altair* 6, Blackwood, SA, Australia, 2000
All the Roads to Heaven, in *Interzone* 156, Brighton, UK, June 2000
Orchids in the Night, in *Interzone* 160, Brighton, UK, October 2000
Watch Me When I Sleep, appeared in *Interzone* 168, Brighton, UK, June 2001; reprinted in *Year's Best Fantasy and Horror*, Tor Books, New York, 2002
Enter the Worms, in *On Spec*, Volume 14, Number 2, Edmonton, Canada, Summer 2002
What the Dead Know in *On Spec*, Volume 16, Number 1, Edmonton, Canada, Spring 2004

About the Translators

With undergraduate and graduate degrees in translation and a doctorate in interdisciplinary studies, **Sheryl Curtis** works as a professional translator. During the course of her career, she also taught translation over a period of 20 years as a member of the part-time faculty at Concordia University, in Montreal, Quebec. More recently, she decided to leave the academic world to devote time to literary translation. Since 1998, her translations of short stories have appeared in *Interzone*, *Year's Best Science Fiction 4*, *Year's Best Fantasy and Horror 15*, *On Spec*, *Altair* and *Tesseracts 8*.

Born in Toronto, Aurora and Boréal Award winner **Jean-Louis Trudel** holds degrees in physics, astronomy, and the history and philosophy of science. Since 1994, he has written two novels, *Le Ressuscité de l'Atlantide* (*Risen from Atlantis*) and *Pour des Soleils Froids* (*Cold Suns*), both published in 1994 by the Anticipation imprint of the Paris-based publisher Fleuve Noir, one collection of short stories, *Jonctions impossibles* (*Impossible Joinings*) (2003), and twenty-two young adult books published in Canada by Médiaspaul. His short stories have appeared in in French in *imagine...* and *Solaris*, and in English in various Canadian and U.S. anthologies, such as *Tesseracts*, *Northern Stars*, *On Spec* and *Prairie Fire*. When time allows, he also does translations and science fiction criticism.

Dominique Bennett holds a Bachelors in Modern Languages from Exeter University and a Masters in Corporate Communication from the Ecole Supérieure de Commerce de Toulouse. She lives in Oxford and currently works for Lafarge Cement.

Ann Cale lives in Reston, Virginia. She holds a Bachelor of Fine Arts Degree from Tulane University. She has published poetry in the Berkeley Poets Co-op Anthology, and in the Anthology of New Jersey Poets. Ann has had exhibitions of her paintings in South America, the United States and France